A Dash of Devilry

Magic & Sorcery Chronicles - Book Three

Marie Andreas

Acknowledgments

I appreciate everyone who has helped get these books out there, bought my books, and told others about them.

To my most awesome team of beta readers/typo hunters who plowed through the entire book and helped tighten it up: Lisa Andreas, Patti Huber, and Lynne Mayfield, And final clean up proof by Ilana Schoonover-thank you! Any remaining errors are mine alone.

My cover artists, Joolz & Jarling (Julie Nicholls and Uwe Jarling), for creating an awesome work of art.

Other books by Marie Andreas

The Lost Ancients
Book One: The Glass Gargoyle
Book Two: The Obsidian Chimera
Book Three: The Emerald Dragon
Book Four: The Sapphire Manticore
Book Five: The Golden Basilisk
Book Six: The Diamond Sphinx

The Lost Ancients: Dragon's Blood
Book One: The Seeker's Chest
Book Two: The Finder's Crown

The Asarlaí Wars Trilogy
Book One: Warrior Wench
Book Two: Victorious Dead
Book Three: Defiant Ruin

The Code of the Keeper
Book One: Traitor's Folly
Book Two: Destroyer's Curse

The Adventures of Smith and Jones
A Curious Invasion
The Mayhem of Mermaids
An Intrigue of Pharaohs

Broken Veil
Book One: The Girl with the Iron Wing
Book Two: An Uncommon Truth of Dying
Book Three: Through a Veil Darkly

Books of the Cuari
Book One: Essence of Chaos
Book Two: Division of Chaos
Book Three: Destruction of Chaos

Magic and Sorcery Chronicles
A Touch of Magic
A Slice of Sorcery
A Dash of Devilry

Chapter One

"I said, no ruffles." Piallen turned around, trying to catch the tiny seamstress. She was at least a foot shorter than Piallen, and now that Piallen was standing on a foot-high riser, she was even shorter. And she was extremely good at dodging out of Piallen's long reach. "I'm not wearing all of this." Piallen waved at the massive pile of lace and fluff masquerading as a dress that swirled around her. She'd agreed to a dress for her Challenge ceremony at the begging of her mother, but this was ridiculous.

Her eldest sister, Lizeth, was a clotheshorse and would have loved this. Unfortunately, her Challenge had started two days early and she was sent off before her ceremony and any chance for fancy apparel.

Her second eldest sister, Nevaine, wasn't a clothes horse per se—but she ended up being kidnapped and barely made it back for the start of her Challenge. No ceremony, no fancy dress.

Which left their parents really wanting their third daughter to have some pomp at her official start. And Piallen felt for them, she did. She was sure with three daughters her mother especially had figured there would be a lot of fancy wear involved with all three ceremonies. Sadly, as the last child, Piallen was her only hope.

Piallen could count on one hand the times she'd worn *any* dress in the past five years. And two of them were at her sisters' weddings.

"Just one more minute, I promise." Drubella darted around her even faster, touching specific spots of the dress as she ran.

"Seriously, when my sisters get here, this dress is done." Piallen had last seen them two months ago, when Lizeth and her husband Finnian left on a grigeen relocation trip. The grigeens who'd appeared when Nevaine completed her Challenge had numbered over sixty thousand at last count. In the past two years efforts had been made to relocate them to the lands and countries they originally came from. Sometimes it worked—sometimes it didn't.

When the people working on it were Lizeth, one of the strongest spell singers in the world, and Finnian, a surprisingly strong sorcerer, the success rate was much higher. Along with Scruff, Lizeth's childhood grigeen companion, they'd been making regular trips to slowly reintroduce this formerly lost species to the world.

Nevaine and her husband Sean had returned from their university studies about that time for a week-long visit. They were both almost done with their advanced degrees in magic and sorcery studies from the University of Luzangberg.

Royals hadn't been allowed to go to university and had been educated in the palace for safety reasons for a few hundred years. Nevaine had used her Challenge wish to say she would be going there to complete her advanced degree—and to keep that option open for future generations.

While it hadn't been as shocking as Lizeth's decree that royals no longer had to wed royals, it had been more upsetting for their parents. Then Nevaine and Sean staged an attack scenario showing them how well they could defend each other. And Clait, Nevaine's childhood grigeen friend, said that she would be relocating a small pack of grigeens into the university town and would be keeping an eye on the couple as well.

Piallen was pretty sure that even as impressive as Nevaine and her fully battle-trained mage husband were—the grigeen support was the deciding push for their parents to agree.

Needless to say, she didn't mention that to Nevaine.

"I'm almost done—"

Trumpets announcing a royal arrival cut Drubella off. Piallen shimmied out of the dress without disrupting the pins and ran out the door. Against Drubella's protests, she'd stayed clad in her fighter workout wear underneath the dress and she now felt vindicated. Running through the palace in underclothes wouldn't have been a great idea. She'd still do it to see her sisters, but not optimal.

It was early, so not many people were in the halls. Probably good since Piallen was running at full speed, and there were few who could match her—or get out of her way fast enough. Her parents were concerned that she hated being inside, but that wasn't completely true. She hated the restrictions that things like walls and doors put on her inside. She was happiest in the woods that surrounded the palace.

Sadly, Drubella drew the line at doing her dress fittings outside.

A tall man, slender, but with his distinctive shaggy rich brown hair was framed in the entrance as he held the door and looked to someone behind him.

Piallen hit her brother-in-law at almost full speed and managed to grab him before they both tumbled into her sister, Lizeth.

"Finnian! Lizeth! You're home!" She stabilized Finnian, he was taller than her, but he hadn't been expecting an ambush, then went and hugged Lizeth.

Lizeth was a few inches shorter than Piallen's almost six feet, and always looked elegant and in control. The only time that she'd looked neither was when she, Finnian, and Scruff returned from her Challenge four years ago.

It seemed like she'd been making up for that ever since.

Finnian looked dusty and tired from their trip. Lizeth looked like she'd just stepped out of a salon.

Piallen tilted her head and looked at her sister carefully. "You stopped and used song magic to make yourself look good, didn't you?"

Lizeth's smile was bright and almost terrifyingly sunny, making her blond hair glow. "Why ever would you say that?" She held the pose, then dropped it and grabbed Piallen in another hug. "More importantly, how are you doing? I can't believe my baby sister's Challenge is in five days!"

"I'm fine. But it seems like I've been waiting for this my entire life." She shrugged. "Okay, I have. But mostly because I want to be able to talk to you and Nevaine about your Challenges. At this point, my imagination has probably exceeded whatever I'll really face."

Lizeth rubbed Piallen's arms and drew her away from the doorway. "How has the training gone?"

Piallen had always leaked magic, it was an odd disorder that showed up in magic users rarely. It meant her magic was weaker than it should be, and she had to wear a magic amulet, a small golden acorn, to keep things in check. Unlike Nevaine, Piallen had no innate ability for sorcery, so that was out. She'd even bugged Gliandra for weeks, asking her to look again. The secretive sorceress who lived in the woods had been gentle, but adamant—there were no sorcery abilities there. Piallen started battlemage training two years ago in the hopes that discipline would work better.

"Still the same." Piallen shrugged it off. The truth was, she was worried about her magic issues. A lot. But talking about them was hard and wasn't happening in the doorway of the palace. "The battlemage training is helping; their spells are much more focused and structured. Plus, many of them combine a physical fighting maneuver—it seems to help. But my magic still leaks. It's as if it doesn't fit right." That was a concept she'd just realized in the last few days, but it still sounded weird. How could magic, something she was born with, not fit?

Lizeth looked sympathetic then hugged her again. "We're not doing any more grigeen relocations for a bit. This last one was successful, but some of the grigeens didn't want to stay. Even after two years, many are having trouble coming to terms that the world they knew a few hundred years ago is gone. Scruff wants to work on more education before they go out."

"There are still an awful lot out in those woods. They've reached the base of the Trulan mountains." The mountains were distant enough that when Piallen's grigeen, Tobias, went to investigate the situation, it had taken him a week to get there and back. From her guess, there were still about thirty thousand grigeens out there.

The mountain range was completely within the kingdom of Astarious, but extremely close to the Northalian kingdom. A realm that had shown to be unfriendly when they tried to destroy Nevaine's chances of surviving her own Challenge. In the past two years, the two countries had mostly ignored each other. Northalian denied having sent people to interfere, just as Laiandra had denied involvement in the attacks that marred Lizeth's Challenge four years ago. Things were tense, but Astarious had enough strength to keep both countries at bay. For now.

Lizeth sighed. "I know. And we'll be talking to our parents. But I agree with Scruff. Forcing them out isn't going to work. Grigeens have much longer lives than us, and things take longer to change."

"Ladies? I believe your parents are calling us for brunch." Finnian stood near the door. He hadn't changed much in the four years since they'd come back from Lizeth's Challenge. He was still slender yet strong. He also had a calming influence on Lizeth and clearly doted on her to an extreme.

Arm in arm, Lizeth and Piallen followed him into the palace. Piallen missed her sisters when they were gone, and was glad they were both coming back for her Challenge. Between her magic issues, and the serious threats that had fallen around both of her sisters' Challenges, she wasn't looking forward to it as she once had.

The Challenge was faced by all young royals before they could be declared officially heir to the throne. Multiple heirs were fine, but only if they all passed their Challenges. Although she hadn't been able to read about any of the past Challenges, including those of her sisters, Piallen understood the Challenge to have always been more of a rite of passage. Perhaps life-changing for the challenger, but not world-changing.

From what she gathered, that had changed with both of her sisters' Challenges.

The palace security had tripled in the past month, and she now felt watched even when she was in the woods. The fear was that the Challenges were far more important to the kingdom than previously thought. The empires of Laiandra and Northalian had both tried to thwart them already.

Unfortunately, the oracles, the beings behind the Challenges, hadn't been helpful. Or so Piallen had gathered from what little Tobias could tell her. Grigeens had their own relationship with the mystical oracles. And while he couldn't break confidence about past Challenges, the normally cheerful grigeen had been concerned enough to give warnings.

He was also determined that he would be joining her.

Up until Lizeth went through with Finnian, at the time he was a woodsman who she barely knew, and her grigeen Scruff, no one ever joined the Challenger. They weren't allowed to. Then Nevaine had gone through with Clait, her grigeen, and her former boyfriend and now husband, Sean. Both times the extras had been approved and sent through by the oracles themselves.

Piallen's last relationship had ended four months ago and she really didn't want him to be the one to join her. Finding the right man to spend one's life with wasn't something she was looking forward to. A heartfelt conversation with her mother a week ago had pointed out that heirs didn't have to be married to claim their rights as heir or queen.

That made her feel better, but watching Lizeth and Finnian, as well as Nevaine and Sean, both couples with extremely different relationships—but both clearly devoted, made her wish for some of that in her life.

She'd done her share of dating. The problem was that bookish men didn't understand her need to be outside, and the more outdoorsy ones didn't understand her innate curiosity. She wasn't nearly as book-driven as her sister Nevaine, but she still enjoyed reading. Her favorites were fictional mysteries. As children, the three princesses had gotten into many adventures by trying to solve mysteries. That they didn't exist really, outside of the three girls' minds, wasn't important.

The three, along with their three grigeen companions, would face deep mysteries in the palace and in the woods.

Piallen hung onto that sense of adventure and wanting to solve mysteries by reading as she grew up. Usually in the forest, but still it was part of who she was. Just like her abilities with bow and sword, and her acrobatics and tree running. Tree running was part of her acrobatics training and helped focus her mind.

She felt that, like her unconventional and unexplainable magic issues, her finding a man who understood her wasn't going to be resolved any time soon.

Tobias came jogging up right before they reached the royal brunch room, also known as their parents' private dining room. Brunch just happened to be a popular meal there.

"Just in time for brunch?" Piallen asked. Tobias had scooted off when Drubella grabbed her for the fitting a few hours ago.

"Sounds lovely." The large tiger striped grigeen grinned and licked his chops. "Sadly, not today. Scruff has news and once Clait gets here a general grigeen council will be called. Then they'll be meeting with the royal family."

Piallen smiled. "And isn't today dried fish day with the pack?" Nevaine came back from her Challenge with little information she could share with Piallen. However, the fact that grigeens loved dried fish had been something she could share. The species had started in coastal enclaves, but over the centuries had moved inland. Clait mentioned their genetic longing for dried fish to Nevaine, and Nevaine set up fish deliveries for the grigeens every few months.

"It might be." He winked. "I'll be back." With a nod to Lizeth and Finnian, he darted off. His roundness didn't slow him down at all.

"Scruff already made his way to their forest. Said he had important things to discuss." Lizeth watched Tobias vanish around a corner.

"We should have known there was food involved." Finnian laughed and held open the door for both sisters.

"Lizeth and Finnian, it is so good to have you back." The king was already on his feet and hugged both, followed by the queen.

As usual there was enough food to feed a battalion. Or a small pack of grigeens.

"Sit, everyone. Nevaine and Sean will be here soon, but I don't want the food getting cold." The queen had a sharp strategic mind, but she also was a mother.

Everyone filled their plates and poured cups of tea.

"Shouldn't they have been here by now? We had a message from them a week ago that they'd be heading up a few days early," Lizeth said.

"We never got that message." The king frowned and looked to the queen.

"They might have been trying to surprise everyone." Finnian got to his feet. "I can get people to track the roads back to the university. They might have just detoured."

"I think we don't need to go that far—not yet." The king looked briefly to Piallen.

"Just because she's finished her Challenge doesn't mean she's not in danger. Remember when they tried to grab me to mess up Nevaine's Challenge? This could be similar." Piallen knew that Nevaine and Sean were a formidable fighting pair, but no one had been able to resolve the portal that the Northalians had used to attempt to grab her right before Nevaine's Challenge.

"I'd say—" the rest of the queen's words were lost as alarms rang throughout the palace. Gliandra had worked with Finnian to set them up, but they could be warning of a number of things. All magic-related, and none of them good.

Fists pounded on the doors.

Finnian was closest and had his hand on his sword hilt as he partially opened the door.

A pair of palace guards stepped back. "We're under attack. There are intruders in the palace."

Chapter Two

"Please stay here." The foremost guard was almost pleading in her tone as everyone got to their feet. None of the royals were good at staying out of things. "Gliandra is on her way in."

"Which is good, please make sure she is escorted here." The king stepped over to the guard with a sad smile. "However, you know we don't do well with people attacking us in our home." He buckled on his sword belt. "We fight."

"I know, but I had to try." The guardswoman, Kilthia, was close in age to the king and queen and Piallen had grown up under her protection. Her short blond-gray hair always stuck up and she was as tall as Piallen.

"I'll need a weapon." Piallen was rarely without a bow, swords, or even a pike when she was outside, mostly because there were always opportunities for training out there. But, unlike her sister Nevaine, she was rarely armed in the palace. And certainly not when going to a dress fitting.

Finnian handed her his sword. "I have an extra one in our things." He refrained from mentioning that both his and Lizeth's magics were stronger and more reliable than hers, but Piallen knew it.

"What do we know of the attackers? Where did they get in?" The queen preferred a dirk and dagger set, but her magical abilities were strong enough that she rarely needed to use the weapons.

"Third floor, near the seamstress's chambers." The second guard looked to Piallen.

"Drubella? I have to go help her." Piallen hadn't liked being pushed around by the tiny woman, but if someone went after her, they had done it to get to Piallen.

"And that's probably what they are waiting for." The king nodded to Kilthia. "How many, and I'm assuming they didn't fly in through the window?"

Yelling could now be heard and the alarms stopped. Gliandra came to the doorway with eight guards around her. She was a small woman, still an inch or two taller than Nevaine, but she always looked the same. Long gray hair pulled back in a bun and an ageless face. Sometimes she walked with a cane—this wasn't one of those times. As a seriously powerful sorceress, she probably didn't need the guards either, but she respected the escort.

"They came in through a portal on the third-floor interior balcony." Gliandra shook her shoulders, but looked agitated. "They shouldn't have been able to even try to get in. They found a hole in my shielding and someone helped them on this side."

Everyone looked to Piallen.

"What? There are other people up there besides Drubella." The seamstress had been with them for a year, and while she wasn't happy about a dress, Piallen had grown to like the tiny woman.

"Not right now. The only people up there are her and a group of fifteen Northalians. I sensed them before a magic user up there blocked me. She might not have been who we thought." Gliandra flashed Piallen a worried glance.

"Something else is out there." Lizeth looked past the guards as more sounds of fighting were heard. They weren't nearby. Yet. She sang a song, soft at first, then louder and more pointed.

Five shapes flickered into place not far behind the guards and charged forward. Tall, thin, and pale. Stiklins. Finnian grabbed Gliandra, and the king motioned for the guards to come in. Two ran back to help and were killed by the Stiklins.

"Get inside!" The queen focused her magic on the closest Stiklins, sending them high into the air and letting them fall. Hard.

Piallen shut the door once everyone was inside the small room. "How are there Stiklins out there? *Why* are there Stiklins out there?" Stiklins were brutal and powerful killers, with enough magic to remain hidden unless exposed by a spell. They could also feed off the magic of others. They had attacked the palace before Lizeth's Challenge, but no one knew how they'd gotten there as their land was on the far side of Laiandra. Which was on the far side of an impassable ravine. "Are they using the same portals the Northalians are?"

Gliandra nodded. "They might be. My alarms picked up the portal, but not the Stiklins. Had they come in some other way, the spell would have noticed them."

"We can't stay hidden in here, your highnesses." Kilthia waved toward the closed door.

"We won't." The queen went to the back wall of the small dining chamber, pressed on two sections of paneling at the same time, and a narrow door slid open. "This will bring us to the main entrance. It sounded like most of the fighting was coming from there." She went through.

Piallen started to follow her mother, but her father stopped her. "This is one of the most secure places in the palace right now. You have to stay here."

"What? I can fight. I'm one of the best fighters in the kingdom."

"And you are probably the current target." Lizeth came to her and held her arms. "There are things that only the Challenger can do and it looks like our enemies have figured that out faster than we have. If they stop you, there could be horrific repercussions."

"Why would the oracles let this happen?"

"They might not have a choice." Lizeth clearly knew more, but even now wouldn't or couldn't say.

Piallen looked around then sighed. "I'll stay here as long as I can. But I don't like it."

"I know you don't." Her mother kissed her cheek, her father hugged her, and then everyone left.

Aside from Gliandra.

"You're staying?"

"Yup. Not just to protect you, but that's part. Especially since those vile Stiklins are involved. But I have a plan, one I'll need your help for and will take a bit of time to set up."

Piallen secured the secret door and nodded. "Okay, what do you need?"

Gliandra took a seat and motioned to the one next to her. "Please sit. This will work better that way."

Piallen paused, then sat. The sounds of fighting could barely be heard now, but she still wanted to be doing something out there to help.

"There you go. Now, I know you were disappointed not to have any abilities in sorcery, and I've been working on figuring out what we can do to determine what's messing with your magic. I had wanted to work through this slowly, as I really am out of my depth here. But I'm afraid that we don't have time for that now." She carefully took out a fragile piece of paper from inside her cloak. A light spell glinted over it, and from its condition Piallen guessed that spell might be the only thing holding the paper together.

"What's that? I don't think a spell is going to strengthen my magic, no matter how old it is."

"No. It won't. But I've realized that your magic is different. Very different." She leaned forward. "Even I can't cast this spell and it was passed down to me from one of the most powerful of my order, Janus, an extremely long time ago. He hadn't been able to cast it either, but knew it was important and must not be lost. But with some help, you might." She grinned as if she'd just solved all their problems.

"We don't have time for this. I know I can't go out and fight, but the palace—my home—is under attack. We have to do something."

"We are. This spell could save everyone out there—well, the people who should be out there. But we need one thing."

"What?"

"A stone from your sister's room. The one she keeps here in a glass case."

It took Piallen a few moments to figure out what she meant. "The one she can't tell me about?"

"Yes. She didn't tell me either, but I now know what it is. And if we get this spell, that rock, and your unique magic together, we might have something."

Piallen dropped her head in her hands. Gliandra had lived in the forest among the grigeens as long as she could recall, but kept to herself until recently. Hopefully, she could actually help. Piallen wanted to do something, but she didn't think sneaking around looking for a rock was going to help. "How do we get there?"

"I figured you might have an idea?"

Piallen started to shake her off, then paused. As kids, she and her sisters had found many secret passages. They were all over the palace and had been created by different generations. "They're going to be tight, but I think I can get us to Nevaine and Sean's room." She fought down the panic at what might have happened to them. Get through this mess first, then find Nevaine and her husband.

"Excellent!" Gliandra got to her feet and tilted her head as if hearing something. "And our help will be arriving soon. Not a secret, but the grigeens are coming." She nodded as Piallen pulled back the panel to the passageway her family had gone out of. The urge to follow them to the right toward the front chamber was strong, but she went to the left instead.

The series of oddly connected hallways and forgotten access tunnels was twisted, but after a few turns it all came back to her and she moved faster. She only smacked her head a few times, but Gliandra was shorter so had no problems.

The accessway they came out of was a few doors down the hall from Nevaine's rooms. She'd kept her original chambers for now since she and Sean had left for university not long after they were married.

Gliandra nudged Piallen aside as they looked out to the hall.

Gliandra squinted down the hall, then shook her head. "I wish we had Lizeth's singing. I have a feeling something might be out there."

Piallen looked down the hall, but couldn't see anything. "I might know a spell, it's a battlemage one and isn't as effective as Lizeth's...but I could try?"

Gliandra turned to her. "Even when I told you that you had no sorcery ability you weren't this self-doubting. Doubt destroys more mages of any type than spells gone wrong."

Piallen shook her head, she was right. Doubt wasn't her thing, usually. "I know, logically, I know. But I'm used to fighting, not lurking about. Let me try this, then we run for Nevaine's rooms." She rolled out her shoulders as if she was preparing for a physical fight, not a spell. Then focused her energy on the hallway and the spell. It was a simple one compared to some of the battlemage spells, and it had a single purpose—to unbalance anything or anyone in its range. If there were Stiklins hiding in the hall, they should flicker when they fell.

Hopefully.

As often happened, when she tried to do magic, the small acorn amulet on her chest felt warm. Growing up, she'd thought of the acorn as a friend, something to help her. With a smile to that memory, she released the spell.

The hall tilted, or so it seemed. And two flickers appeared at the far end of the hallway.

Piallen grabbed Gliandra's arm and ran for Nevaine's door. The door was locked but they'd added magic-responding palm panels to all three sisters' doors two years ago—it swung open at Piallen's touch. She pushed Gliandra inside and slammed the door shut behind them. Pounding and the flare of the reinforced shielding on the door told her she'd been right about those flickers.

"That was impressive," Gliandra said, as she picked herself off the sofa. "And I knew there had been security improvements beyond mine, but the palm unlock and shielded door are very impressive. Sean's work?"

"Yes, he put both up the day after the attack on Nevaine when they returned from her Challenge. He copied the spell to all of our doors." She looked around. "I don't see that stone." She wasn't sure what a stone could do unless it was thrown at someone, but they needed to do something.

Gliandra wandered the room. "It's here. I can feel it. She might have hidden it." Holding her left hand out, she slowly went along the wall. "She has many hiding spots, but I think this one is it." She flicked her fingers, and a piece of paneling popped open, revealing a small cubbyhole. She pulled out a glass case.

"Never did understand what was so special about a rock." Piallen looked down at what looked like a normal, palm-sized stone.

"Neither did I until I dug out this spell while thinking of ways to sort your magic. But I think it is a connection to a magic long lost." She gently removed the glass covering. "Take it. She'll understand."

Piallen knew her sister better than Gliandra, and she knew Nevaine was exceedingly touchy about her possessions. However, if there was a chance that this could save people she cared about, she'd deal with Nevaine when the time came. She picked up the rock, expecting it to be cold. And it was for a moment, then started warming.

"It's warm and almost purring." She didn't drop the rock or fling it, but it was a disturbing feeling.

Gliandra touched it, then pulled her fingers back. "It contains a memory of a person, a very powerful one. I believe this will help."

"The stone is a person?" Piallen wasn't squeamish, but if this rock contained a real person, that was going to weird her out a bit.

"Not really. He has gone on. More that it's an echo of who he was. The rock will help you focus when you read the spell. But you need to maintain control, too much power and you'll hit everyone."

Piallen started to put the stone back. "I'm not trying anything that might kill my family."

Gliandra stopped her and folded her hands around the stone. "You wouldn't. This spell will simply make everyone not touching you unconscious. It's a massive sleep spell in a way. But I don't think your parents would appreciate being knocked out. Nor your sister and her husband."

The pounding against the spell-protected door stopped but that didn't mean that the Stiklins, or whoever else was invading, were gone. And there were still sounds of fighting echoing from the ground floor.

"You said you could sense where the attackers, and Drubella, were—can you still do so?" This was the fourth floor. Piallen would probably need to get them back down to the bottom floor through the hidden ways they came up, but she wanted to see whose side Drubella was really on if she could. She was a good judge of character, usually, but she'd sensed nothing wrong about the seamstress.

"It's harder now. I think there are more Stiklins out there and their foul magic muddles things." Gliandra closed her eyes for a few moments, then opened them. "I can tell there are beings gathered together on the floor below us, but beyond that, no."

"I have to see what's going on, and we're going to have to go to the main floor anyway."

"I was actually thinking of your casting the spell from here." Gliandra held the ancient spell paper up. "But we can see if she's there first." Her eyes said she didn't hold hope. If Drubella was still alive she was most likely on the side of the attackers.

Piallen ignored her. "Do I need to carry this stone in my hand? Is it safe in a pocket? And shouldn't I at least look over that spell?"

"It's fine in your pocket, but I think you'll need to take it out for the spell. As for reading it beforehand? Normally, I'd say yes, that reinforces a spell. But this one is different. Our best chance is for you to first read it, while holding the stone, with me assisting the moment you cast it."

"What if it doesn't work?"

Her smile was small. "Then we go with plan B." She patted Piallen's arm. "You'll think of something, I'm sure."

There wasn't time for debate, but Piallen was going to have a long talk with Gliandra if they survived. "Fine, we'll take the hidden way to the third floor, see about Drubella, then hopefully cast this spell." Piallen wasn't as set in her ways as her two older sisters, but she did like consistency. She'd never heard of a spell that was only read the first time as it was being used.

She listened at the door but heard nothing, so she carefully opened it and let loose her battlemage spell, but there were no flickers this time. She and Gliandra were almost to the entrance to the hidden passages when a guest bedroom door swung open.

Drubella was surrounded by Northalians and Stiklins on *this* floor, not one lower. She wasn't a prisoner—she was holding a bloody knife as she ran forward.

Chapter Three

Gliandra threw a sorcery spell at Drubella, managing to shove her into the people behind her. But then Gliandra grabbed the side of her head and bent forward. "The Stiklins are pulling my magic. You'll have to cast the spell now."

Piallen took the spell page she shoved at her. "I'm not feeling a magical drain." That was weird and something to deal with later. She shoved Gliandra behind her. Then pulled out the stone, and read the page. It wasn't in any language she even recognized, but somehow the odd words made sense.

Drubella and her people were on their feet running toward her when she cast the spell. Dark words echoed the spell in the palace, then everything went silent as Drubella and the other attackers dropped to the ground.

Piallen felt a tugging on her foot and looked down to see a wincing Gliandra hanging on to her ankle. She'd pushed up Piallen's leggings a bit so she was touching skin.

"Well done. And you supported my theory, but that was a brutal spell. I have a feeling everyone down below is unconscious." She didn't look like getting up was going to be easy. "I might need some help. Even holding on to you, that spell nicked me."

Piallen tucked away the stone and the spell and helped her get up. She was wobbly but stayed on her feet. "How long will they stay unconscious?" She didn't want to leave Drubella and her cohorts untied but she also wanted to find her family. The silence coming from below indicated she had knocked out everyone. Hopefully that was all she did.

"If I translated it correctly, at least an hour—possibly longer. Let's go down the normal stairs and see to your family." Gliandra moved slowly, but she seemed to get stronger with each step.

There were unconscious people everywhere they looked when they got to the bottom. Kilthia was dropped in front of the king and queen. Piallen ran to them, but they weren't injured, just knocked out by her spell.

Finnian and Lizeth were in similar positions not far from them and both were breathing slowly as if asleep.

"I'm glad they're all fine, but how do we wake the ones we want to wake? We need to tie up the attackers and lock them up. I can't do that myself."

Gliandra studied her closely. "How do you feel?"

"Fine. Worried, but fine. We need to focus on them though."

"That spell, or one of that strength, would have drained even Lizeth. And she's one of the most powerful magic users I personally know. Yet, you are fine. Not even tired." She shook her head and muttered under her breath.

"What's happened?" Nevaine's voice behind them was a welcome sound.

Piallen ran toward the open front doors and hugged her sister. Nevaine was two years older than her, but a lot shorter. Her feet dangled in the hug but she hugged her back.

"Good to see you too, but what happened?" Nevaine looked around as Sean slowly approached the nearest unconscious guard.

"This one is just asleep. These too. There are Stiklins?" His hand had been on the hilt of his sword, but he now switched to holding a spell. "What's happened?"

Gliandra patted his arm. "It's okay. We were under attack, but Piallen took care of it. Now we just need to wake up our people."

"Piallen? How…" Nevaine stopped herself. Instead of getting better as Piallen had gotten older, her magic had gotten worse. It wasn't a secret, but the family rarely spoke of it.

"It was some trick Gliandra pulled with an ancient spell. Oh, and I borrowed your stone." She pulled it out to hand it back, but Gliandra stopped her.

"Might need you to stay in contact to wake up your family and the guards. Hold it in one hand and touch the skin of the one you want to wake with the other."

Piallen knew the look of confusion on Nevaine's and Sean's faces was probably reflected on her own. But she shrugged, held the stone, and touched the nearest guard on the hand.

He stirred immediately, stretching and giving a huge yawn. "Your highness! How did I…" He tried to scramble to his feet, but his legs were sluggish. Sean reached down to help him up.

Gliandra nodded. "Don't worry, might take a few moments to feel all there. Move slowly for a bit." She looked up to Piallen. "Well? Carry on."

Piallen ran back to her parents and Kilthia, leaving Nevaine to help them up before going to Lizeth and Finnian. Lizeth was on her feet the fastest and helped Piallen go through the rest of their guards.

The king and queen ordered the attackers to be bound and taken down to the former dungeons. They were used as magic training rooms now, but would work to keep them contained.

"I still don't know what happened, but we can wait until a private meeting." Nevaine looked around as guards hauled off unconscious, and some dead, Stiklins and Northalians.

Piallen turned to her parents. "Drubella was working with them and it seemed that both groups were working together."

The queen frowned. "She'd been vetted well. I'll get some people looking into it."

They all followed the king and queen into their council chambers, but Piallen stopped. "Weren't there supposed to be grigeens coming to help?"

Gliandra looked around. "There were. That's odd; there's a faint spell overlaying the castle." She turned and ran for the back.

Her running was enough to get everyone else to and they ran out the back of the palace.

There were hundreds of grigeens all frozen in place. Some in midair as they'd leapt forward.

"Did my spell do that?" Piallen had put the stone away but started to bring it back out.

"No." The queen spoke a few spell words and all of the grigeens snapped back into movement. "That was done by one of the people inside."

Scruff, Clait, and Tobias chittered to the rest of their people behind them, then came running up. The rest faded back into the woods.

"Thank you. I felt the spell hit us, but it was aware of our magic and disabled us." Clait looked around. "I assume everyone is okay?" Although Scruff was the oldest of the three, Clait often took charge.

"We believe so. Unless you need to report to your people, we'd like you three to join in our meeting." The queen nodded to the grigeens.

Tobias came to Piallen and sniffed her. "Something has changed."

"Things always change," Gliandra said before Piallen could respond.

"We can go with you." Scruff started jogging toward the palace. Everyone followed his lead.

Piallen walked back slower than the rest, thinking about what Gliandra did. She must have found a way to work that spell through her. But why? If Gliandra had that kind of power, she could have done it directly. Unless she was hiding something.

Sean dropped back to walk alongside her. He was a striking looking man with dark, almost black hair, blue eyes, and a quick grin. Right now, the grin was struggling. "How goes the battlemage training?"

"Slow. It does seem to work better for me than other magic, but I still am better with the lower-level non-augmented magic, than augmented." She held up Nevaine's stone. "What is this? Without breaking any Challenge rules. I felt it warm and almost speak to me."

"It belonged to someone Nevaine and I met. But I think we'll need to wait until we get to the council chamber. That's interesting that it helped you." He looked at the stone, but made no move to touch it.

Piallen was going to ask more, especially when he refused the stone when she tried to give it to him, but then they were in the palace and almost to the council chamber doors. She could wait.

Tobias had run ahead with Scruff and Clait, but he waited just inside the door for her, then walked alongside her until they sat.

"What? Do I still smell weird?"

"Hmm, no. But there has been a change. Fear not, I still adore you." Tobias was the youngest of the three royal companion grigeens, and many thought he was too flippant to be a royal companion. Piallen loved growing up with him, as he was more than willing to join in whatever adventure she dreamed up, but he'd gotten more serious in the last four years.

Before Piallen could ask him more questions, Kilthia pulled shut the chamber doors.

"I am impressed and grateful at that sleep spell, Gliandra, but I'm not sure how it was done. I didn't sense sorcery in it. Or even magic," the queen said.

"That's because there wasn't either. Nor did I do it." She looked toward Piallen. "Show them the stone and the spell page. We might as well get this over with."

Piallen narrowed her eyes but put both items on the table.

"Nevaine's stone souvenir and an ancient spell?" The king was closest but shook his head after a moment of trying to read the page. "It's not in any language I know."

"Me either, aside from a few words." Gliandra looked like she'd just invented the wheel. "But Piallen was able to."

"I thought you were doing something to help me read it. What language is it?"

"Here's where it gets tricky, as I think the oracles are holding to their rule of silence. It's not to punish non-Challengers, it's to keep future ones from second guessing their actions and muddling things up that need to happen." Gliandra waved her hand. "That being said, that is a wizard's spell, in an exceedingly old wizard language."

Nevaine darted over and nodded slowly. "It appears like it. At least based on the very few examples I have found. How did you read it?" She turned to Piallen.

"I have no idea. We got your stone, Gliandra handed me the paper, and we were attacked. I didn't have many options."

Lizeth leaned forward and sang softly. A light glow appeared around Piallen, then vanished.

"That's not possible." Lizeth leaned back shaking her head. "They've been gone for a thousand years. Tell them, Nevaine."

"Who's been gone, and what was that spell song?" Piallen had felt an odd tingle at Lizeth's spell.

Nevaine shared a look with Sean and Lizeth, then nodded. "The wizards. They all died out long ago. That stone is related to one and that spell is one of theirs, as Gliandra said."

"What trick made the spell work?" Piallen felt like she was on the bad end of a joke. Looking around the room, even the grigeens were watching her carefully.

Aside from Tobias. He jumped off his chair and sat in her lap. "You did. You've got wizard magic." He got as close as a grigeen could to a full smile. Long canines made the look a bit less friendly than intended.

"Don't be silly..." Piallen's words died when she saw the looks on the faces around her. "How? Wizards were crazy hermits. Violent hermits. They ended up killing each other. I can't be one."

Her mother came and hugged her. "It's shocking to us as well. But it does explain a lot. There's not much we can do before your Challenge, but we'll figure out some training."

"And the reason they were solitary, was because they chose to be," Nevaine said. "You'll still be you."

"But with wild deadly magic." Sean shrugged and looked around. "Just saying it. However, I think that between us, we can train our wizard. Might need to bring up some books from the university library though." He shared a look with Nevaine. She'd have them in the palace within a few days at the most.

"Where did you get that spell, Gliandra?" Nevaine was still looking at it, but didn't touch it.

"From a friend." She smiled to Lizeth and Finnian. "An old member of my former magic order, Janus."

Both Lizeth and Finnian looked surprised, but didn't say anything.

Piallen shook her head and absently scratched Tobias' head. "Am I the only one who's not okay with this? I mean, how did this happen?" She liked physical challenges and enjoyed learning new things. But this was beyond anything she'd even heard of before.

"It will be okay." Her father came closer and took her hand. "We have the best minds in the land right here—we'll sort this out."

"Now we just need to deal with the attack." Finnian was quiet, but often got to the heart of a situation. He was former military and had a good mind for strategy.

A soft knock came from the door. Finnian answered it and Kilthia came inside.

"We've gotten everyone locked up. They'd managed to get people on every floor. Eight of our own were killed, all guards. Many of the housekeeping staff were beaten and tied up to keep them quiet. There are twenty Northalians alive, ten dead, fifteen Stiklins alive, five dead. And Drubella the seamstress."

The room went silent. Then the queen nodded. "We need to question the Northalians, I doubt we'll get anything from the Stiklins. Did Drubella appear to be working with the Northalians or on her own?"

"She was with a group of both and appeared to be leading them." Piallen wasn't happy about being so wrong about Drubella, but she was more disturbed that they were all working together. "If this move was related to my Challenge, I don't understand why they did it so early. The other attacks have come closer to the date." She was still five days away at this point, both of her sisters had been closer when the attacks came.

"Unless they are *trying* to move the date forward," Nevaine said. "Think about it. In both Lizeth's and my Challenges, attacks around us made the oracles bump up our Challenge dates. Since there are no records of focused attacks like this ever occurring around a Challenge before ours, we have to believe that whoever is behind these attacks is aware of the impact these Challenges make and how they function."

"So, we don't let the oracles move Piallen's date? Or maybe they need to?" Finnian didn't look happy about either option. "We don't have enough information."

Gliandra and all three grigeens shook their heads. "That is a muddle you don't want to go down. Trying to second-guess a future action can leave you with a splitting headache and no solid answers." The grigeens were silent but nodded in agreement.

"For now, Kilthia, triple the guards on all entrances to the palace—no matter where they are. Gliandra, can you, Sean, Finnian, and Nevaine work on increasing the sorcery protection around and within the palace and adjacent grounds. Lizeth, you, your mother, and I will layer some augmented spells as well. Hopefully the combination will make it harder to break in." Everyone nodded and got to their feet except Piallen.

"And I just sit here? You know I don't do that well." What she really wanted to do was go for a long run in the forest, followed by an hour of archery. She knew that under the circumstances, that wouldn't be an option.

"You are going to work with the three of us. In your room." Tobias nodded to Scruff and Clait. "We have some innate spells, ones far more linked to the wizards than any other type of magic. We can train you to use them."

Piallen looked up but the others were all discussing their plans. "I guess that's better than hiding. But can I use Nevaine's knife stable? I really need to be outside right now." Any spells on the palace would be extended to the stables, even the one Nevaine had converted to a knife throwing practice area. Since she'd been gone, Piallen had gone out there for her own practice from time to time as it was long enough, once hay bales were moved, for crossbow practice.

Nevaine shrugged. "I'm fine with it. Oh, I do have one wizardry book out there, in the hidden cupboard behind the smallest target. Maybe you can read it. I never could. And I'll get more sent up from the university."

"Just be wary," Gliandra said as she paused in the doorway. "Don't read any of the words out loud. Especially if they ask you to."

Chapter Four

"They might *speak* to me?" Piallen got to her feet. She was fond of books, but having them speak to her wasn't something she'd like.

"You can never tell with wizards." Gliandra shook her head. "The shenanigans they pull! Just be aware of whatever the book does. In fact, after we get these shields around everything done, I might come out and just have a talk with it."

Piallen waited a moment to see if she was joking. She wasn't. "I promise to ignore anything the book tells me to say or do." Going to the modified stable wasn't her first choice, but better than being stuck inside here. Her mind worked best when she was doing something physical.

Everyone dispersed except her and the three grigeens. "Don't you need to warn the others? There's no way this shield over the palace can reach all of the grigeens."

Clait shook her head. "We already did. They'll pull in as many of the ones near the Trulan mountains as they can, but they might not get them all. Aside from us three, all of our people will stay in the forest until your Challenge."

Piallen made a short detour to grab some throwing knives and a crossbow. She preferred the longbow, but the stable was too short for that practice. Tobias sighed as they walked to the stable.

"What's that about?" She looked down at her furry friend. Clait and Scruff were ahead of them, chittering to themselves.

"I was just remembering running in the woods for hours with you as a wee child. Those were good times." He looked up and shook his head. "Now you're going to be a wizard. Things change."

"I'm still the same person, you know." A tiny part of her was actually pleased that they might have found why her magic had never been normal. The other part wasn't happy at all. There were children's stories about wizards, and none of the wizards were good people. "At least I hope so." She'd said the last part under her breath.

She had been looking forward to her Challenge, but now this bit of being a wizard, and a seriously untrained one, was marring that. Should she even go on her Challenge? What would happen if she refused? The oracles could still send her—that was clear. They'd grabbed Lizeth as she, Scruff, and Finnian raced through the forest before her Challenge even started.

"Why has no one questioned the oracles about this Challenge?" she asked as they went into Nevaine's stable. "I know the grigeens have a different type of relationship with them than we do, but why do we follow them?" She was certain the long answer was buried somewhere in the exceedingly dry history books that her various tutors tried to make her read instead of her mysteries. But she wanted a short answer.

"That's a long tale," Clait said as she jumped onto a hay bale and curled up.

"The short version is that when this kingdom was being created, the first queen was saved by an oracle," Scruff said as he went to find his own hay bale. "This was over a thousand years ago and the oracles were already fading as beings of worship in most lands. After they saved her, the oracle asked for a boon, one that would be claimed against her family line at a future point."

"And they claimed it a few hundred years ago by demanding these Challenges?" Piallen watched as all three grigeens nodded. "Didn't anyone think it was a strange request and why did they wait hundreds of years to ask?" She'd simply accepted the Challenge as a part of her life—but looking at it now, there was a lot of mystery around it. And it wasn't something that she felt would be answered once she completed her own.

"Because..." Tobias' furry brows lowered and he looked to the other two. "She really does have some good questions. You're both older than me, what are the answers?"

Scruff shrugged. "You'd have to ask the oracles, I'd guess. Our interaction with them is different than yours, but still limited. I, for one, believe they knew exactly what had happened to our people. Yet, they never told us." His tail lashed a bit.

"I have a theory." Clait looked around and motioned to the stable door. "Can you shut that first? This goes no further than us four for now."

Piallen shut the door, then she and Tobias both took hay bales to sit on.

"I believe that the oracles control far more than we know, but that their power isn't all reaching. They created these Challenges when something went wrong that they couldn't fix and they needed help." Clait nodded solemnly.

"What's out of their ability?" Piallen didn't think about the oracles much beyond an acceptance that they were there, somewhere, and somehow held sway over certain things. But she'd never thought of them as being unable to do anything. The Challenges were more of a ritual of passage—even if not all young royals returned from them.

"That's what I don't know," Clait said. "As I said, this is simply my theory, based on going on Nevaine's Challenge and reading about Lizeth's. I've read about others, and most weren't as...impactful as your sisters'. I'm sorry, I can't say more."

"I understand. But I still think that we need to find this information. It's not good that our enemies are aware of something that happens during this time and are trying to take advantage of it. We can fight off the Northalians, the Laiandrans, and even the Stiklins separately, but not if they join forces."

"I didn't see or hear that any Laiandrans were in this group," Tobias said.

"They weren't. Unless my seamstress was a Laiandran spy. But they have been involved in the other attacks. We can't discount them, or their potential threat." Piallen walked to the four targets, adjusted them, and started crossbow practice. The small bows fired shorter distance than a longbow, but used far more powerful bolts. "I think we have to look at what has changed in the past four years; five, if we want to include the time before Lizeth's Challenge. What has happened that is causing this change?" She quickly fired off a group of four bolts that each hit the bullseye in their target.

"You do love a good mystery." Tobias grinned.

"I do indeed, but I'm not sure how I feel about ones that I'm in the middle of. I almost wish the oracles would push my Challenge up; I'm not sure I can handle five days of this waiting for another attack."

"You probably won't have a choice one way or another. But maybe you could try reading that wizard book of Nevaine's? I know it's not as much fun as shooting things, and I'm not sure if your wizardness is part of the current situation, but it could prove important." Clait looked like she wanted to say more, but couldn't.

Most likely she'd been about to say something about this mysterious wizard who'd somehow given Nevaine a rock with his memory in it during her Challenge. When she came back from her Challenge, Piallen was sitting her sisters, their husbands, and their grigeens down and having a long conversation.

Piallen put down her crossbow and went to the smallest target. The bookshelf under it was tiny and well protected against accidental weapon incursion. The book was small, not much larger than her hand, and covered in a thick, carved, tree bark. One that was obviously protected as it looked like it had just come off the tree.

The pages inside were old, the paper was turning yellow. But they were in better shape than the one Gliandra had. Another question to ask after her Challenge, who was this Janus person and why did both Lizeth and Finnian react to his name? How did an old member of whatever order Gliandra belonged to come into contact with her sister? So many questions that she'd have to wait on answers for.

"Any of them catch your eye?" Tobias climbed down from his hay bale and wandered over.

"I did just open it, you know." Piallen had been mostly studying how the book was made, but paused on one of the spells. The words looked like ancient shape writing, symbols more than words. Like things explorers found in distant ancient caves.

At first.

As she held the page open, the symbols shifted around until she could read them. She barely refrained from throwing the book. The words in Gliandra's spell most likely had done the same thing, but she was focused on saving lives at that point. Calmly standing in a stable, the effect was far more disturbing. "Are the letters and symbols moving or is it something in my head?"

She shut the book quickly, but kept her thumb on the page she'd been on. Then she flipped it open quickly. "Hmmm. They remained how I saw them." She shut it again, then opened to another page. "Yup, those weird symbols are there...and now I can read it again. It's something in my head I think." She closed the book and looked to Clait. "Are we sure this is a good idea? Maybe something's invaded my brain."

"I don't think so," Clait said. "Your magic has always been odd, and it's only gotten worse as you grew up. I think this is the secret, you were born a wizard. Or with at least wizard-like potential. Had Gliandra not realized that might be the case, no one might have ever known."

Piallen tapped the wizard book in her hand. "And had this Janus person not given her the ancient wizard spell, and had Nevaine not gathered the rock." She nodded. "It was the oracles."

Tobias had gone back to his hay bale. "How did you make that connection?"

"Because the oracles sent both Lizeth and Nevaine on their respective Challenges. I know no one can say anything yet, but what if part of their Challenge was to make sure those two things came my way? Maybe the oracles want me to be a wizard?" She started pacing. "That sounds daft even to me."

"No, that could be part of it." Scruff had appeared to be dozing but was clearly paying attention. "We don't know the mechanics behind the oracles and these Challenges, and I think Clait's theory is sound. Which could mean they are trying to make you a wizard. For some reason."

Piallen wasn't sure how she should feel, but mildly frustrated wasn't it. It was hard to think that someone like herself, whose magic was barely beyond the non-augmented magic level—more generally common—might possibly be a wizard. One of the almost mythological users of the highest levels of magic.

"I'd kind of gotten used to the idea that magic just wouldn't be my thing. I don't need it to be declared third heir."

"No, you hadn't." Tobias gave her a sideways look. "Oh, you made it sound like you were fine with it. But I saw how long you trained in the forest after each magic failure."

Piallen couldn't deny it. "Yes, I was bummed. A family of serious magic users and the baby was a dud." She allowed a bit of the self-pity she usually kept to herself to show. "But if I'm really meant to be a wizard?" A thought hit her and she held up her acorn amulet. "I was a baby when they put this on to keep my magic from leaking. Do any of you know where it came from?" She'd never asked before, just grew up knowing that she could never take it off.

Tobias looked to the other two, then nodded. "Actually, it was gifted to you by Gliandra. It was the first time she met the three of you, but she'd been living in her cottage in our forest for about fifty years or so by that time. She gave little trinkets to your sisters, long since lost. But your parents were already concerned about your magic leaking. She said that amulet could help with that."

"And I believe it did work." Gliandra had quietly opened the stable door and stood there. "Wasn't trying to eavesdrop, but my ears perk up when I hear my name."

She closed the door behind her and went to claim a hay bale. "Now you want to know if I always knew you were meant for wizardry." She shook her head. "Not at all. That acorn you wear was a spelled relic from a long-ago time. I am far older than I look, and no, I won't tell you how old. But when I'd heard that the baby princess was leaking magic, I knew you needed it. And before you ask, no, the items I gave to your sisters were not magical. And also, no, I don't think you should remove it until after you're back from your Challenge. Once you are fully trained, you might find that the magic leak stops automatically. But even if it doesn't you should be able to control it better on your own by then."

Piallen let the amulet drop to her chest. "It did seem to warm, sort of like the stone did, when I cast the wizard spell. Am I going to need that stone in my hand every time I try to do wizardry?" She was grateful for whatever the stone had done to help her connect to the spell, but that was going to be awkward if she had to carry it everywhere.

"I don't think so. Once you start your training, you won't need it."

"Who is going to train me? The wizards are all dead, right?"

"They are. Of that I am certain. But I think the grigeens and myself can cobble together some training for you. Once we get more books, that will help as well." Gliandra's smile faltered a bit. "Okay, you might need to hold on to the stone for a while."

"Can we at least make it smaller?" Piallen took it out of her pocket. It wasn't huge, but was noticeable.

"Hmmm. Not sure. Clait? Do you want to try?"

Clait lashed her tail. "Not sure what I can do." She jumped down and walked over to Piallen.

Piallen leaned down and held the rock closer to her.

"Hello, old man. Not sure if you can hear me from where you've gone. But your stone is helping a very important person. Nevaine's little sister. However, it is a bit large for everyday carrying about. And she will be needing it. She's apparently the first new wizard." She leaned close to the rock as if listening, Piallen couldn't hear anything, but Clait could. She laughed.

"It could be! You did a good thing."

Piallen almost dropped the stone as it shrunk to the size of a pendant and grew a hole in the middle.

"Thank you. Now go back to your rest."

"You spoke to a dead wizard?" Gliandra smiled. "Even I am impressed by that."

"He had been dealing with some issues. And was the one responsible for the grigeens being hidden and coming back. I thought I felt a part of him in the stone." She pointed to her collar. "And he gave me this. I think it helped with the connection."

Piallen held up the rock pendant. "Looks like I'll need another chain."

Gliandra reached around her neck and unclasped a delicate silver chain. "This has no magical abilities—that I know of—but I think it would go nicely with your new stone. It will also hang lower than your acorn amulet. I don't think they'll have trouble with each other, but better to be sure and keep them physically apart. And I'd make sure you have both on when you go for your Challenge."

The rest of the discussion wandered down to things of more interest to the grigeens and Gliandra. Mostly about seasons and the grigeens who were heading further into the Trulan mountains.

Piallen went back to crossbow practice and even switched up to knife throwing. She wasn't as talented at that as Nevaine, but she was better than average, and the workout felt good after the recent stress. After an hour or so, the grigeens bid her farewell as they left to meet with their pack. Gliandra looked at Nevaine's wizard book and pronounced it safe to read. But she again admonished about reading any of the words out loud. At least not unless she intended to use them. Then she, too, left.

The stable seemed lonely after they were gone, so Piallen took the wizard book and went back to the palace. She was crossing the main floor, lost in thought, when yelling came from behind her. It was the stairway down to the former dungeons, where the prisoners were now being held. She ran over to see if she could help when Drubella charged up the stairs, freezing guards as she went and ran after her with one of the guard's swords.

Piallen had put Finnian's sword back on as she returned to the palace so she wouldn't forget to give it to him. She drew it and blocked the attack. Like the guards, everyone around her was frozen.

"You were supposed to be my way into the dark arts circle. I waited on you for a year! The magic leaking princess would have gotten me in! Why don't you freeze so I can kill you now!" Drubella was almost foaming at the mouth, but her swordplay was calm. Whatever else she was, she was an excellent swordswoman.

Piallen thanked whichever amulet was keeping her from freezing under Drubella's spell as she fought back. She didn't want to kill Drubella, they needed to find out what she was talking about, but she might not have a choice. Piallen's advantage of having a longer reach was matched by Drubella's speed.

Everything slowed down after she'd blocked a slice and Piallen feared that Drubella's spell was finally getting her. Then she realized it was a spell thrown by Nevaine and reinforced by a song spell from Lizeth—one so soft it was barely audible. They and their husbands were moving toward her, slowly, but the spells reduced Drubella's movements as well.

Suddenly, Sean sped up, tackled Drubella, and held his hand against the back of her head. Piallen kicked away her sword as she fell and everyone else returned to normal speed.

"Your highness!" The guards from the stairwell came running up along with her parents. "We don't know what happened."

"This one has a strange magic." Sean sat on Drubella but didn't remove his hand from her skull. "We need magical restraints and a spell bag. Whatever she is, she's strong."

Drubella stopped trying to move the moment his hand went to her head, but the look on her face was pure murder.

Two guards came up with a full jacket made of magic-blocking material and Nevaine came forward with a spell bag. "Good thing you kept this." She smiled to Sean then slipped it over Drubella's head as five guards fought to get her into the jacket. Sean didn't let go of her head until she was fully enclosed.

"She was almost too strong for me." Sean shook out his hand but it looked red.

"She wanted to kill me because she failed to get something she thought I could give her." Piallen looked around. "Anyone else want to make sure that dress she made for me is destroyed? Maybe at sea?" She hadn't been fond of the thing and that was before she knew it was made by someone who wanted to destroy her. Who knew what that thing would do?

"Agreed." Her father nodded as he and a group of the strongest mages in the palace came forward.

"We will interrogate her, but it might not do any good." The foremost mage, an older man who mostly kept to himself, nodded to Piallen.

"I understand." Piallen knew that meant this prisoner would be killed if they couldn't gather information. Piallen had no problem killing someone if they were trying to kill her, her family, or innocent people. It was harder to stomach killing someone like this. But the image of fury on Drubella's face as she was pinned by Sean was going to linger in Piallen's mind for a long time.

Chapter Five

Once Drubella had been contained and locked up in a new heavily magically sealed room, Piallen gave Finnian back his sword and wandered back to her room. Her sisters and their husbands were getting things adjusted in their own rooms and the plan was to meet later.

Piallen was not one for napping, but she found herself drawn to it now. Her room was sparse compared to either of her sisters'. She felt more at home outdoors. But right now, shutting her door behind her felt wonderful. She was exhausted. Her front room held a sofa and a huge comfy chair, one that she could tilt back as she liked. She fell into that with a sigh.

One that felt echoed by her jewelry.

She pulled out both amulets. The acorn was short enough to be visible usually, but the longer chain on the stone kept it hidden. The acorn felt cool, but the stone was warm. "Are you in there?" Even though she was alone, she felt odd speaking to a stone. But Clait had spoken to something. "I don't know your name, or rather what your name *had* been when you were alive. But I think you and I are going to be friends." The stone warmed more, but didn't say anything. "You'll warn me if things are about to go wrong, right?" Again, the stone warmed a bit, then cooled back down. "Okay. As long as we understand each other. This wizard business is kind of freaking me out, just so you know." She dropped the amulet back inside her shirt. It had been a long morning, and a nap was called for.

She'd just dozed off, already having an odd dream where she was being chased by giant rocks armed with sewing scissors, when she heard a rap at the door. Or it might have been in her dream, but it woke her up.

Then it came again. Given what had happened that morning, she didn't feel paranoid about grabbing a dagger from her desk before she went to the door. "Who is it?" That wasn't paranoid either.

"Your sisters. Thought we'd come by and see how you are," Lizeth said.

"Why don't you let yourselves in?" Piallen shifted the dagger in her hand and stood ready. It sounded like Lizeth, but there had been a lot of magic going on. Her sisters could use the palm lock. If it was them.

"Really? I'm usually the suspicious one," Nevaine said as the door lock audibly retracted and the door opened.

"Not that I blame you after the events of this morning, but who are you and what have you done with our sister?" Lizeth asked as they both came in.

Piallen put the dagger down and reclaimed her chair. "Sorry, just everything has thrown me for a loop. I thought you two were getting settled?"

"Eh, Finnian can handle it. I was worried about how you are holding up."

"Same, although I think Sean was going to see if he could help with Drubella." Nevaine sat on the sofa.

"I have to say, this entire thing is disturbing. My possibly being a wizard actually more so than being attacked in the palace. By my seamstress, no less." She wasn't sure how much to tell them about Clait's theory, at least not yet. In a few days things might have settled down more.

"That is enough to shock anyone. Wizard. Wow," Lizeth said with a huge grin. "You'll be more powerful than me. Which is kind of wonderful."

"You're not upset? I thought you liked being the most powerful princess in our kingdom." Lizeth had never been snotty about it, but there was no doubt she relished being so strong. But when she'd come back from her Challenge, her spell singing was noticeably weaker—and it took over a year for it to really start coming back. But she'd been okay with it. Whatever she'd done to damage it had been worth the cost in her mind. And, as it was related to her Challenge, she couldn't talk about it to Piallen.

"I did." She shrugged. "But I'm older now and have realized there's more to life than power and plans."

"Besides, being sisters to the first wizard in a thousand years is pretty great," Nevaine said. "Did the spell book make sense? There are other simpler ones coming up from the university. I will warn you, once it gets out that you're a wizard, academics from all over will be coming to ask your advice."

"Yes, it did. I didn't try any spells, but I could read them. You'll protect me from the academics, right?" It wasn't that she didn't like them, but sitting around debating theories was not on her list of enjoyable things. Once it got out that she could read those books, Nevaine was right, she'd be hounded.

"Not a worry. Consider Sean and I your academic defense guards."

The next hour was spent with both Lizeth and Nevaine sharing their adventures of the past two months.

Nevaine's were mostly about research for her final paper and how she and Sean were both happy and sad that they were almost through school. They both would be graduating soon, with doctoral degrees in different magic and sorcery studies.

Lizeth's information was far more interesting. The repatriation of the grigeens was being met with resistance on both human and grigeen fronts. Some of the grigeens were happy to relocate and start new packs, others were less so. The spelled status they'd been in for the last few hundred years was taking longer to mentally work through than anticipated. The original plan had been that they'd all be relocated within the first year. It was nearing the end of year two, but many countries, and grigeens, still weren't sure it was a good idea.

"Oh! I almost forgot. I'm going to have to borrow your stone a bit longer." Talking about the grigeens had made Piallen think of the wizard behind their disappearance and reappearance. She pulled out her amulet to show Nevaine.

"Looks a bit different now." Nevaine reached out for it and smiled. "But it's still the same. Good. I didn't want to leave him behind when we came back, so I'm glad he might help you on your path."

"Who was he? I know you're limited in what you can say about your Challenge until I finish mine. But was he a good person?" Not that she had much of an option if he wasn't, but it would be nice to know.

"I think he was." Nevaine smiled. "He was a wizard, and they were extremely solitary—not that you will be. I think it was just the way they were back then. And I think that was what destroyed them. That stone is also connected to me, since it was my spell that made a connection for the mage and the rock." She grinned. "And that's about all I can say."

Piallen really wanted to know how a long dead wizard came into contact with Nevaine, but, like all the interesting information, it would have to wait.

"Ignoring all that happened today, how are you feeling about your Challenge?" Lizeth's eyes went wide. "Oh, and we need to figure out what you'll wear! Our parents had the dress made by Drubella magically and physically incinerated. Clearly, we'll need a new dress made. You should keep your training leathers on underneath though, those Challenges can be rough."

Piallen leaned back in her chair with a sigh. "I know you and our mother want me to wear a dress, but it's just not me. Maybe the betrayal of Drubella was a sign."

"I told you she didn't want one." Nevaine laughed and nodded to Lizeth. "Lizeth is under some misguided idea that you secretly love dressing up."

"What? Where did that come from?"

"At Nevaine's wedding. You were enjoying the attention, don't deny it. You're stunning no matter what you wear, but a fancy dress? It really got people noticing you."

"That was a year ago and I haven't worn one since. And I felt so uncomfortable it wasn't funny. I have days to worry about my wardrobe." She held up the wizard book. "I think my focus should be on this. What if my becoming a wizard is vital for my Challenge?"

Lizeth shook her head. "And it has nothing to do with wearing a dress. Wizards can dress up too."

"This one won't be. Too bad I don't have a future significant other to go with me on the Challenge though." Piallen knew that would get Lizeth off the dress focus, at least for now.

"Now, I barely knew Finnian existed, maybe there's a secret one out there for you." Lizeth rubbed her hands together. She loved couples, love, and romance.

Piallen started to answer when the room dimmed around her. She blinked her eyes, and everything came back, but both of her sisters were on their feet reaching for her. She couldn't speak and the world dimmed again and then vanished completely.

A moment later, Piallen's vision cleared. She wasn't in her room anymore or even in the palace. She was sitting in a thick forest, and not the one that surrounded her home, and no one was in sight.

"Nevaine? Lizeth?" She knew it wasn't likely that wherever she was, they were with her, but couldn't hurt to try. Silence greeted her as she slowly got to her feet. Her dagger, her sword, and sword belt were near her in the dirt. She felt for her amulets and relaxed when both were there. Had she been taken for her Challenge this early? Five days early? There should be some warning for that kind of thing.

Looking around and listening for any sounds, she put her weapons on.

The wind was strong and masking some noises, but she still heard the stealthy footsteps behind her. She drew her sword and spun around.

A tall, hooded man stood before her with his sword also drawn. "You won't get away with this. I will bring you back to stand trial." He charged forward but Piallen met his move with one of her own. He was a few inches taller than her, but it was hard to tell anything else since he was wearing a bulky cape with a deep hood.

"I have no idea how you brought me here, nor who you think I am, but I haven't done you any wrong. Now send me home." They were well matched, which seemed to surprise the man. His hood fell back, revealing a sharply tapered face, high cheekbones, red hair that dusted past his shoulders, and rich hazel eyes. He'd be stunning if he wasn't in the process of trying to kill her.

"I hadn't heard that you knew how to fight with swords, but if your powers can change what you look like, mayhap they can also give you gifts for the blade that you haven't earned." He darted forward for another strike and again she held her own.

"I don't know what you're talking about, *friend*. But I'm pretty sure I look like I'm supposed to; and I came by this skill with years of hard work. You're the one who brought me here—send me back." She had been staying on the defensive, but wanted to prove her point. Her charge forward was met with equal skill, but confusion marred his handsome face.

"I called the dark witch forward to stand for her crimes. You are her. I call you, Drubella, show yourself!" He waved his free hand in an intricate move.

Piallen felt the spell he cast flow over her, but she couldn't tell what it was or even what type of magic he was using.

"Still me. I'm not sure why your spell grabbed me, but we had a magic user named Drubella—short, tiny thing, strong magic, bad attitude—who recently tried to kill me and my family. She's in a magically shielded cell right now."

They locked swords once more, this time their faces mere inches from each other. His face was expressive, and it went from fury to confusion to hope before they broke apart.

He held his hand up in truce. "You speak the truth. But I have no idea why you were pulled here instead of her. Even if, as you say, she was contained magically. My spell shouldn't have targeted another person. I apologize and will send you back." He sheathed his sword.

Piallen nodded. "Trust me, Drubella will never be free."

His grin took years off his face, to where he looked only a few years older than her. "That is good to hear. There will be many people in my land who will be pleased. Again, I apologize." He waved his hand and a feeling not unlike his prior spell flowed over her. There was a slight shimmer, then nothing.

"I'm still here. Are you sure you're the one who brought me here?" She didn't want to insult him, but his magic didn't seem to be very strong. She didn't think even Lizeth could pull someone from one place to another. This man could fight with a sword, but the magic was lacking.

"Yes. I did. I had a bit of help, but the spell was mine." He closed his eyes and lifted both hands. Dirt and pine needles flew around her and she held onto her sword.

Instead of her leaving, Tobias came slamming into the ground in front of her. Then the wind increased and everything went dark.

Chapter Six

Piallen woke to a solid furry paw patting at the side of her face. She expected to be in the palace, but the farmland around her wasn't at all familiar.

Tobias peering into her face, was. "We have a problem."

"Where are we?" The deep voice just out of her range of vision belonged to her red-headed former opponent.

Piallen had a splitting headache and was just trying to sit up when chimes echoed in her head. *You have begun your Challenge. Be fleet of mind, gentle of foot, and strong of heart. Blessings of the oracles be upon you.*

"No. No, no, no." The words had been in her head, but she still looked around. "You can't do this; I had more time. You need to take it back. Take me back. I'm not ready."

The only people around her were the red-headed swordsman and Tobias. Both looked concerned.

"This is my Challenge? *THIS?*" She knew that the swordsman wouldn't have a clue, but Tobias would.

He nodded with a frown, then looked to the man. "Who's he?"

"I was going to ask the same about both of you and where you brought us."

Piallen dropped her head in her hands. There had to be a way to reach the oracles and change this.

"She's Piallen and I'm Tobias. We're from Astarious. But I can assure you, neither of us did this."

"Astarious? I don't believe I know of that land. I am Kendric and I am the caretaker for the Fleli province in the kingdom of Ceredigion." He leaned down. "Are you a magic cat?"

Piallen laughed as Tobias huffed.

"I am a grigeen. I am not a *cat*." He managed to spit the final word out like a swear word. Piallen knew he actually was fond of cats, but one didn't call grigeens cats.

"Sorry, no idea what a grigeen is, nor where you two are from, nor why your friend was yelling and still looks ready to break something." He kept a few steps back from Piallen but at least didn't have his hand on the hilt of his sword.

"I received some disturbing news; something that wasn't supposed to happen for at least five days, has happened. And you have been pulled into it. And I have no idea where we are." She got up, dusted herself off, and looked around. "Please tell me this land looks familiar to you."

They were definitely in a farmland, that was clear. But the land was divided by large stone walls, not green hedges such as they had in Astarious. Not to mention, the mountains surrounding the farmlands were higher than anything she'd seen or heard of back home.

And, if the voice in her head was to be believed, she was on her Challenge. With a complete stranger from an unknown land. The odds of them being in Astarious were slim. Her only hope was that they were still in Ceredigion, wherever that was, it didn't sound familiar at all, she could get Kendric on his way, and she could get on with this badly timed Challenge.

A breeze ruffled his hair as he scanned the area, then shook his head. "Not at all. Ceredigion is a flat valley, and while we do have farmlands, they aren't like this. Now what exactly is going on? This isn't home to any of us, yet, you're more annoyed than upset."

Piallen looked to Tobias, but he just shrugged. She ran her fingers through her hair, then finally nodded. Keeping things secret might have been a better idea, but for good or ill, this man had been looped into her Challenge. Hopefully the oracles would send him home when it was done.

"Okay, this is going to sound weird, but my name is Princess Pi-allen. I have two older sisters so don't think about kidnapping me, or any crazy idea like that. I'm not important to running the kingdom. All royals must go through a Challenge, a rite as it were, where we get sent somewhere to do something by these mystical people called the oracles. If we survive, we are returned home and are allowed to be counted as heir to the throne. My Challenge was scheduled to start in five days. Earlier today, or whatever day I was in, your friend Drubella—who had been living in our palace and was making my dress for the Challenge ceremony by the way—staged an attempted coup with help from the Northalians and a group of Stiklins." She had been pacing as she talked but turned to look at Kendric as she mentioned the attackers.

He was angry about Drubella. "We know of the Northalians. They are far south of us, but were aggressively trying to spread about a hundred years ago. For the others, do you mean Sticklants? They're an ancient race that were created by the wizards long ago. In the stories my people tell their children. They aren't real."

"Tall, pale, suck out magic?" Piallen nodded when he did. "Yup, they're real. No idea why the oracles pulled you along in this."

"The oracles work in mysterious ways." He gave a small smile. "My sister is one of their priestesses. If they put us here, they had a reason."

Tobias had been cleaning his tail, but turned around. "Your people still worship the oracles? Few countries do anymore."

"We do. Not as we used to; but obviously your land still has a connection to them as well."

"Mostly it's just the royal family, to be honest." Piallen looked past him as a rolling black cloud came swiftly from the furthest mountain. "What's that?" All three royal sisters had extremely good vision, but Piallen's was the best. However, the cloud was traveling so fast, it was within normal eyesight range by the time she asked about it.

"That's a cloud?" Kendric said.

"When have you seen one move that fast? It came from that distant mountain." Piallen felt a chill go up her back at the approaching darkness.

Kendric sent a spell toward it, then started backing up. "That's nothing we want to deal with, head for the trees." He waited until both Piallen and Tobias were ahead of him before following. There wasn't a proper forest here, but the clump of trees they ran to might give some shelter.

If it was possible to hide from a rampaging cloud.

Explosions in the air behind them sounded like lightning, but increased a hundredfold.

Tobias darted ahead of her and stopped. "There's something wrong with that. I can feel it in my fur." He shivered and looked physically ill.

Kendric joined them and looked as ill as Tobias. "It's a wizard cloud. We might not be in my land, but I know those. They were eradicated in most of our kingdom, only the open deserts have them now. Remnants of the wizard wars that almost destroyed us."

"You still have wizards?" Piallen patted Nevaine's wizard book in her inner pocket. She wasn't certain if showing it, and her potential wizardness, was a good thing or not.

"There were two left in the Cyithan mountains. A man and a woman who hated each other, and pretty much everything else. They vanished twenty years ago and their caves were closed off due to the potential danger of anything left behind. Drubella was found hiding in their caves a few years ago, practicing dark arts. She attacked two small villages in the mountains, managing to kill most of the people, before she escaped."

Piallen kept her eyes on the cloud, but it seemed to have slowed down. She doubted it was because they were hiding under the trees. "There were no other wizards?" She'd gotten her hopes up when he mentioned them.

"No. And aside from whatever arts Drubella created, their magic is gone as well. Most of our mages use standard magic; wizardry, and the horrific dark magic Drubella created, isn't used there." He looked her up and down. "You're an excellent fighter, but I'd guess you have some magic of your own to have survived against her."

"I have some talent." She forced a smile. Bringing up the wizardry issue wasn't going to happen for a while. Kendric obviously wasn't a big fan of wizards.

"Why is it sitting there?" Tobias had stayed closer to the edge of the trees while he watched the cloud, but his tail was lashing. "It makes my skin crawl."

"Not sure why it's not moving now, but it's foul wizardry that you're feeling. When it goes bad, other magic users sense it." Kendric studied the still cloud.

"So that cloud is the remains of wizard magic gone bad, and it's smart enough to hunt us? How do we stop it?" Another thing Piallen would be avoiding mentioning—she didn't feel anything about the cloud at this point. She'd felt a chill when she first saw it, but that left quickly. But she didn't think that going out into the fields right now would be a good idea.

"I've never heard of them hunting people with clouds, but they have killed people before. Our kingdom was the site of many wizard battles a few hundred years ago. The guard mages were formed, and with the help of those two wizards who hated what their people were doing, stopped them. Actually, the rest of the wizards eventually destroyed themselves, with our help. Solange and Hilth, the wizards who lived in the mountains, helped protect everyone else from them. Those were the two who vanished twenty years ago."

Piallen squinted her eyes and tried to figure out if there was any-thing she could tell or feel from the cloud. Not a single thing. "We don't even know where we are. I know this isn't my kingdom, but could this be part of yours? Maybe a place far from you?" Finding where they were would be the first thing to do after this cloud took off.

Kendric looked out over the rolling farms and high mountains. "No. I've done some traveling within my country during my mage training; this isn't home."

"It doesn't feel like any place where my people have been." Tobias looked sad and worried as he glanced over. Neither look was some-thing common to him. The fact that grigeens had never been here wasn't good.

Piallen was about to take out the wizard book and hope there was something to chase off that cloud—if it upset Kendric, so be it. It wasn't moving now, but kept sending out nasty lightning strikes. Anything it hit burned immediately.

The cloud darted closer to their clump of trees, but before any-one could react, it turned and vanished back over the mountains.

"Was that normal?" Tobias turned to Kendric. "I felt like it sniffed us."

"And, what? Decided we were too dangerous to attack? I doubt that." Piallen's chill came back, but it wasn't at the cloud. She also felt like it had been sensing them. Or rather, *her*. There was a spark of almost recognition before the cloud vanished. Finding out that she was a wizard, or at least had the ability to become one, and seeing what they left behind were massively different things. She was having serious second thoughts about it.

"I'm not sure, but I'm glad it left. We'll need to find supplies and shelter until we figure out how we get to our homes. Am I right in thinking this isn't normal for that thing you were supposed to be do-ing?" Kendric asked. "Maybe this isn't even it."

"No, this isn't normal. At least I don't think it is. Unfortunately, people who have gone through the Challenge can't speak of it to anyone who hasn't gone through it. But I heard a distinctive voice in my head when we arrived. It spoke words I've seen in some older journals. This is, or should be, my Challenge." She wished she knew why the oracles had pulled in Kendric. Yes, both of her sisters ended up meeting their husbands on theirs, but he wasn't from Astarious and was from somewhere so far away she didn't even recognize the name of the kingdom.

Long distance marriages probably weren't what the oracles had in mind. Which meant they pulled him along for another reason. While she welcomed the help, she didn't think that someone who appeared to justifiably hate wizards was a good choice to work with her.

"So, they just grab people and toss them somewhere and let them sort it out? The oracles my sister follows are less hands on, but kinder." He started looking around. "These woods aren't at all like home, we need a better place to sort things out."

"Ours either. But I agree on finding better shelter and figure out what we do next." She stood and listened. With all the time she spent outdoors, listening to the woods was second nature and one she welcomed after the stresses of the day. She finally pointed toward the north. "I think we might find something that way. It's close to sunset, so shelter first, then food."

"Watch out!" Tobias yelled and grabbed her legs to tackle her as something large flew by. He didn't pull her completely down, but did get her to duck.

Kendric wasn't as lucky.

Chapter Seven

Three packs, two large and one small, slammed into Kendric, bowling him over. Piallen was impressed at how quickly he jumped to his feet and looked ready to magically blow apart whoever was attacking. Even Nevaine's battlemage husband Sean would have been impressed.

"I seriously doubt that is normal." Tobias sniffed at the smallest pack. "Can you imagine either of your sisters having to dodge their packs?"

"Someone threw these at us? From where?" Kendric now had his sword out and his fingers curved for a spell. Whatever magic he used appeared to be a combination of magic and sorcery.

"If I'm right, the oracles. They provide supplies so that the Challenge isn't basic survival based—at least not food and water." Piallen opened the first bag. Food, water bags, and some of her clothing. Plus, a slim pair of books that she'd never seen before. A quick peek showed their pages to be like the one Nevaine gave her, but the covers were like regular books, not the odd wood type of Nevaine's book. She buried them under the clothing. "That pack should be for you. If you were supposed to be here." The fact that there was a third one was interesting. The fact that they'd been forcibly flung at them was disturbing.

Kendric scowled, but put away his sword, released the spell, and picked up the pack. "I don't see how even the oracles could have brought me into this." Shaking his head, he pulled out the same food and water she had. Then he froze as he pulled out a shirt. "This is mine. It was in my cabin back home. And these are my daggers. The rest of the clothing is mine as well. How did they do this?"

Piallen shrugged. "Ask your sister the priestess when you get back. But it does tell us that you're supposed to be here. And that Tobias better not go for that third pear." Grigeens loved fruit but Tobias' favorite were pears. Clearly the oracles had helped secure him some and he had been munching since he opened his pack.

He dropped the pear he was about to bite into back in his pack. "I've been through trauma. Not to mention that they gave me Clait's collar, even though I told her I didn't need it. She better not blame me that its missing. It's too small for me." He then looked past her into the forest. "What's that?"

Piallen turned to see a familiar looking bow sticking out from behind a tree. She ran over to find her bow and a full quiver of arrows behind the tree. "I'm glad they didn't throw these, and I'm glad to have them."

"You're an archer and a swordswoman?" Kendric looked suitably impressed.

"She's the best archer in our kingdom. And one of the best swordspeople in the land." Tobias was now snacking on a piece of travel bread.

Piallen tested the string on her bow. However the oracles had gotten it here hadn't damaged anything. "Okay, unless they want to give us something else, I think we'll go that way." She looked up into the treetops while pointing toward the north— it still felt right. She had no idea what all the oracles could or couldn't do on a Challenge.

But the fact that some Challengers came back broken in mind and body, or didn't come back at all, indicated that the oracles' control over the situation was limited.

"I don't think they have anything more to add." Tobias had tucked away his food and shimmied into his pack. He looked quite comfortable in it.

She shrugged and put on her pack with her bow and quiver over it.

Kendric nodded and put on his pack. "I still am not sure what is going on, but I don't argue with mystical beings who tossed me into a foreign land and can pull my belongings to me. Even if they were a bit rough with getting them here." He gave a smile and a half bow and motioned toward the trail. "Lead the way, *Princess* Piallen."

Piallen felt herself blush at the way he said her name. She needed to put that thought out of her mind immediately. Yes, he was handsome, extremely so if she were honest. But he was from some distant land and hated wizards. That was not going to be a relationship that worked. Besides, he might have a wife and five kids back home.

The trees grew thicker as she made her way up the trail. There were a few diverging paths, like the one they were on, and all were slightly overrun with tree roots and bushes. But with a pause at each split, she felt the direction to go.

"And an expert woodswoman. Are all the princesses in your kingdom so multi-talented?" There was no judgement in Kendric's voice—her last boyfriend had looked down on spending time in the forest. That should have been her first clue he 'wasn't worth the gravy' as old Margie from the kitchen would say.

"Actually, yes. I have two sisters, both extremely talented. We're all different, but we each have our skills." She dodged around a tree root. "What about you? Any other siblings besides your priestess sister?" She hadn't thought that she'd be getting to know a random handsome stranger on her Challenge, but it did look like he was along for the trip. At least for now.

"I have two younger brothers. They'll be good guys once they grow up a bit."

"And I believe that is what you are looking for?" Tobias had stayed near Piallen but ran ahead as a hill came into view. More importantly, a small cave in the side of the hill. Tobias darted inside before Piallen could say anything, then came racing out. "Run! Fox-spiders!" He spun around as soon as he got past Piallen and Kendric, claws extended and teeth bared. His tail was massively poofed.

"Fox, what?" Piallen drew her sword, but had no idea what Tobias was chittering about.

"Fox-spiders! Don't you remember those awful fairy tales Lizeth would tell you and Nevaine once she started to read? Until your mother took the book away from her?" He paused as nothing came out of the small cave mouth. "I swear that's what was in there. Three giant, creepy, fox-spiders."

"If you two don't mind, might I check?" Kendric took off his pack. The entrance to the cave was a good size for Tobias, but not for Kendric or Piallen. He'd have to crawl to get in.

Piallen wasn't a huge fan of small places, so she nodded. There were a lot of things she did well; she wasn't going to worry about the things she didn't.

"I didn't make it up. They were just like your sister's stories. Eight legs, fur, fangs. Bigger than me." Tobias shuddered and Piallen picked him up.

"I believe you. I don't remember them, but you wouldn't make something up like that."

A yell and sound of fighting from inside the cave cut her off. She put down Tobias and ran to the cave. "Kendric! Answer me!"

"No spiders but I'm being attacked by bats—killer bats!"

Piallen reached out with her magic; it wasn't strong, but she could usually detect other magics being used. "There's a really weird magic coming from that place. Did you ever get frightened by bats?"

"No! Wait, yes. When I was five." Kendric let out a loud breath. "And these aren't real." He crawled back out. "Nice defense this place has. Once you pointed it out, I felt the nightmare spell. It's old, but focuses people's fears so they run away. By the way, the place opens up nicely inside so there's plenty of room to stand."

Tobias lashed his tail, then shrugged. "Annoying, but those spells are often used when there is something to protect. How do we keep it from happening again? I can't sleep if I have to keep telling myself fox-spiders aren't real all night long."

Kendric nodded. "Not to mention that I've heard of these nightmare spells, and they can pick up on something else you fear if you work your terror out for the original item. I say we find somewhere else to stay."

Piallen looked around. The mountains were still quite a way off and anything else nearby looked to be just roughing it on the forest floor. "With none of us knowing where we are, or what we're facing, outside might be more of a threat than inside. But we need a way to hold the spell off."

"Maybe we could camp out here and only go inside if we need to?" Tobias wasn't happy about those fox-spiders, even if they hadn't been real.

Piallen ruffled his fur, then set him down. "The point of staying inside the cave would be to hopefully keep any predators, on two legs or four, from knowing we're here. It would be better to be inside if possible."

"I can mask our entrance into the cave so it won't be visible to anything passing by, but I'm not sure if my spell will hold against that nightmare spell." Kendric didn't look afraid to spend the night there, but Piallen wasn't sure how things would work out for her and Tobias. She also didn't know what dark terrors the spell would drag out of her, and she didn't think she wanted to find out.

Her own words were true, though. Especially if he could make it less noticeable that they'd gone inside. She sniffed the air then walked closer to the cave mouth. "Did either of you notice any scents of animal droppings?" That could call this entire thing off.

Both shrugged.

"I was busy." Tobias scowled and his paw twitched toward his pack.

"I could go back and check." Kendric offered.

Piallen shook her head. "I should be the one. I don't smell anything around here and most animals mark their territory. But it would be bad if we set up camp in there and someone large, furry, and not in our heads, came home." She took off her bow, quiver, and pack, took a deep breath, then crawled inside. The entrance opened to at least a few feet taller than her almost six-foot-tall height immediately. She called up a light spell that she'd leaned from Nevaine, a slender rod that worked to illuminate larger areas. She felt a slight warming from her acorn amulet, but the light bar held.

There was a painting on the walls. Old, but still done well. A hunt of a deep russet colored stag with heavily clad men and women following on horseback. More of what one would see on a tapestry than inside an obscure cave.

"Piallen? Are you okay?" Kendric's voice seemed to echo as if he was far away and not just outside the cave mouth.

She blinked. "Yeah, sorry, I got distracted. There's a painting on the wall in here." She sniffed a bit. "No smell of wild animals though."

"And no fox-spiders or bats?" Tobias also sounded further away than he should be.

Piallen had been moving closer to the painting and pulled back with a start. "Not a single one." To be honest, she'd been focusing on the painting and forgot about the spell on the cave. She pulled the wizard stone necklace out from her shirt. It was glowing slightly. Very faint and hopefully Kendric wouldn't notice once it was hidden again. But she had a feeling the stone was blocking the nightmare spell tied to this cave. Hopefully, it would block it for all three of them.

Tobias stuck his head in, but looked ready to run out if needed. His nose twitched with each forward step, but then he was inside the cave. "I don't see any fox-spiders." He motioned to the stone with his paw but didn't say anything.

Piallen gave a half shrug-half nod then dropped it back under her shirt. "I think the shielding spell connected to my light spell is blocking it." As she spoke, she also released her shield spell. It was mostly to block light, and would keep the light from leaving the cave mouth, but it would also work as an excuse as to what happened to the night-mare spell. Hopefully.

Kendric crawled in and looked around. "Shielding spell? Interesting idea, but it seems to be working, I'm not sensing any bats or anything else. Stay there, I'll push in our packs." First Tobias's pack, hers next, then his all came through the crawl space, followed by Kendric himself.

"That really is amazing." He walked to the wall with the painting. "And familiar. There's a tapestry back home that this reminds me of. It's a lot larger though. The detail..." His pause lingered as he froze in front of the painting.

Piallen had to shake his shoulder twice before he stepped back. "It did that, sort of, to me too. I don't think any of us should look at it for any length of time. I take it that the one back home doesn't do that?"

"Not that I've heard of." Kendric rubbed his eyes and took a few more steps back. "It hangs in the main audience chamber of the royal castle. It would probably be noticeable if it stunned people who came to gain an audience with the king."

"Why would this be here if it's like one in his land?" Tobias scowled at the painting. "It doesn't seem to affect me though."

Piallen looked down at him. "You're too short. I'd say there's a trigger for whatever spell this thing is doing that is aimed at a taller victim. It might be connected to that nightmare spell, or something completely separate."

"I don't suggest we test it to find out. I'm as curious about magic and spells as the next mage, but not inside a cave that we might need to stay in." Kendric moved his pack away from the painted wall and set some of his own magic lights. Between those and Piallen's light bar, the cave looked almost cheery.

She gave the painting one more glance, but it didn't pull at her as it did when she first came in—nor how it had pulled Kendric. But she wanted to know what it was doing and why. And also why, according to Kendric, it was the same as a tapestry in the castle back in his homeland.

However, sometimes answers couldn't be found. At least not now. It was a good thing this hadn't been Nevaine's Challenge, she would have taken the cave apart trying to figure out what the painting was doing and why. Piallen was better at holding off curiosity for survival.

They set up bedrolls around a pile of the small magic lights that Kendric created. It almost felt like being around a fire, without the risk. Luckily the food in their packs was all travel rations and didn't need to be cooked. Not exciting, but sustainable. When she was sixteen, and Lizeth had just vanished on her Challenge, Piallen had taken a pack of food and water and gone to live off the land for a week.

She'd left a message for her parents, and she hadn't gone far, but they were still furious when she was finally found. After they calmed down, they admitted they were also impressed that she'd hidden that well. It didn't stop them from grounding her for a week.

Kendric was putting his food back when he started swearing. "This just refilled." He held up the water bag. "I was just wondering how I'd find a stream to refill it before we headed out tomorrow and it just...filled." His sharp face showed an interesting cross of curiosity and wanting to throw the bag. He eventually shrugged and put it back in his pack.

"Really? I'd heard of that, vaguely." Tobias shook his paw as he dove into his pack. "More pears! The food refills too!"

"That doesn't mean you need to eat all of the pears they give you. You probably have some jerky in there too." Piallen knew what too much fruit did to her little friend, and this wasn't the place or time for it.

"Fine." Tobias gave a long-suffering sigh and bit into a piece of dried meat. "Fish!" He crammed the entire piece in his mouth and started purring as he chewed.

"Dried fish?" Kendric looked in his pack and tried a piece. "Odd, but tasty. So, they provide magically refilling water and food, but no clue as to what you're supposed to do or where we are? Not to mention grabbing strangers to join you?"

"Sounds weird when you put it that way, but yeah." Piallen finished her food and looked around the cave. Aside from the painting on the one wall, there was nothing to indicate prior residence of animals or people. Nor anything of any real interest.

She'd grown up in a palace where she knew everyone except visiting nobles. And she usually avoided those by staying outside. Small talk with a stranger wasn't one of her gifts. Had Lizeth been here, she would have already had Kendric's entire life history, full list of likes and dislikes, and his family names back to his great-grandparents. Unfortunately, that wasn't Piallen's way. She sighed and looked through her pack again. She really wanted to look at those two new books, but she had a bad feeling they were wizardry ones. If Kendric was with them for a reason, she didn't want to mess that up by annoying him.

"What was the sigh for?" Tobias had built a nest out of blankets next to her and finally stopped eating.

"Just thinking how Lizeth might handle things. Or even Nevaine." Nevaine wasn't near as social as Lizeth, but she was more comfortable with it after two years of higher education and lots of mingling.

"Eh, they sometimes wish they were more like you." Tobias adjusted his nest. "You're all different. It's fine."

"Those are your sisters' names?" Kendric smiled at her nod. "My brothers are Rhys and Donall. Rhys is nine going on eighty—never seen someone so cranky at such a young age. Donall is sixteen. Quiet, bookish, a good kid." The affection for his brothers was clear.

"So, just what does a guard mage do? We have battlemages, more of a specific fighting magic training program. They're sort of a military trained spell user."

"That's close to ours. The guard mages are specialized in spells that protect and defend. They also go out on travels through the land acting as roaming rangers. I was just a few months short of finishing my first tour when Drubella attacked."

"Will you be able to finish when you get back?" Piallen asked.

"Hopefully. Our ranger days, as they're called, are overseen by the king. Once completed we're given a special status. Maybe they'll count this toward my time. Although it would be better if I could bring in Drubella."

"There might not be anything to bring in but her body. Her attacks were such that my parents might order her execution. I'm still trying to figure out why I got pulled through when you called for her, though. Only the oracles can move people around like that in my land."

"You said she had been your seamstress?" He got up. "Maybe she tagged you with something while fitting a piece of clothing. A magical marker to make you appear as her—magically. The spell I used to pull you to me isn't common, nor easy to do. But she would have known of it, even if it was outside of her abilities." He motioned for her to stand. "Let me see if I can pick up if she tagged you with something."

Piallen stood but she'd never heard of a spell that could make someone else appear magically as another. But it was clear that whatever land Ceredigion was, it had a different type of magic than what she was used to. It had to be very far away for it not to have ever been included in her diplomatic lessons. She'd never even heard of it.

Kendric stepped right in front of her and closed his eyes. His left hand slowly raised and moved across her but stayed inches above her. He paused near her amulets.

"I have a magic leak; the amulet helps with that." Piallen was glad his eyes were closed; she didn't lie well. And it was only a partial lie anyway—more of an omission.

He nodded and kept going. Then he did her left side and back. When he got to her right side, he froze. "It's on your right shoulder. Damn she's good. Normally a marker like that would be noticeable to the victim when placed. Let me guess, she kept you distracted?"

Piallen thought of how annoyed she'd been at the dress, and how fast Drubella had darted around her while fitting it. "Yes. Their attack must have been planned in advance and she wanted to make sure no one from your kingdom could grab her. I get why she fled your land if everyone was after her. But she'd been in my country for a year. How was she in both places?"

"That's a good question. The last attack she made was three months ago. I was called back, but it took a while for the information to get to me. She hasn't been seen since then."

"Three months ago?" Tobias had looked asleep but was now sitting up. "Wasn't that when she went to visit her sick aunt? Or was that her dying uncle?"

Piallen shook her head. "I didn't pay much attention to her until two months ago when she started that horrible dress. Can you get her marker off of me?" She wanted to know why Drubella picked Astarious to attack, or maybe she was hired by someone, but the skin-crawling feeling once Kendric pointed out the marker was getting worse.

"I should be able to." Kendric stepped back, said a few words under his breath, and then held his left hand up over her shoulder.

"It's burning!" Piallen grabbed his hand to stop him.

"It shouldn't do that." He glared at the invisible marker on her shoulder. "My spell is being blocked. Do you have any type of protection spells on you?"

"Not that I know of." She let out a breath. The pain had been sharp but vanished once his hand moved away. "Try again." She tried to mentally communicate with the wizard stone. If it was trying to protect her, this wasn't the time.

He tilted his head, then shrugged and stepped forward again. The pain was lesser this time but still there.

"Stop."

He stepped back without her grabbing him this time. "I'm going to have to work on something else. The good news is that unless someone does the same spell I originally did, and there are very few who can do it, no one should be able to grab you again."

Piallen rubbed her shoulder and sat back down. "Thank you for trying. I'm even more grateful that the dress she made was destroyed."

"That was good thinking. I didn't pick up on any other markers from her, but she would have put something in the dress."

"Which would indicate she was planning on me wearing it. Yet the attack she was a part of, and might have been leading, was five days before the event where I'd have worn it."

"There could have been multiple plans," Tobias said.

"I think there were," Kendric said. "Drubella is evil, but also extremely smart. I hope your family is vigilant. She won't be easy to destroy, even if she's currently captured and magically bound. The wizard information she stole from the home of Solange and Hilth have made her deadly." He shook his head. "Even though Solange and Hilth once helped my people, anything to do with wizards isn't to be trusted."

Chapter Eight

The conversation drifted off at that point and Kendric lowered his lights. Tobias curled back into a ball and was quickly snoring. Piallen was thinking of what might be happening with her family if Drubella really was that dangerous, and she had no idea what Kendric was thinking. He was unmistakably good looking, but he looked like the troubles of the world were floating around behind those hazel eyes.

She'd drifted off as he stared contemplatively into the pile of mage lights that he'd dimmed. She thought about telling him to rest, this cave was safe, but she doubted he'd listen.

The enticing smell of breakfast brought her out of a sound sleep. Cooked breakfast. Neither Tobias nor Kendric was in the cave, and the magical glows were gone. She'd released her light bar spell when she went to sleep, but there was enough light coming in from the cave opening to see.

She got out of her bedroll and went out to see how they were making a hot breakfast from fruit, jerky, and travel bread.

The fire wasn't surprising; the cooking equipment, including a heavy skillet nestled comfortably on rocks over the fire, was. Tobias was focused on the food and almost drooling. There looked to be eggs, mushrooms, tomatoes, and some sort of sausage.

None of which had been in their packs. She hadn't gone through the pack Kendric had, but perishables would have been noticeable.

"There's enough for all of us. Even some toasted bread, and look, tea!" Tobias was almost jumping in excitement as he pointed to the battered metal teakettle on the stones near the fire.

"How...where did this come from?" Her stomach took that moment to rumble at the wonderful smells. She'd always eaten more than her sisters, or most people. Just a fast metabolism. Or maybe *wizards* burned through a lot of food—she'd have to look into that when she got home.

Kendric pushed the eggs around a bit before looking up. "I woke up early. Once Tobias was awake as well, I went to see what is around us. There's a small homestead and farms not more than a half hour to the north. Not terribly friendly folks, but I was able to buy supplies off of one with a gold blank." He nodded to a new pack behind them. "We can divide the new supplies after we eat."

"A gold what?" Piallen's attention was really focused on the wonderful food. Access to food other than the travel provisions they'd been given would go far to make her life better.

"A gold blank." He set down his spatula, reached into his pocket, and tossed her a small gold coin. One without any country, ruler, or denomination. "We use these when we travel to avoid any issues with people outside of our kingdom. The farmer was suspicious at first, but after he tested the coin, he gave me all that I wanted." He laughed. "He got the much better of the deal."

"That's actually brilliant. And would probably be a good idea for future royals in Astarious who have to go on a Challenge. There's no rule against buying things, but since the Challenges are usually not in our land—that would be an issue." She tossed the coin back to him and he got her a beat-up tin cup of tea.

"Nothing is fancy, but it'll work." He pulled out three battered tin plates and divided the food, adding a piece of toast to each before handing them over.

"Do all of your guard mages know how to cook like this?" Piallen got out after her first bite. It could be that she was just exceedingly hungry, but everything tasted amazing.

Kendric's laugh was a good one. Piallen always said you could tell a lot by a man's laugh—and Kendric's was relaxed and honest. "My brothers hate my cooking. But after almost a year on the trail, I had to step up my game, just for myself."

"That's tasty food there." Tobias had already cleaned his plate and was chewing on a pear. "Glad you came along. She can't cook." He grinned at her as he said it.

Piallen shrugged. "It's true. I am fond of eating, almost as much as Tobias, but my kitchen skills aren't great. Lizeth is the only one of the three of us who even tried cooking. But she got bored after a few months."

"I like seeing people enjoying my food. My brothers aside, I sort of wish I could go into the restaurant business after my training is done. They don't need guard mages to be constantly waiting for something to happen—we get lives. But we promise to protect when needed."

"So why can't you?"

"Family business. I'm obligated to go into it when I'm finished with my training and route. What about you? Do princesses in your land get a say in what they do?" There was a wistfulness in his voice. Clearly he wasn't looking forward to whatever life had planned for him.

"Luckily, yes. Well, within reason. This Challenge is just to prove I'm able to be counted as heir. But with two older sisters already confirmed, I'm mostly able to follow what I want to do."

"Does the eldest rule once your parents are gone, and you two are the extras?"

"If all three of us are declared heirs, we could divide the kingdom once our parents pass on. Or just have the other two and their husbands rule how they want, and I'll go live in a forest."

Tobias snorted as he drank tea out of the flat bowl from his pack. "That's what I'm afraid of—she'll go feral on us."

Piallen watched him, then shook her head. "Not that I'm complaining, but most grigeens leave when the royal they're assigned to is fifteen."

"And when you turned fifteen, I did leave, just as Scruff and Clait did. Then when things in the world got weird, we all came back." He gave a shrug. "It appeared that you needed me. Us."

"I was just teasing you. I'm grateful that you and the rest of them hang around more. I like you being in my life. And seeing more grigeens in the palace."

Tobias smiled. "Good to hear."

"Did you get any clue from that farmer as to where we are?" She knew asking the farmer directly would probably raise suspicion, especially if they weren't near any borders.

"Not at all." Kendric shrugged. "He could have been a farmer in any land. But he did say there was a town no more than four hours walking up the road, that might be a place to start."

"Four hours?" Tobias' eyes went round. He wasn't quite as lazy as Scruff, but he definitely enjoyed lounging. Racing through trees with Piallen was one thing, but from the look on his face, trudging on a path for four hours was not the same at all.

"You can ride on my pack if you get tired." Piallen had heard comments about Scruff riding on Lizeth's pack during much of her Challenge, and from the grin on his face, Tobias knew that as well.

"We can take turns, if you get tired he can ride with me." Kendric gave a small bow to Tobias. "I'm saddened that my land doesn't have your people in it, we are the poorer for that loss."

Tobias lifted his head proudly.

Piallen narrowed her eyes. Kendric's speech was normally plain, but that had more of a ring of nobility to it. She couldn't figure out why he wouldn't claim to be royal or noble if he was though—especially after he found out she was a princess. She wouldn't pry, but she would keep an eye, and ear, out on him.

Once the food was finished and the dishes cleaned, using their refilling water bottles, they went to get their packs. Kendric tried to get Piallen to leave the cave before him, but since she was fairly certain that it was her wizard stone blocking that nightmare spell, she declined.

He took one more look at the painting. "I still wish I knew the story behind this and why it looks like the one they keep in the castle back home."

"Maybe when you get home you can find your answers there." She watched him as he looked at the painting. If he started looking stuck, she was grabbing him.

He shook his head and left.

When she came out, he'd divided the extra supplies and put his pack back on. He also pulled up his hood.

"Why do you wear a hood?" Tobias beat her to the question.

"This red hair is too noticeable in the woods. You're dark and blend in. Piallen's hair is lovely, but also dark, and better suited to dark forest areas. My hair isn't extremely bright, but it's too noticeable." He smiled then tugged his hood a bit lower.

Piallen glanced to Tobias and he shrugged. Yes, Kendric's red hair would be more noticeable than her own, but not enough to make a difference. Not to mention, he'd had his hood up when she met him and while they were in the woods, he wasn't trying to stay hidden as he attacked her.

"Lead on." She motioned toward the trail. Yes, this was her Challenge and once she had a clue as to what she was supposed to do to resolve it, she would do so.

First, they needed to figure out where they were.

For all of his worry about traveling, Tobias kept up easily and seemed to enjoy veering off the path to investigate an odd flower or shrub, then bouncing back to her side. He never went out of eyesight and, while grigeens looked like adorable bundles of fluff, they could hold their own against animals far larger than themselves.

They did stop at a pond fed by a wide stream. Rather, Piallen made them stop. She was used to roughing it, but she was self-conscious being around Kendric. True, there was no way he could be a romantic interest, but it was still uncomfortable to be wearing yesterday's clothes. That she slept in. Especially when she had clean clothes in her pack.

They went in shifts, even Tobias took some time to play in the water, even though he mostly cleaned his fur like a cat. Then, refreshed and changed, they continued on.

Even after changing clothes, Kendric still wore the same cloak over them and kept his hood pulled up. Piallen made a mental note. Affectations usually started for a reason—or so Nevaine always said when as girls they used to run around looking for mysteries among the palace staff. He was wearing it for more than simply covering an unusual hair color.

They'd been walking for two hours and still no sign of outlying farms that might be surrounding a town or village. She was starting to wonder if there was anything out there, when an arrow shot to the left of her head.

"Stand where you are." The voice was female and had a rough edge to it.

Kendric froze and raised both of his hands to show they were empty. Not that it meant much with a magic user. Piallen did the same. Tobias was nowhere to be seen. Hopefully he'd ducked into a shrub and not been grabbed.

Piallen slowly turned around. "Wouldn't warning us before you tried to shoot me in the head have been more sporting?"

There were six people behind them. All, except the woman in the front, were wearing dark hoods similar to Kendric's. The woman stood a few feet in front of the rest and her bow was almost as long as Piallen's legs. She had long dirty blond hair on her right side. The left side of her face and scalp was scarred and hairless. She snarled. "Get your man to turn around and pull back his hood or I'll drop him where he stands. And don't think of reaching for your swords, either of you."

She was dressed in mostly dark browns and green—same with the three men and two women standing a bit behind her. All of them had small silver pendants over their clothing.

Even with her eyesight, Piallen couldn't see them well, but she thought they looked like the fake magical protectors sold by some Northalian vendors when she was young—before that kingdom decided to cause problems with Astarious. Lizeth had scoffed at the collection when they went to the market, and with a light spell song she turned over the cart holding them.

If these were the same, they wouldn't protect anyone from spells.

She heard Kendric slowly turn behind her and judging by the way the woman's eyes narrowed, he'd dropped his hood. "You're too pretty to be out traveling about. Maybe I won't kill you yet."

"What do you want? You have us at a disadvantage." Piallen tried putting a combination of Lizeth's imperiousness and Nevaine's snark in her voice. She also mentally went through the wizard spell Gliandra had given her. Since they weren't touching her, and she wasn't sure how else to control it, she'd also knock out Kendric and Tobias. But she might not have a choice.

"You're pretty too. I bet we could get a lot of coin for the two of you."

"What do you want?" Kendric managed to sound bored. "You attacked us long before you decided we were pretty."

"Your coin, your gear, your weapons. You both. Standard. And if you two are magic users, don't even think of it. These work." The woman held out her pendant and a light flicked across it.

Kendric took a step forward. "Nice. Did you get those at a fair with candy included?"

Piallen heard him take another step, mutter some words, and a blast of light came from behind her and hit all six pendants. Their attackers stumbled back, but none fell.

Not good.

"You're not worth as much at the markets if you're damaged. Now, stand down and toss us your gear." The woman didn't look as cocky as before and all five of them were rubbing where the pendants sat on their chests. Kendric's spell hadn't disabled them, but it had done something.

Piallen had no intention of becoming a robbery victim, or anything else, but she didn't trust the wizard spell, especially without pulling it out to review. She'd figure something else out.

"Look what I found!" One of the men dove into a bush and came back holding Tobias by the scruff of his neck. "Bet we could get a lot of coin for this one—alive or dead."

Piallen didn't think, she just spoke the words for the wizardry spell, made the finger movements, and released it.

The pendants on all six attackers exploded, the people collapsed, and she heard Kendric swear then collapse as well. Piallen ran to Tobias and pulled him free of the fallen attacker.

"Are you okay?" At her touch, Tobias twitched and then opened his eyes.

"I am now. Thought I was hiding well enough." He dropped his voice and looked around. "You did the one from the palace that I heard about?"

"I did, but we shouldn't talk about it." She and he ran to Kendric. He actually looked like he'd started to draw his sword when he fell. He should have fallen immediately. It said a lot of his own magical ability that he was able to fight back against the spell, even briefly.

She touched his hand and jumped back as his movement with his sword continued.

"I! Wait, what happened?" He got to his feet and sheathed his sword. "You killed them all?"

Piallen shrugged and turned the leader over with a stick. So far it had seemed that it took skin on skin/fur contact to break her wizard spell, but now wasn't the time to test that. There was damage where the pendant exploded, but the woman was only unconscious.

"I think they're still alive."

Kendric nodded then started patting them all down and taking their coins and weapons.

"That's thievery." Tobias didn't sound concerned, just making a statement.

"That's fair payment for attacking us." He looked over to Piallen. "I know that I didn't do that spell, my magic was blocked by those pendants."

"My magic is different. We had Northalian vendors selling those trinkets in the market when I was a kid." She shrugged. "They didn't block magic in my kingdom. Probably just a difference between our magical styles." She held her breath and smiled. Lying was not one of her strong points.

He watched her, then moved on and picked the pockets of the rest of the gang. He divided the knives and daggers and put the swords in a pile. Then he held up the longbow the woman had. "Do you mind if I keep this? You have one already."

"Fine by me. Are we just leaving them here with their swords?" Piallen's heart had raced as she cast the wizard spell this time, and it still wasn't slowing down. Her acorn amulet also felt a lot warmer than usual. Neither had happened when she cast the spell the first time. She might have remembered it a bit off but she hadn't had time to pull it out and read it.

"Nope." Kendric reached for a coil of rope that he'd had at his side. "I'd intended this to hold Drubella, but it will work on them. I don't kill unless I have to, but we also can't leave them free behind us." He quickly nudged the people together and bound them hand and foot.

Tobias went to the one who'd grabbed him and kicked his hind legs, flinging dirt and leaves on the unconscious man. A sign of serious disrespect from a grigeen.

Piallen stood back as Kendric tested his ties, then turned to the swords. His spell called forth something in the back of Piallen's mind, but she wasn't sure what. The swords flashed brightly, then vanished. Or so it looked. A pile of twigs was left in their place.

"What did you just do? Where are the swords?" Transformational magic was nothing more than a theory. At least anymore. There were fairytales of it happening long ago in some distant kingdom, but nothing real. As far as she knew anyway.

"They're right there." He smiled and pointed to the twigs. "I take it your magic can't do that? We might have much to learn from each other."

Piallen nodded. She didn't want to upset him with the wizard magic issue but there was a good chance that she could pass it off as just a difference between their magics. As long as this Challenge didn't go on too long. She sighed.

"What was that look for?" Kendric pulled his hood back up and returned to the trail.

"I was just thinking that it's been a day and I still have no idea what my Challenge is."

"Piallen isn't known for patience." Tobias jogged between them. He acted like being grabbed by that man hadn't bothered him, but he was staying closer to them both now.

"How long does this Challenge thing last? I'd think it would take a while to sort out if the oracles aren't giving you instructions."

"It's supposed to be a week. But it can range." Piallen tried to look through the trees, but she didn't see anything as they were now extremely close together—yet she couldn't shake the feeling of being watched. "Did that farmer know you had more coin? This isn't a well-trod path and those people found us quickly for just happening to be here." She dropped her hand to her sword. Reaching for her bow would be more noticeable if they were being followed.

"No. I made a point of digging through pennies before I found it, and made it seem like I was desperate for food and supplies." He slowed down. "But I do think we're being watched."

Piallen tried to reach out magically, but while her acorn amulet did warm up, she didn't sense anything. Unfortunately, the only wizardry spell she knew was the one to knock everyone out. She wasn't sure if repeated attacks could damage someone, and she didn't want to take a chance with Kendric and Tobias.

"You two are making me nervous." Tobias came to a stop in front of her. "I think I'll ride on your pack if you don't mind."

"You'll be a target if someone shoots at us again." Piallen came to a stop for him to climb up, even though she wasn't sure it was the best idea.

"I'll take my chances. I don't want someone grabbing me like that again." He shook his fur and scampered up to the top of her pack.

Kendric came to a stop as well. "I'm not sure if there is someone or something behind us, but if all three of us are feeling it, chances are good we're being followed."

"And are we just standing here until they shoot us?" Tobias adjusted himself deeper on her pack.

"There's another trail to the left. I noticed it at the last branching. I really can't sense anyone though," Piallen said. "There's a chance that whatever new direction we go, we could be walking into a trap."

"Let me try something." Kendric looked right at her, then closed his eyes and reached his arms out.

Piallen didn't feel anything, then ten copies of him all took off running in different directions. Magically, they didn't feel the same as he did, but if someone wasn't a magic user, they might fall for it. It was extremely disturbing.

Then he vanished.

"What?" Piallen started, but Tobias tapped her head.

"It's okay, we're just shielded." He kept his mouth right by her ear. "He's good. Extremely good."

Piallen stayed silent but she really needed to question Kendric. His magic was extremely different than magic *or* sorcery back home. Maybe her Challenge *was* to learn from him.

Kendric reappeared and started leading them off the trail. "There were people following, and they're now following a ghost, but they'll be back. Those images fade quickly."

He was moving quickly and soon left the thin trail he'd been following. Piallen could tell he was leading them east, whereas before they'd been going north, but that was about it.

"I still want to go to the town, but I don't think we should come from this direction." She stayed close behind him and kept her voice low. They needed to find out where they were.

Kendric nodded and moved faster. He also slightly adjusted his direction.

Piallen was a fast runner, even in a forest. But she was working hard to keep up with Kendric, and almost lost Tobias once when she misjudged how low a branch was.

They'd been racing through woods for almost an hour when Kendric slowed and held up his fist.

Piallen slowed as well and assumed he was motioning for quiet. Sean had done that a few times when he was training her to scout with battlemage skills.

Then he darted to the right and dropped behind a mass of bushes. Piallen followed but her quick drop rocked Tobias and this time he did tumble off.

She grabbed him as he fell, but both stayed silent.

They stayed there for almost ten minutes by her count, and she was about to ask Kendric what was going on when two guards jogged past.

They were running at a speed that must have been augmented by magic or sorcery and seemed focused on getting wherever they were going.

They were also wearing the gray and red tabards of the Northalian army.

Chapter Nine

Piallen kept her swearing inside her head, but Tobias was chittering softly as he spotted the distinctive uniforms as well. Unless whatever country they were in had been recently invaded by the Northalians, she'd just figured out where they were.

Unfortunately, Lizeth had been the only one of the three sisters to visit Northalian. She'd said it was boring, but gave little information beyond that. The last time their parents visited, when Lizeth's Challenge was about to begin, they were delayed coming home, and the Northalian borders closed as soon as they left. Communications between the two countries had dried up at that point.

Piallen wasn't as up on other kingdoms' geography as she possibly should be. But she knew their army's clothing.

"Damn it." She kept her voice low, but Kendric tilted his head in question. "Those were Northalian soldiers. Using magic to travel faster—magic my parents' intelligence people never implied they had access to. We're probably in Northalian now." While she was glad it was no longer a mystery, this wasn't where she wanted to be. Were those guards after her? Did they know who she was, and where she was? Northalian was weaker both in military and magic than Astarious, but holding a princess hostage would go a long way in leveling the field.

"I take it your people don't get along with them? They're too far south for us to deal with, really. My kingdom is small and well-guarded against outsiders." Kendric kept looking around as he spoke, but wasn't acting like he heard anyone else.

"Just not enemies from within," Piallen said, then shrugged. "Sorry, Drubella fooled us as well. I can't believe that the oracles would drop me here—what kind of Challenge can I do? I can't broker peace or anything like that. And neither of you can say who I am, to anyone. Even if they seem like a friend." She picked Tobias up off her lap and made sure he nodded in agreement. She knew he wouldn't mean to say anything but sometimes he could be a bit scatterbrained.

Kendric looked ready to say more, but then nodded. "Do you still want to go to that town?"

Piallen looked around. What she wanted to do was wait out in the forest until her Challenge became clear, complete it, and then go home. She assumed that since the oracles grabbed him, they would return Kendric to his homeland once this was done.

If they all survived, anyway.

She shook her head. "Not yet. Maybe once things are sorted out, but right now, I want to hide. Maybe go up into those mountains?" There weren't any large mountain ranges near the palace, but she'd gone on a few trips to ones further away with friends as a kid. With escorts of course. It should be harder for anyone to follow them in the heavily forested mountains that loomed above them. Hopefully.

Kendric looked toward the mountains. "I know I can jog for a few hours to get there, what about you?" He turned to her with a grin.

"She can run circles around you!" Tobias said from her lap.

"So says the one who's adding weight to me as I run." Piallen gave him a scritch. "But I do believe that I can keep up. And I really don't want to linger here and find out if there are more military coming this way." She'd wait until they found a place to hide before asking Kendric about those spells he'd used. If they were something he could teach her, it would come in extremely helpful. And perhaps it would be something the other battlemages could learn. There was a mirror spell used to copy people, but it wasn't one she'd ever mastered. This one had seemed more realistic than the mirror spells she'd seen demonstrated by her teachers. And as far as she knew, no one had a spell to turn invisible. But those spells could prove helpful. There had been a subtle increase in the training for battlemages in the past few years.

Her parents hadn't mentioned it, but the disturbances in the Challenges, and attacks that appeared to be tied to them, were making the Astarious military nervous. As well as her parents. Nevaine pointed out that something was going on when attacks came up near her Challenge. But when she, Clait, and Sean had returned, nothing more happened.

They sent out people to try and find any connections, including spies sent to Laiandra and Northalian. But nothing had been found.

"Okay, I'll get us up to those mountains. Keep up." Kendric got to his feet, waited until Piallen was also up and had placed Tobias on her pack, then started toward the foot of the mountains.

Kendric set a good pace, and even took Tobias on his pack halfway through. He seemed extremely comfortable once they reached the mountains and Tobias didn't slow him at all. Piallen smiled as she watched him run. It was rare to find someone who could not only keep pace with her in the mountains, but make her work for it. Kendric was an interesting man—even if she did think he was keeping secrets.

Even if no one was still following them, it would be a good idea to keep the talking down, so Piallen let her mind wander as they went. She also tried reaching out to the oracles. Maybe the Challengers who never came back just never found out what they were supposed to do and remained lost in a foreign land. That was not a cheery idea and she almost tripped on a tree root as she thought it.

Kendric kept going as they made their way up the mountain. It was massive and the trees covering it were old and thick. They didn't feel threatening, but Piallen swore she saw lower branches reaching out toward Tobias as he and Kendric passed under them. Watching where Kendric went took a lot of her focus, but part of her was still wondering what her Challenge was.

And what would happen if she just tried to make her way home? If she was in Northalian, then it bordered her kingdom. She wondered if anyone had abandoned their Challenge and just gone home.

And her third magic instructor's voice, Fillia, popped in her head. She had been the first teacher to really work with Piallen's magic leakage and not just ignore it. She'd also been the one who'd taught her more about the Challenge. And the importance of not trying to take shortcuts or cheat.

Fillia wasn't royal, so she couldn't have read past Challenger's journals—but she had some solid ideas about what took place.

Most likely, if Piallen did turn around and head home, the oracles would find a way to stop her. It was tempting though. Tobias was right about her not being patient, it was hard to wait to find out what she should be doing.

"I think we can rest here," Kendric said as he finally stopped. "Or rather, there." He pointed through the trees to an abandoned cabin.

"It's missing the front wall." Piallen wasn't complaining, just observing.

"True, but it does make it easy to see that no one is inside." He grinned and motioned for her to go ahead of him.

Piallen plucked Tobias off Kendric's pack as she went by and went up to the cabin. Or the remains of it. The front wall might be missing, but the rest seemed stable enough. At least for a night or two.

"How'd you find this?" She was good in the forest and had eyesight that was far better than most people, but she hadn't seen it until he pointed it out.

"I told him." Tobias jumped out of her arms and paraded around the single room.

"And you knew…how?"

"The trees told me. They recognized what I am and wish my people would come back." He frowned. "It's not good to be a tree in a land without grigeens."

Piallen took off her pack and looked around. "I don't think the Northalians are going to let us reintroduce your people. Not if they've been involved with those attacks around our kingdom."

Kendric also dropped his pack and looked thoughtfully at Tobias. "I wonder if your people were ever in my kingdom. I don't recall hearing any stories, but maybe they left long ago."

"They did. All of my people vanished a few hundred years ago, except for my pack. Long story." Tobias had already removed his pack and was digging for food.

"When we get through this, and I get home, I'll look into it. It sounds like our countries are far apart, but maybe someday we can be friends." There was a sadness in his eyes that Piallen only briefly caught. Then he smiled and it vanished. But then his eyes widened. "What's that?" He looked pale and pointed to the wall behind her.

Piallen turned but she'd looked at the three blank walls when she came in. Except this one wasn't blank anymore.

There was a faint painting there. One that had been painted directly on the wood of the wall long ago. Most of the colors were faded and exposure from the missing wall hadn't helped. However, the russet stag was almost as bright as if it had just been painted. He looked ready to dash off the painting and into the forest.

"Is that the same painting we found in that cave? The one that you said was like a tapestry in your homeland?" Piallen didn't get bothered by too many things—aside from having to dress up and attend formal events—but this was disturbing. That hadn't been visible when they came in, she knew it. She took a step closer. "Are the horses and riders closer to the stag now?"

Kendric didn't say anything, but walked up to the painting and touched it. Some flecks of paint came off, but the image was definitely the same, although it was modified.

The closer she looked, the more she was certain the riders were closing in on the stag.

She realized she was staring and took a step back. "Watch it."

"This one doesn't have the same power. Not like the other one. But it's old." Kendric wasn't staring blankly at it, but he was starting to stoop over.

"And you both should step away." Tobias walked in front of them and started pushing them back from the wall. "Magic paintings are never good."

Piallen would have said the painting hadn't done anything to her, but she felt happier the moment she pulled away from it. She tugged Kendric's arm and he blinked and moved away.

"I don't understand how this is here, why it was also in the cave, or what it all means." He stumbled back and sat on the floor.

"What are the odds that the two places we stop, one I chose and one Tobias and you did—have this same painting?" Piallen looked down to Tobias. "Can you pick up anything from the painting?"

He shrugged. "My connections are mostly with trees, not weird paintings. But there is a similar magic to the other one. Reach out and see."

Piallen could sometimes sense magics but she didn't think this one would give her anything. She closed her eyes and reached out anyway. A mass of images, lights, colors, and sounds slammed into her when she tried to figure out what magic might be there. She blinked and then she was sprawled out on the floor.

"What happened?" Kendric ran to her, but Tobias sat back shaking his head.

"She forgot to shield when she reached out is my guess."

Piallen rolled to her feet. "I did shield. There is something massive behind that painting. And it stomped on my shield." She stalked closer to the painting but didn't touch it. "Not behind the wood it's painted on, but the paint itself. It's hard to explain. Wait, is this one of those portals? Like Nevaine saw before her Challenge? The one you guys shut?" She'd not been able to see it, but two years ago, right before Nevaine's Challenge, someone had opened a portal. Piallen was attacked but fought back. The attackers fled through the portal once the grigeens arrived.

Mages had been studying the area for the past two years and still not found anything. At the time, Piallen hadn't sensed or seen anything, but Gliandra, Nevaine, and Finnian had seen it. Perhaps not only was it visible to sorcerers but also wizards? She thought about the wizard stone under her shirt. Rather, wizards-in-training with assistance. If Gliandra was correct, Piallen was always meant to be a wizard, and Nevaine's stone was helping her.

She certainly saw something when she reached out magically this time. And she didn't want to do it again.

Tobias continued to scowl at the painting. Finally, he lashed his tail and stepped back. "I'm not sure. Mostly, at the time, I was focusing on copying Scruff and Clait and shutting down that thing. This feels different. That being said, I don't think we should get too close—nor stare at it." That pointed comment was for Kendric who'd moved away from Piallen and back toward the painting.

"You think there's a portal behind this? One you've seen before? Your magic is extremely different than ours then." At Tobias' continued tail twitching glare, Kendric moved away from the painting.

Piallen filled him in, briefly, on the portal. Mostly that it hadn't been created by her people, and after two years they still weren't able to resolve where it came from—nor had it opened again, which was good.

"I saw images, colors, and heard sounds just now when I tried to reach out to the magic behind the painting. I'm not sure what caused it—but it can't be natural."

"We don't have anything like that or this portal you mentioned. But there has to be a connection to the tapestry in the castle back home." He twitched like he wanted to turn back to the painting, but instead pulled out cooking supplies.

"Is that a good idea? I like hot food as much as the next person, but should we risk smoke being seen?" Now that she knew they were in Northalian, Piallen felt like a massive target had been put on her back. She didn't want to do anything to make that worse.

"I can disburse the smoke; a simple spell will send it a good distance away." Kendric stepped outside the cabin and gathered wood. Nothing large and all from the ground. "It's one of the first spells we learn when we start our training."

"The trees appreciate that." Tobias nodded to the gathered branches. "I appreciate the food."

"Your magic seems to be different than ours. We have magic and sorcery, although there are far fewer users of the latter. But I've never even heard of most of the spells you've used." Piallen still had no idea what her Challenge was, but learning new skills along the way couldn't hurt.

"We have closed magic and open magic. Closed is heavier magic, more like what I've heard of as sorcery, but not exactly the same. Open are easier learned spells but you still have to have an inborn gift for them. Rangers have to be able to use both. If there were true sorcerers in our land, they're nothing more than ancient history now. I can try to show you some of the open spells, they're easier to pick up quickly."

Tobias had turned back to the painting since the preparing of food wasn't as interesting as eating it. "Do your people have any myths about stags? I feel there's a point here—it almost seems alive.

The stag in the cave painting was more noticeable than the rest of the painting as well, but not like this one." He hadn't moved any closer, but the cabin was small enough that the painting was visible from any point inside it. Now. It hadn't been at all when she walked in.

Piallen had been watching Kendric, so she saw the brief look that crossed his face. A combination of fear and embarrassment that quickly vanished as he turned completely.

"Nothing more than children's stories. My people appreciate nature and what we can learn from animals. I don't think the stag has any more meaning than it being the focus of the hunt."

"But is it a hunt?" Piallen didn't reach out to the painting, nor get to her feet. "None of the riders have weapons."

Kendric's eyes narrowed. "They do on the tapestry at home. If this is some weird copy, why don't they?"

Piallen tried to recall if the painting in the cave had shown them with weapons. Her mind thought she'd seen bows on the backs of the riders, but it could be her mind filling in what she expected to see.

"It's something to ponder for certain." Tobias took a pear out of his pack and bit it, then looked at Piallen. "We're going to have to disguise you before we go back out, you know."

"Me? If we avoid being seen it won't be a problem. Not to mention that I doubt those guards were looking for me to be roaming around their land." She'd had that thought in the back of her mind, but now that it was out loud, it seemed daft. Even if people working against Astarious had found out things about the Challenge, they couldn't have a way to find out where the Challengers were sent. Not unless the oracles themselves had been corrupted.

Kendric continued with his fire but shook his head. "You said this country had tried to interfere with these Challenges before. Maybe they do know you're here. You are extremely noticeable." He flashed a grin. "In a good way. You're tall, stunning, and unique. We need to change what you look like."

Piallen wasn't used to men looking at her like he was. Or rather, she didn't notice. But Lizeth had been trying for years to get her to be more aware of her looks. "I can't change my height, unless you have a spell for that too?"

"No, can't change that." He tilted his head and studied her. "Maybe red hair like mine, or even lighter. I do have a spell that will help with that, by the way. Sadly, it doesn't work on my own hair. But I know plants that will remove your natural color. Then some more to give it a nice shade. You can be my sister."

"What are we going to do about her eyes, though?" Tobias clutched his pear as he peered at her carefully. "If people *are* looking for her, they'd make a note about those too. Granted, they'll be less startling without that mass of black hair."

"That is harder. Let me think about that." He went about getting the meal started.

"Don't I get a say?"

"No." Tobias smiled as he said it.

She gave him a slow smile back. "You know, if they do suspect that I'm out here, they might know about you too. We need to change *your* looks."

Tobias' green eyes went huge and he patted his fluffy chest fur. "Change this? But I look great."

"And you look like what you are—a grigeen. Especially if this land doesn't have your kind, you're going to be noticeable even if they don't know what you are. What can we make him look like that will fit in better?" She wasn't fond of disguises any more than she was of fancy dresses. But if she had to do it, so did Tobias.

Kendric started to laugh, then froze. Piallen heard the sound as well. A low rasping sound like a snake sliding over leaves.

A massive snake.

Chapter Ten

Piallen's dagger was closer than her sword or bow, same with Kendric's weapons. Both silently grabbed their daggers. Tobias hadn't said anything, but the fur on his back and tail was fluffed up and his canines were showing more than usual.

Piallen had heard of a few larger species of snakes, but they were mostly from the jungles of the far southern lands. Nothing she knew of that sounded that large should be in a dense forest in the mountains. She took a deep breath and adjusted her grip on her dagger. Snakes could move quickly once they decided to attack.

Tobias was still more to the back of the cabin, but he charged forward as a large reptilian head appeared in the open front of the cabin.

The snake's eyes widened as Tobias jumped on its head and Piallen leapt forward with her dagger raised.

"Kendric! Call them off!" The words came out of the snake's mouth but Piallen had no idea how, since the shape of it was all wrong.

Then her mind caught up with the words. "You know this snake?"

The snake shook his head, sending Tobias tumbling off. Piallen held her dagger over the snake's left eye. "I'd hold very still if I were you."

"Gareth? What are you...*why* are you here?" Kendric didn't ask Piallen to stand down and Tobias had recovered his feet and was scampering back for another try.

"It's a long story. Call them off, please?"

Kendric turned to Piallen. "If you wouldn't mind, I know this snake." He definitely wasn't happy about either of them knowing it.

Piallen removed her dagger from near its face, but didn't put it away. Tobias glared at the snake as he stalked past and sat down next to her. "Explanations would be good."

"I agree. Gareth, how in the world did you get here and why are you in snake form?"

Piallen pulled back at that. Snake form? As in this was a shifter? She almost laughed at the joke, but caught herself when she saw Kendric's face. She might not recall Lizeth telling her stories about fox-spiders, but she did remember the horrifying stories of shapeshifters. For weeks when she was five, she kept trying to get Tobias to change back into his human form.

Then the snake, Gareth, shimmered, and instead of a large snake, there was a tall, skinny man. He was clothed, thank goodness, but was moving slowly.

"Oy. I've been traveling in that form for days. My back might never get back to normal." He had been on his stomach, then rolled over to his back, took a long stretch and didn't look like he was planning on getting up.

The more interesting bit was Kendric's complete acceptance of the snake and the man. And that they obviously knew each other.

"Hello, Gareth, is it? I'm Pia." She'd almost said her full name, but while it seemed as if these two were friends, it was better to be cautious. "You've been traveling for days as a...snake? How are you a snake? And traveling from where?" Aside from kids' stories, there were no such things as shapeshifters.

At least she would have said so up until two minutes ago.

Kendric let out a long sigh and ran his hand through his hair. "Might as well tell her, you kinda already gave it away."

Gareth shrugged but still didn't get off the ground. "I'm a clystike—a shapeshifter. Had I known that Kendric was hiding out with a beautiful non-shifter, I would have changed before I approached. I could sense your fierce little friend, but not you. Nice to meet you by the way. Thank you for not killing me." He sighed and turned back to Kendric. "I was scouting down here on your father's orders. He thinks something is wrong with the Northalians and that they're getting ready for an invasion of some sort. Then I heard your voice and thought you'd been sent down as well."

"He what? There are two kingdoms between us and them. He's just looking for a fight." Kendric's hazel eyes flashed a bright green, but it was so quick Piallen wasn't certain what she saw.

"You know him, neither Pax nor Cholred have a good army, nor do they have much magic. His fear is that the Northalians could plow right through them to get to us." He twisted his head. "Do you have any food? Eating as a snake isn't enjoyable." He moved into a sitting position.

Piallen tossed him a piece of fish jerky. "What are you two not telling me? Kendric said he barely knew of Northalian and they were too far south for his people to be worried about. Now you're saying that your country is ready to defend itself from them? If the Northalians attack, it will probably be Astarious—a land you said you'd never heard of." She folded her arms and glared at Kendric. No idea what the oracles were up to, nor why he had been included, but she hated liars.

"Not heard of it?" Gareth was focused on his jerky so he missed Kendric's increased glare. "He's been studying Astarious for months. But I don't think they'd be the first target, at least not a direct one. They'd want to get us first, add our strength, then go after Astarious. Lots of magic users down there."

"I'm from there." Piallen waited until Kendric looked her way. "Has anything you've told us been the truth? Is that even what you really look like?" The stories said that shapeshifters had one animal form and one human form. But considering that she thought they didn't exist, who knew what the truth was.

"This is what I look like. The snake over there can verify that. I am from Ceredigion. I am a ranger, a guard mage." He glared at Gareth when he snorted. "I was hunting Drubella when I pulled you over instead."

"He magically grabbed you from that far away?" Gareth let out a long whistle. "I told you that you just needed to get mad enough to make the spell work. Since you're here and Drubella isn't, I take it she escaped? How'd you get here anyway?"

Tobias had been silent but stalked toward him on stiff legs. "You still smell like a snake."

"Because I am one. Shapeshifters can never be completely free of their other selves. The snake is as much of me as this form is. And you can talk?"

"This is Tobias, he's a grigeen. Also from Astarious. Yes, they talk." Piallen was trying to figure out a way to ditch both of these men. She and Tobias could figure this out on their own.

Kendric shrugged. "Drubella found her way to Astarious for more mayhem. She managed to tag *Pia* with a mark and when I got the spell to work, Pia came through instead of Drubella. As far as we know, Drubella is still in a cell down south." He turned to Piallen. His look said friend or not, he wouldn't spill her secrets to Gareth. That was one good thing.

"How we got here is complicated and it involves some things that I need to take care of. Things that you don't need to know about." Explaining the Challenge was hard enough when people knew who she was. Keeping her royal status a secret would make things too complicated to even try. Not to mention, hopefully she wouldn't be around long enough for him to question it.

Clearly, he was one of those people who would just keeping poking for answers, as he opened his mouth. The as yet unspoken questions were clear on his narrow face.

"Don't." Kendric got there before she could. "Trust me when I say both Pia and Tobias are good people, and we don't need to know anything more than that. What have you found, oh great master spy?"

Gareth smiled at Piallen then turned back to his friend. "Not much, honestly. There's something going on, that's for certain, but I couldn't take a chance on getting closer to find out. I was heading toward the massive plain on the other side of this mountain when I heard you a bit ago."

"What's there?" Tobias still didn't look happy, but he no longer looked like he was going to try and kill Gareth in his sleep.

"That, my fine furry friend, is what I intend to find out. There seem to be a goodly amount of people and supplies going there through a pass north of here. I figured going where they weren't exactly crossing would be the better idea." He paused and looked past Tobias. "What's that?" He stumbled a bit getting to his feet but made his way closer to the wall—and the painting.

Piallen got up also. "Do you recognize it? We also saw another version in a cave yesterday." She watched Kendric, but he didn't get up.

"Recognize it? How could I not? Grew up around a version of it. But why are the people closer to the stag?" He turned to look at Kendric who was studiously fixing sausage in the skillet on his small fire. "What have you been doing?"

Piallen wasn't sure what the connection was with the paintings, but Kendric's look of anger at his friend wasn't the reaction she'd thought they'd get.

"Nothing. I've done nothing. I told them how there is a version in the castle of our kingdom, there's nothing else to tell."

Tobias snatched a piece of sausage, then scampered back to Piallen. "You're a bad liar. *Pia* isn't good, but you might be worse." He chewed on the sausage contentedly.

"You've been lying to this lovely lady and her friend? That's not very royal of you now, is it?" Gareth scowled at the painting then turned back. "I won't give his highness' secrets away, but yes, he is a bad liar."

"Your *highness*?" Piallen folded her arms. "Why didn't you tell us?"

"He probably was doing that whole humility thing. Does it every once in a while." Gareth sat by the fire. "Sorry, old man, she seems bright and probably would have figured it out. And look, she's not even swooning at your feet."

Kendric looked ready to say something, most likely why Piallen wouldn't be impressed with him being a royal, then looked at her and shook his head. "Gareth, you can be a total jerk."

"I don't swoon in front of royals." Piallen gave a tight smile "It just gives them airs. Better to let them live like normal people, right?" She didn't want to push Kendric too far but considering that she'd told him up front who and what she was, his keeping it a secret irked her.

"So true. I work for his father by the way. King Brae. Nice guy, looks sort of like Kendric, not the red hair of course, but the face and build."

Piallen caught the red hair comment, but judging by the grimace on Kendric's face as he violently speared the sausages, this wouldn't be the time to ask.

"It's disturbing that the images are following you. I told you those two wizards came down here to Northalian. No one believes me, but I think they're here." Gareth took a fork and grabbed a sausage before Kendric could snatch them away. "Hilth and Solange helped saved our kingdom from the other wizards. Then took off somewhere. Kendric here was just a wee boyo then. But finding the missing wizards was one of his games."

"Even if they are here, what good would it do? They can't help us."

"That sounded important. Help you do what? I thought you hated wizards?" Piallen was trying to unravel his prior words to see if there was any truth there—so far, not much.

"I do. A tenth of the people in our kingdom are shapeshifters. Genetic curses passed from generation to generation *because* of wizards. As a kid I thought if Hilth and Solange came back, they could change it."

Gareth's joviality vanished and his voice was soft. "Not all of us hate who we are, Kendric."

"Not everyone carries a curse, either. Eat the food, I need some air." Kendric got to his feet and was lost in the darkness outside the cabin.

"Why is he so touchy?" Tobias asked before Piallen could hush him.

Gareth looked sad. "He has his reasons. Justified or not to us, they are in his head. That painting can't be putting him in a good mood." He shook off his sadness, divided up the food and handed plates to Piallen and Tobias. "Might as well eat, he won't be back for a while."

The talk mostly centered around what it was like to be a snake shifter and what Gareth had seen on his way down. "Most of the north is empty. There were villages and small towns, but no people. Didn't look like a plague, but like they'd moved out."

"Where to?" Piallen asked.

"No idea. Nothing was left. We might have been wrong about the Northalians first plan of attack." He looked pointedly at Piallen.

"I think they'd be coming after us first and that confirms it. They've already made stealthy attempts in the past few years, but we are still larger and more powerful. They could be clearing the north for battle or to bring the fight to the south. The mountains between here and Astarious are twice this size, but if they find a way around them…it wouldn't be a good battle for anyone."

Gareth nodded silently and returned to eating.

Kendric still hadn't returned by the time they were going to turn in, so they put out the fire.

Gareth looked out into the darkness. "We can do guard shifts, and mess up all of our sleeping, or I can go back into snake mode and guard on my own. If you trust me. I rarely need to sleep that way."

Piallen had come to trust Kendric with her life, even if she didn't trust his words right now, and he trusted Gareth. "I'm okay with it. Tobias?"

Tobias stared at Gareth for a few moments, then finally nodded. "I'm a light sleeper, snake. Don't forget that."

"I won't." Gareth didn't laugh but there was a small smile. "Sleep well." He moved outside, then turned back into a snake and curled around himself at the front of the cabin.

Piallen got out her bedroll and dropped into it. She still had no idea what her Challenge was, but it was proving to be interesting. Kendric was obviously hiding more than just being a royal, she'd have to see if he told her in time. She'd decided that sticking with the two men for at least another day might be prudent.

Besides, she wanted to see what was on the other side of this mountain too. If they were planning an attack, she needed all the information she could get to warn her family.

She woke the next morning to Tobias poking her in the shoulder. At first, she thought something was wrong, she never slept in, then realized he was just trying to get her to move over. The sun was just barely up but it had gotten extremely cold during the night and Tobias was trying to burrow into her bedroll.

"Come on, we should get up now anyway." She got out of her bedroll only to have Tobias, and his own small blanket, take over her spot.

"Fine, you sleep, I'll eat your food." She was surprised that Kendric hadn't made breakfast, in fact his pack and belongings were right where he left them the night before.

Gareth looked up from his spot near the front, then shimmered and turned back into a man. "Kendric is out near that ridge. He asked that you go speak to him." His voice and face were decidedly neutral.

Piallen nodded and went outside. She wasn't usually affected by the cold but was kicking herself for not grabbing her cloak out of her pack before she went.

Kendric didn't seem to be bothered by the cold as he stood looking over a small rise. He looked like one of the tortured ancient poets in the books Lizeth was always reading as he turned around to face her.

"I'm sorry that I didn't tell you I am a royal. Obviously it wasn't because I was afraid you'd throw yourself at me." He gave a crooked grin. "Even though you said you hadn't heard of our kingdom, I thought you might have heard of the cursed prince." He paused. "No, apparently you haven't. You have an honest and expressive face. Anyway, I am the cursed prince of Ceredigion. Like Gareth, I'm a shapeshifter. Unlike him, I am the only one of my kind. I am primarily a stag, but can also shift into nine other animals. And it was foretold that I would be the one who would destroy our kingdom."

Piallen had startled at the mention of the stag—that explained his reaction to the paintings they kept finding. "How can anyone say what you will or won't become or do?" Yes, the oracles made royals go through the Challenge, but a royal could opt out and simply not be declared an heir. The thought of prophecies controlling someone's life was foreign to her.

"It's not like someone is forcing me to do it, they just said that was what would happen. Okay, there were more words that that, lots more words, I've read them dozens of times. But that's the basic gist of it. I will destroy our kingdom."

Piallen watched him. "And yet your parents, other family, even townspeople didn't try and kill you when this was announced? Sorry, but in the stories I read as a kid, that's usually what happens."

"The oracles wouldn't let them even if someone had wanted to. My sister is older than me and joined the oracles' priestesses when they proclaimed my curse. I can defend myself now quite well if anyone changes their mind."

Piallen shook her head. "Who claimed this of you? I know you said it's written down, but where did the words come from?" How could someone grow up with that hanging over them? "Did they say when?"

"You're probably not going to like this, but it came from the oracles themselves." He shrugged. "As for when? Not a clue. Even my sister can't get them to narrow down when or how."

"That stag in the paintings is you?" She still had no idea how or why. Both of the paintings she'd seen looked far older than Kendric, but his reactions, and the new information, put things together.

"I don't know that I look that regal when I change, but I have to think it's meant to be me. Someone is trying to tell me something and I don't think it's good." He folded his arms. "My friend is a snake, I'm a stag and a cursed prince. Do you still want to travel with us? Don't go by what the oracles did by bringing us together—there's no way to know why they do things. How do you, Princess Piallen of Astarious, feel about it?"

She shrugged. "I'm more pissed about the lying, to be honest. Not a big fan of that. But Tobias and I have to talk it over. For now, I want to see what's over the top of this mountain." She held out her hand. "Partners at least until then?"

He smiled and shook her hand. "Agreed. But we do need to disguise both of you before we head out. It'll be quick, just enough to throw off casual observers if we're spotted. And we should get back before Tobias starts eating the sausages cold." He nodded to the cabin. Even from there it was clear that Gareth wasn't having much luck with starting a fire.

"He's really a spy? Not usually out in the wild though, I assume?" She could see where if he were careful, he could get into places people couldn't, but he didn't seem great at being an outdoorsman.

"He is and yeah, usually in towns. He claims to avoid them, but he manages to hide well enough to gather plenty of information." He walked back to the cabin and quickly started the fire.

"Your little friend has had four pears by the way." Gareth nodded toward Tobias.

"I am not taking care of you if you get sick." She grabbed the one he was about to eat and tossed it to Gareth. "Have a pear."

He almost bit into it, then paused. "I don't want him to kill me in my sleep for taking his last pear."

"It's not." Piallen laughed as she and Kendric spoke at the same time. If they ended up staying with them, she'd explain about the packs to Gareth. If they separated, Kendric could explain. She wondered how long they would keep refilling, but assumed it was until the Challenge was done.

Food taken care of, Kendric and Gareth worked on disguising her and Tobias. Tobias was quick. A few swipes with some dark plant-based mixture and he looked like a round raccoon.

"This will come out, right?" He patted the dark mask on his face. "Nothing against my raccoon friends, but I like the way I look normally."

"It will, just remember that raccoons can't grab things with their tails," Kendric said. There had been an issue when they first started as Tobias kept grabbing the bowl of dye with his tail. "And they don't talk."

"I'll remember. Now fix her." He grinned sharply at Piallen; his teeth even brighter against his darkened face.

The work on her hair was the main thing, as nothing could be thought of to change her eyes except for covering them with a cloth. Piallen drew the line at that. Especially in the woods, she needed to have access to her full vision.

Within an hour her hair was lightened to a shade blonder than Nevaine's. No red was added, as they needed to get moving. She smiled as she looked at the color. As the only dark haired one with two older, blonder sisters, she'd always wished she had lighter hair.

"Nope, leave the hood down," Gareth said as she pulled up the hood on her cloak. "It just makes it look like you're hiding something." He shot Kendric a look that Kendric ignored.

"Is that why you always have that thing up?" Tobias nodded. "I figured you were hiding from a life of crime."

"Nope, just the cursed prince. Royals, eh?" Gareth grinned.

Piallen looked to Kendric and he nodded. If they were going to hang around, Gareth needed to know about her. He'd been fine with helping to hide them, but he needed to know how serious it was.

"Actually, I'm a royal too. But you can't say anything outside of this cabin."

Gareth rocked back on his heels. "Did figure there was something going on, obviously, but not that. Pia. *Princess Piallen*?" He grinned and gave a low bow. "Your beauty is as legendary as your fighting skills. Thank you again for not killing me yesterday."

Kendric laughed. "Now who's swooning? Shall we get going?" He grabbed his pack and weapons then stepped outside.

Tobias shimmied into his pack and jogged after him. "Should a raccoon carry a pack?" Gareth watched him go.

"Probably not, but raccoons don't talk either and the likelihood of him staying silent is slim." Piallen got her pack adjusted and added the bow and quiver over it. Her sword was under the cloak. That had been a bit of debate—Princess Piallen's primary weapon was a bow. But there was no way to hide it, and she wasn't leaving it behind.

Although he'd been chatty in the cabin, Gareth dropped into silence as he followed behind them. She'd caught him twitching at lower tree branches from the corner of her eye when they started. It must be difficult to go back to being tall and bipedal after a few days as a snake.

Tobias had dropped behind her, walking between her and Gareth. It was almost as if he was acting as a guard against the shapeshifter.

Kendric would stop like he was listening to something in the woods, then after a moment or two he'd move on. They stopped once for dried food and water, then an hour later started up the final stretch to the top. As there were plenty of trees, and even large boulders and dense shrubs, they shouldn't be seen by anyone looking up from the other side.

Kendric stayed in the tree shadow as he went up to the edge. He got there a moment before she did.

He swore low under his breath, but Piallen couldn't even do that.

The massive plain below them was covered in troops.

Chapter Eleven

Piallen started her own swearing when she realized that there were banners for the Laiandran army as well as a smaller group under the Offialian flag.

"You know who those others are?" Kendric said softly.

"I do. And I'd guess she and the raccoon do too, judging by their reactions." Gareth stayed low to the ground as he came up, almost to Tobias' level.

Tobias was chittering and lashing his tail.

"The Northalians don't have that many fighters, even removing the other two groups, there shouldn't be that many down there." Gareth scowled at the plain. "We know they don't."

Kendric pulled out a collapsible looking glass, used it to watch below, then handed it to Piallen. "What do you see?"

Piallen focused it on the closest group. Then moved it to the Laiandrans, then the Offialians. Then back to the main group. "The Laiandrans and Offialians look like military, trained military. The Northalians don't. At least not most of them. But there is some spell on their people to look like what they aren't. I had to work around the spell to see through it." She figured that the wizard stone was breaking the spell for her, but it had taken a bit. At least they knew where the people from those empty villages had gone. But making them look like fighters wasn't the same as them actually being able to fight. She started to hand the glass back to Kendric, but Gareth held out his hand.

Gareth muttered a few spell words and his fingers flicked as he looked through the glass. Their magic really was more like sorcery, which was interesting. "They want people to think they have a massive army? What's the purpose? I'm sure the wild animals are extremely impressed."

"What would your kingdom do if this army showed up on their borders?" Kendric retrieved the looking glass and seemed to be focusing on specific sections.

"Knowing my parents, fight. But they'd be vastly overwhelmed—if those were all actual fighters." She shook her head. "It doesn't make sense though—it would be clear that over half of those people aren't fighters and, in many cases, they appear to be illusion." Which was another spell her people didn't have. Short term illusions were possible by powerful magic users, things like the mirror spell. But nothing like what was going on before her. "How are they doing that?"

"There are some bad things going on down there. Bad." Tobias kept chittering under his breath.

"I was hoping you might know; that's not a spell we have," Kendric said without turning.

Piallen felt movement under her shirt and looked down. The wizard stone was rising on its own. "What in the world?" She pulled it free of her shirt, but it was radiating a soft, pulsing glow.

"What's that?" Gareth noticed it first, as Kendric was still studying the crowd.

Piallen watched the stone and thought quickly. Bringing up wizards and a wizard stone wasn't a great idea, but it was reacting to something down there and as soon as he turned, Kendric would notice it. "It's a stone my sister had; I believe it ties into wizardry." She watched Kendric closely as he slowly turned.

"Your sister is a wizard? I thought you said they were dead in your land?"

"She's not. She's a mage and a sorcerer. She brought this back from her Challenge—the one that she couldn't talk to me about."

She turned to Gareth. "I'll explain later, when we aren't dealing with some bizarre army."

Kendric scowled then went back to looking over the plain.

Piallen's amulet twitched toward the front of the army below them. "Is there something there? Near the front on the left?"

Kendric lifted one eyebrow but looked where she pointed. "Nothing that I can...see. Damn it. You were right, Gareth. Hilth and Solange came here and they're working with the Northalians. I can see Solange and Hilth looks to be behind her."

"Those are the wizards that helped your people? Can I see? Why would they be working for the Northalians now?" She was so excited at seeing real wizards she almost dropped the glass. She held it carefully and looked through. A dark-haired woman in a long dark dress stood talking to two higher ranked Northalians. There was a tall heavyset man behind her, wearing similar clothing. Neither were looking directly her way so she couldn't get a good look. "How old are they?"

"They're wizards. Probably a thousand or so years?" Gareth looked like he wanted to take a peek, but didn't grab the glass out of her hands.

Good thing, because she saw the woman turn her way and lift her hands. "She's cuffed. The woman at least is in chains or cuffs. I can't see about the man...wait. Yup, he is too. His chains go to a collar around his neck." She handed the glass back to Kendric. "They aren't helping the Northalians, they're prisoners. My stone can tell too." She didn't know how to explain it, but as soon as she saw the chains, the stone almost became frantic.

"How did they capture them?" Gareth kept looking down even though without the glass he couldn't see much.

"I have no idea, but Pia is right, those are the two wizards."

Piallen stepped back and sat on a boulder. "That army, completely real or not, plus two wizards? Even if those wizards are working against their will, they're obviously doing something. My kingdom wouldn't win the fight." As someone who'd been training with weapons most of her life, Piallen was proud of Astarious' defenses. But she knew when they were outmatched.

"Now what do we do?" Tobias climbed up on the boulder next to Piallen and he looked as scared as she felt.

"We have to go home and warn them. I don't care what I'm supposed to do, I'm not sitting by and letting that army destroy my home." She had no idea how she was going to get there and more importantly, cross the massive Trulan mountain range that divided the countries. Somehow she doubted that Northalian would unblock the road that used to cut through. "Is there any way that you can magically send Tobias and I back? Maybe swap with Drubella if she's alive?"

"I can try, but the odds of my success are minimal and could end up stranding you farther away." Kendric turned to Gareth. "We need to warn my father also."

"I can get back to them in six days if I move constantly and don't get caught." Gareth was obviously speaking of traveling as a snake.

"Could you go into Astarious? Please, my country is closer and if that army wins, no land is safe." Piallen fought down the panic of what could happen if those two wizards attacked her kingdom. Whether acting on their own or not, obviously Northalian was using their abilities.

"And a land with no shifters is going to believe him?" Kendric stepped away from the edge. "I'm sorry, but I've heard the stories of what our neighbors tried to do to my people when we first were cursed. Before we closed our kingdom off. Aside from a few like Gareth here, we don't leave our lands for a reason."

"Then I'll go on foot." Piallen stood and pointed a shaking finger at the army below. "With the power of two wizards, they can blast apart anything they want. Maybe even the entire Trulan range. If you won't help me, get out of my way." She stepped closer to him to emphasize her point.

"Um, Pia...llen? Pia? Look at your necklace?" Gareth took a step back.

Piallen hadn't noticed that while she was still holding the chain the stone pendant was on, it was no longer around her neck and the stone was glowing.

"It feels angry." Tobias rose up on his back legs and sniffed. "Very angry." He looked down to the plain. "At them."

Piallen wasn't sure what to do. Charging down and fighting the entire army wasn't reasonable and while she was supposed to be a wizard, that didn't mean she had much in the way of wizard powers—not yet anyway. "Wait a moment." She went back to the boulder, sat and dug through her pack. All three wizard books were together. "Let me see if there's something I can use..." she flipped through the pages. "If I find what I'm looking for, you two are going to have to get us somewhere safe. Fast."

Kendric didn't look at the books, not after his first glance at the covers. But his jaw tightened as he turned back to viewing the plain.

"Okay. This might work." She jumped to her feet. "Tobias? Do you have that collar Clait gave you?"

"What? Yes, I can't wear it, it's too small. No idea why the oracles sent it to me." His tail lashed as he went through his pack, finally pulling out the green and white collar. Nevaine couldn't explain what it did, but she'd been glad when Clait gave it to Tobias for the journey—even if he hadn't been. Even more glad when the oracles included it in his pack. There was a good chance that it and the stone were somehow connected.

Piallen held out her hand for it, then held it over her stone. A small ball of crackling energy encased them both. "Don't ask what I'm doing, I'm not sure, and it could blow up." She read the spell again. It seemed simple. On paper. Many things seemed that way but proved to be vastly different in practice. Nevaine loved the printed word, but Piallen wanted to see things work before she believed them. "You might all want to step back a bit." She looked up and while Gareth had moved a foot away, neither Kendric nor Tobias had.

She shrugged, held the stone and collar tight, and chanted the spell, pointing down to the two wizards in chains below. Ideally this spell should remove their bindings—she was counting on them destroying that army once they were free.

If this worked and she didn't blow them all up that was.

An odd force flowed through her hand that held the stone and collar as she repeated the spell. Then there was an explosion, one that threw all of them a few feet back down the mountain.

And dropped two tall, cloak-clad wizards in front of her. The two wizards looked as surprised as she felt, then both collapsed.

"Did you kill them?" Gareth scrambled forward the fastest but smiled when he checked their pulses. "Alive. Still bound though." He held up the woman's wrists.

"Was that what you meant to do? Not very good for a wizard." Kendric's voice was as flat as the look on his face.

Piallen shrugged at his anger. She would have tried it again if she had to. "No, that wasn't my plan. I was trying to get their chains to come to us, not *them*. I shouldn't have been able to grab them with that spell. And I'm not a wizard. Someone thought I might have the ability for it, but I was ripped from my home before they could do much training." She glared at him. She had no idea if the oracles pulled her to start her Challenge five days early due to the attack on the palace, or in reaction to Kendric's dragging her to his country. But she would have appreciated those five days of training. Not to mention, without more information, she didn't fully understand his hatred of wizards, especially since his friend and countryman, Gareth, didn't seem to feel the same.

Hilth, the male wizard, groaned and reached out for the woman. "Where..." He held her hand and looked toward them but didn't sit up. "How did we get here? Which one of you is a wizard with a glamour spell on?" He looked beaten up but there was still a fire in his eyes. He had short gray hair and a scruffy beard and if he hadn't been a wizard, Piallen would have said he was in his eighties.

"There are no wizards here." Kendric shot her an odd look. "At least that's what she says. She's the one who pulled you up here."

"I don't know if I'm a wizard or not, but aside from my hair, this is what I look like." She held up the stone and collar—the ball of energy around them had vanished. "I'm not sure how I got you here, but these two things helped. And we probably want to find somewhere to hide?" There was a lot of yelling echoing up from the plain and she didn't think they wanted to be found.

The woman, Solange from what Kendric had called her, stirred and Piallen helped her up. Her hair was still dark, but like her companion she looked to have been in her eighties if she weren't a wizard. Something about her eyes reminded her of Gliandra.

Kendric nodded, and with Gareth, helped the male wizard to his feet.

Tobias waited until they were both standing before running forward and sniffing them. "Yup. Wizards. Blocked wizards though. Need to get those chains off." He turned to Piallen. "That spell you used neutralized the control from the chains, but not sure for how long it will last."

"A grigeen?" Solange smiled and almost looked ready to cry. "We feared your people were long lost."

"It's good to be missed, but we are back." He grinned his toothy smile. "Which is a tale for a safer time. Okay, forest people, find us somewhere to hide."

Kendric looked ready to say no, then nodded to Piallen. "Neither of us know this land, but maybe together we can find some place that will work?" He didn't sound happy, but was still keeping his face neutral.

Piallen had been around her sisters enough to recognize the royal shut down. She gave it right back. She usually didn't think about being a princess, but there were times it was called for. "I agree." She smiled to the two wizards. "Will you two be okay to walk down?"

Hilth patted Gareth's shoulder. "With this strong clystike to lean on, we should be fine."

Gareth smiled and held out both arms. "I am happy to serve."

Kendric and Piallen led the way down, with Tobias following, but closer to Gareth and the wizards.

Piallen wasn't sure if Kendric's silence was in concern of someone already coming up from the plain, or due to anger at her wizardly connections. Right now she didn't care. Ever since she'd pulled the wizards up the mountain, she'd felt an odd tingle in the back of her mind. And it was getting worse. It was as if whatever was making their chains block their wizard magic was also reaching out for hers. They needed to get those chains off and somehow destroyed, quickly.

She'd put the chain for the wizard stone back on her neck and dropped the stone under her shirt. She kept Clait's collar out though. Unless he wanted it back, it might be better with her than Tobias at this point.

They'd been walking for about twenty minutes when Kendric froze and tilted his head to the left.

"You might pick up things better in your stag form, Prince Kendric," Solange's voice was soft and sad.

"I'll do fine like this." Those words were sharp enough to cut through the rocks he was glaring at. "Can you two crawl over these?" He pointed past the large rocks. They didn't go far, maybe a few feet, but they would be awkward moving over.

"If it means we stay safe, we'll crawl over shards of glass," Hilth said. "Just get us hidden. Please."

Kendric said nothing more, but started over the rocks. Piallen motioned for Tobias to go before her—he had no trouble and got to the other side a moment before Kendric. With Piallen helping Solange, and Gareth helping Hilth, they made it across.

"This way." Kendric barely waited before heading down a narrow, almost-not-there path.

Piallen wondered if he really wanted to see if she'd punch him because he was being a jerk. Nevaine was more prone to physical violence when angry, but right now Piallen was agreeing with that stance.

Gareth continued helping the two wizards. Tobias stayed near them, leaving her to glare at Kendric's stiff back. It took a moment to realize that he hadn't pulled his hood up since they left the mountaintop.

They walked another ten minutes, then he led them off the trail and toward a tree-filled hollow. The coolness and the water that was there flowed over her mind.

"This will have to work for now. Once we get your chains off, you can go to my father and explain yourselves." Kendric dropped his pack near an indentation in the hill above the grotto—not really a cave but it did go back a few feet and would provide some shelter. A small stream fed a pool at the bottom of the grotto.

"Please, sit, welcome to our new home, and ignore the prince-jerk." Gareth shook his head at his friend then smiled and motioned to the two wizards.

"I'm...never mind." Kendric shook his shoulders and gave a polite royal smile. "You already know who I am. This is Gareth, a snake shifter from my kingdom. Our two guests are Tobias the grigeen and Pia from Astarious. These are the wizards Solange and Hilth." He nodded first to the woman and then to the man. "They were *once* of Ceredigion."

Piallen was impressed that he didn't out who she was, but if these two could help her and her kingdom, they needed to know everything.

"I am pleased to meet you, Solange and Hilth. Kendric is trying to protect me, and I do appreciate it. I'm Princess Piallen."

"I thought there was more to you than simply Pia." Solange smiled.

"You were wrong about us, Prince Kendric." Hilth sat up fully. He was roughed up, but his bulk was mostly muscle. And he looked ready to throw some of it around. "We are still citizens of Ceredigion. We were taken against our wills and kept in stasis when you were only a child."

Kendric's jaw tightened, but he simply nodded his head. Piallen recognized that move too. When her father was letting one of his councilors know he heard them but wasn't quite agreeing with them.

Tobias sniffed the chains on Solange's wrists. "Not sure how to get these off. Strange magic on them."

Kendric stomped closer to Solange and held out his right hand, palm down over the chains. He pulled back as if Gareth had changed into a snake and bit him. "It's not strange. I recognize it. Chancellor Mertil, first advisor to my father. He's been the Chancellor for my father since before I was born. Why is his magic on your chains?"

Chapter Twelve

"That's an exceedingly good question, Prince Kendric." Solange kept her hands still. "We never saw who captured us, but it was done while we were in the castle." The implication was clear.

"I thought the wizards were all powerful, and also all gone. No offense. How did the two of you get taken by a Chancellor? My understanding is that even the highest-level sorcerers couldn't take out one of you." Piallen now wished that she'd paid more attention when Nevaine was visiting last year. She'd brought her sorcery books with her.

"Normally they couldn't." Hilth stood up. "Are you certain, without a doubt, whose magic you sense?"

Kendric stepped closer to Hilth and put his hand out as he had to Solange. After a moment he nodded. "Whether by truth or elaborate ruse—that is Chancellor Mertil's magic. Although it feels odd. There's a twist to it that I've never felt from him."

"Let me check." Gareth came over. "I'm not nearly as strong magically as our prince, but I was on the receiving end of some of the Chancellor's magic as a kid." He put both hands over Hilth's chains and closed his eyes. He looked like he wasn't noticing anything, then snapped his eyes open and took a step back. "It's him. But there is something odd, too, like Kendric said. Something that's being blocked by another spell."

"Since neither of us know him, we can't tell anything except it's not normal magic." Tobias sniffed them both again, but then shrugged.

Piallen stepped closer. "We had a problem with our Chancellor four years ago. It looked like he'd been working with the Laiandrans and possibly Stiklins. He killed himself when he was found out. But afterward, it looked like he'd been up to something secretly for a long time—and working with unknown sources. Maybe that's what's happened in Ceredigion."

"Something happened." Solange snorted. "And I will be paying back whoever did it. We were beaten after we were captured, and then locked in stasis. Taken out, forced to cast spells, beaten again, and dropped back into stasis. I've had many years to dream of a proper punishment." She leaned into Hilth's shoulder with a sigh. "Don't forget, husband, I get first shot."

Piallen smiled. Even with all they'd been through, these two obviously adored each other. She turned to Kendric. "I thought you said these two hated each other?"

Kendric shrugged. "I never knew them; the stories were that they didn't like each other and probably killed each other when they vanished." He gave the first real smile she'd seen since the mountaintop. "Sorry about that. It's what everyone, including my family, believes."

"Bah. They spread that rumor so no one would look for us. Regardless of who did it, could one of you remove these please?" Hilth rattled his chains. "If we're found, it would be better for everyone if we can defend ourselves. And you."

Gareth shook his head. "That's over my level of magic."

Tobias did the same.

Piallen held out her hands. "I did grab you two, but I was trying to take those chains off so you could fight back. Obviously, that didn't happen. I leak magic and that might have messed up my attempt at a wizard spell." She held up her acorn amulet. "This helps contain my leaking—mostly. But I just found out that I appear to have wizard abilities. As in, a few days ago found out, so I'm not trained. I got you two away from the army with a spell from a book and these two things." She pulled out the stone and Clait's collar. She wasn't sure what to expect, but Solange and Hilth leaned forward anxiously, then passed out.

"What did you do to them?" Kendric and Gareth were closest so they got both off the ground with their backs leaning against the rocks they'd been sitting on.

"I didn't do anything." She dropped the stone back into her shirt and stuffed the collar into a pocket.

Solange recovered first and let out a deep breath. "That Pantiar. He was always causing problems. Crazy dead old man."

Hilth started laughing and shaking his head. "Gone a thousand years and still knocks us both out. Now, to be fair, if we didn't have these on, we'd probably have been fine. Where did you get those relics?"

Piallen didn't take either item back out. "My sister." She briefly explained about the Challenge, and more importantly, the secrecy around the Challenge, and her really having no idea who this Pantiar person was.

"He was a powerful wizard in a distant land." Solange laughed as Piallen leaned forward for the story. "And if the oracles don't want you knowing more at this point, we are not going to be the ones to muddle that up. It's a distant land, leave it at that. He must have found a way to tie himself to something—he died a thousand years ago. He must have thought kindly of your sister to give her those items."

"The collar was actually given to Clait, her sister's grigeen companion," Tobias said. "The oracles sent it along with me."

"Oh, I so want to see the grigeens." Solange looked to Hilth hopefully.

"After we're free, we've warned King Brae, and saved Astarious." He nodded to Piallen. "That army on that plain is meant to bring your kingdom down. Be a bit harder now though."

"Without you two?" Tobias grinned.

"Aye. They'd found a way to tap magic. Those wretched Offi-alians brought the secret of pulling magic from others. They're still dangerous, but without us and our power they will be slowed down and far weaker. The spells they have on the non-fighters and illusions will vanish quickly." Hilth held up his hands again. "But could some-one try to get these off? My bet would be our wizard-in-training-princess. Along with some support from Pantiar."

"A ghost is going to help?" Gareth took another step backwards and looked paler.

"No, there's just an echo of him in those objects." Solange gave a sad smile. "He found his peace. But even an echo of a master wizard has power. He was one of the strongest of us all."

Piallen really was going to enjoy talking to Nevaine about her Challenge. A wizard ghost? That was providing she figured out her Challenge, stopped the possible invasion, and survived. "I have no idea what to do."

Hilth looked to Kendric as he looked everywhere except Piallen. "Not sure what's wrong with you two youngsters, but I think you two need to work together on this. Prince Kendric can remove the chains, but he needs a wizard to give his spell enough power. Now, be nice and work together."

Kendric closed his eyes, gave a sigh, then opened them. "Follow what I do. Probably hang on to those two wizard artifacts while we do it. It'll be close to what you were trying when you brought those two to us—but done right." He winced as even he caught the snarky tone in his voice. "Sorry, I didn't mean it like that." He held his hand out to her.

Piallen held the stone and the collar in one hand and took his hand with the other. The spell she'd tried before was still in her mind, probably because it had been short. But she wouldn't be calling on it—just working with Kendric to give power to his spell. Lizeth used to do that when they were kids. She'd push Piallen's spells with her own power.

Kendric drew in power for his spell, and Piallen felt her magic, or her wizardry rather, lending support. It was odd, but she felt power running from the stone and collar in her right hand through her and into her left hand and Kendric. There was a pleasant warmth coming from the connection that she hoped was a good sign.

The pressure in her left hand increased and Kendric's eyes narrowed. Then first Solange, then Hilth's chains dropped.

Hilth removed his collar, took both of their chains, and blasted them into oblivion without saying a word.

Piallen felt a brush of wind as the chains vanished, but that was all.

"Now, we need to get back to Ceredigion." He nodded to Kendric.

Piallen dropped his hand. "That army is reduced, but it's still dangerous. I have to warn my kingdom."

"And I need to warn my father. Who knows what else the Chancellor has been doing? My father trusts him about everything." Kendric folded his arms but didn't glare. He also didn't look like not going to Ceredigion would be an appropriate answer.

Piallen shrugged. "Then we go our separate ways in the morning. I don't think trying to get home is my Challenge, but I need to try to warn them."

"And we need to notify my people." Tobias briefly explained about the grigeens reappearing to Solange and Hilth. "We've relocated some, but many of the newcomers have settled in the Trulan mountains. They're in that massive mountain range between Northalian and Astarious. I have to advise them."

"I'm extremely happy to hear that your people are back, the world needs you." Solange nodded to Tobias. "But if we can get the people of Ceredigion behind us, and if the king agrees, obviously, we could help defend Astarious."

"But you'll be leaving here, going north, then what, cut back through Northalian, and then cross to Astarious? I don't think either my kingdom or the grigeens have that much time." Piallen wanted the wizards to help—both her with her wizardry, and in defending Astarious. But she knew time was important. Even if the wizards had been funneling energy and magic into that army—there was still a good-sized fighting force down there.

"We have ways to travel that will expedite things. You really should come with us, both of you." Hilth looked to Tobias as well. "We will be taking down a well-loved Chancellor and disrupting a kingdom. The more support we have the better. We can use the chorogh path."

Gareth smiled broadly. Kendric scowled.

"That's not a safe way to travel. And in case you didn't notice, Tobias and Piallen aren't shifters." Kendric's jaw was going to get locked if he kept clenching it like that. He turned to Piallen. "The chorogh path is a magic trail that supposedly clystike, shapeshifters, can use to cross vast distances quickly. Except it doesn't always work, has killed many who have tried it, and can't be used by non-shapeshifters."

Solange looked to Gareth. "Has he always been this cranky? He was such a happy baby." She sighed.

"Since he became an adult, he has. Moments of fun, the real him is in there somewhere, but often difficult. Takes himself too seriously. That whole cursed heir to the throne bit." Gareth shrugged and ignored Kendric's glare.

"Now, the thing is that if a clystike is carrying the non-shifter on his or her back while on the path then the non-shifter is fine to travel it. And having both wizardry and magic fueling the spell will make it stronger. It will work." Solange shrugged. "Hilth and I are both clystikes, but our only forms are birds."

"I can carry our wee raccoon." Gareth continued to ignore Kendric.

"This sounds great, but what if there are problems in Ceredigion that delay us? I need to warn my family." Piallen was ignoring Kendric's lack of suggesting that he could carry her. She had no idea what his other forms were, but she hypothetically could ride a stag if he were large enough. She was an excellent horsewoman. But she had to admit it would be extremely odd.

Not to mention the nagging urge to get home.

"I think you and Tobias need to find your way home. Prepare your people. If we can," Kendric gave the two wizards a glare, "we will send troops to support you."

Solange and Hilth turned to each other. It was as if they were talking but not speaking. Then both turned back.

"It's getting late, you all must be tired; we're exhausted after our troubles. No one can go anywhere until daybreak, yes?" Hilth waited for both Kendric and Piallen to nod before going on. "Then we make dinner, get some sleep, and deal with things in the morning." He turned to Piallen. "I'd love to see what wizardry books you have sometime. Solange and I did write a few of them a long time ago, maybe you have one of ours."

Kendric nodded first, followed by Piallen. She was starting to feel the fatigue from the spell she'd cast. Resting would be better than trying to find her way off a strange mountain in the dark. She had very good night vision, but better not to push things in an unknown forest.

They made a fire after Tobias spoke to the surrounding trees and Hilth put a small spell of protection around the camp. The spell felt similar to one of Piallen's magical ones but had an odd power running through it.

"I do a magic spell like that. Blocks light and sound. Not sure that I could cover this entire area though." She looked at the shield. It was barely visible, but gave a soft shimmer in the firelight.

Hilth nodded. "Why don't you give it a try, but reach deep inside and tap your wizard skills. Whoever told you that you had wizard abilities was right. And I can't recall the last time a wizard was born."

"It was a sorceress named Gliandra. She's not from Astarious but has been living in the grigeen forest since before my father was born. How did I become one? Neither of my parents are wizards, nor, as far as I know, anyone further back in the family line." She would have thought that something like a wizard in the family tree would have at least been mentioned. Unlike Kendric and his hatred of wizards, her people just didn't think of them since they'd been gone so long. There were no good or bad perceptions about them.

"Oh, it would have been there. But long lost, I'd assume. You said you leak magic?" At Piallen's nod he continued. "I'd say that was the first tipoff. Wizardry will push out the other magics and must be worked with to make it stop doing that. But that will be a talk for another day, I'm afraid. Right now, cast your shield spell, but tap into the wizardry side."

She started to take out the wizard stone but he stopped her. "Try it without old Pantiar's ghost weighing in. Guard his relics well, but you need to rely on yourself."

Piallen released the necklace then focused on the feeling she got when she'd cast the wizard spells and the spell for the protection shield.

She ended up dropped on her behind a few feet from where she'd been standing and a rock-like shield covering the area, "Did I do that? How'd I end up here?"

Hilth helped her to her feet.

Tobias was trying not to laugh. "You did your spell, then gave a yelp, flew back, and then dropped down. The rock is protective, but maybe a bit overkill."

Kendric and Gareth were just silently watching.

Piallen shook her hands out. She needed to think of this the way she learned any new skill. Because of her magic leaking, she'd never done a lot of magic training. But she'd done plenty of weapons and athletic training. "Let me try again." She closed her eyes and focused on the rock over them changing into her normal shield. She didn't drop this time, but neither did the rock change.

"Get rid of the rock completely first, then cast again. Your magic is still trying to help." Solange looked on encouragingly.

Piallen nodded and shook out her hands and shoulders this time, then again closed her eyes. The spell was there, she could feel it, she just needed to release the wizardry holding it in place. There was a popping sound and her stone shield was gone. So was the one that Hilth had put up, which hadn't been her intention.

With a long, calming breath, just as if she were pulling back the string of her bow, she released the correct spell. The wizardry felt wild and untamed, but when she looked again, her shield was in place. And then she tilted sideways.

Gareth caught her first, but only because Kendric had been further away. He looked pensive but had definitely reached out for her.

"Thanks." She patted Gareth's hand as he steadied her. "I can't feel it the same way I do my magic-based version. I can see it better, but how do I know if it will hold or not?"

"That will come," Solange said. "But it feels solid to me. Nicely done."

Tobias patted her knee, Gareth gave her a smile, and Kendric still looked mildly annoyed. Then he shook it off.

"Due to many circumstances," he looked to the three wizards, "which might have been in error, I haven't trusted wizards. I could have been wrong. Please forgive me."

Gareth's jaw dropped but he stayed quiet.

"I accept your apology." Piallen felt like she should say more and had she been Lizeth or even Nevaine she probably would have. But that was really all she needed to say. He wasn't a love interest, not even a friend. Kendric was good looking, there was no doubt of that. But he had a kingdom to run. And even though he was standing down a bit on his wizard stance, if he felt that wizards were responsible for the prophecy the oracles said about him destroying his kingdom, he'd never truly trust them.

Or her.

The rest of the evening passed quickly with food and Hilth and Solange sharing stories of some of their past adventures and why they turned against the other wizards in their kingdom.

"Not all wizards hate and distrust each other. For example, we've been married for hundreds of years. Pantiar was a good one, and there were others around the world that we counted as friends when the world was newer." Hilth shook his head. "But there were three who were friends to no one and only wanted power. I won't even say their names. The kingdom of Ceredigion is unique in many ways, including geographically. It's located in a shielded valley. The mountains are special in the world of wizards and amplify power. Those three wanted to make the people slaves and mine the mountains for their power."

Solange nodded. "We took exception to that."

"And your people created the clystikes." Kendric's jaw wasn't clenching, but he didn't look to anyone as he spoke, simply stared into the fire.

"Those of us who have been blessed with multiple forms aren't cursed. As we mentioned, Solange and I are such. The clystikes existed in the northern realms long before your kingdom was even more than a hill fort and huts. The wizards didn't create them. However, some did try to take advantage of them."

"To be fair, the combination of the power of the mountains surrounding your valley and the results of the wizard fights to get those three bad ones out, might have compounded the issue." Solange leaned forward until Kendric finally looked to her. "You being a clystike is not what caused the prophecy. Nor do prophecies always mean what they appear to mean. I know much of the oracles and some of their work with Astarious. I doubt they would have risked one of their royal challengers by exposing them to a dangerous prince. You need to live your life and stop worrying."

Gareth nodded. "Thank you! I've been telling him that for years. Never listens to me."

Like many redheads, when Kendric blushed it was noticeable. Even in the dim firelight. "Apparently I have a lot to think about. Do we need to set guards?"

That he was asking it, knowing that wizardry held the spell in place, was a step forward, Piallen hoped. She'd never had a prophecy on her, plus, being the third princess meant a lot of the pressure of ruling wasn't on her. If she completed her Challenge and was declared third heir, she still could choose not to rule.

"What do you think? This is your spell." Solange's smile reminded her again of Gliandra. "Kendric? What does it feel like to you?"

Piallen reached out in her mind for the spell. "The spell feels solid. I'd say no guards."

Kendric closed his eyes briefly, then opened them. "It is solid. And the more rest we can all get, the better tomorrow, whichever way people go, will be." He took his pack and moved back a bit out of the enclosure. "I have two blankets if you'd like." He held up the blankets to Solange and Hilth.

Hilth laughed. "Thank you. However, the day I can't provide bedding for my wife and myself is the day I don't roll out of bed." He made a small movement with his hands and two full bedrolls appeared.

Kendric nodded and tossed the blanket in his hands to Gareth.

Solange turned toward Piallen. "Hilth is simply showing off. Using wizardry for bedding is a bit gauche. Not that I'm complaining at this point." She winked and set out her bedroll.

Piallen set up her roll across the fire from Kendric. Only Solange and Hilth were actually in the small cave until Tobias dragged his blanket over and made a nest near them. He was purring and neither wizard complained.

Even though they'd said they didn't need guards, Kendric was still awake and watching the woods around them when Piallen finally went to sleep.

Piallen rarely dreamed and almost never had nightmares. But they hit her quickly that night.

Chapter Thirteen

At first Piallen thought she'd been transported back home. The woods felt real as she stood near one of her archery targets. Then the screams came.

They were coming from the palace and flames were visible through the trees. Piallen ran toward the palace, but she couldn't get any closer. No one was running past her as they should have been if the palace was on fire. Not even animals. It was as if she could hear people, but she was alone in facing whatever was going on.

Or she would be if she could move from this place. She'd get a few feet ahead, but then her feet were just running in place no matter how hard she tried.

The screams coming from the palace were horrifying and through the woods came a massive troop of armored soldiers that was flattening everything in its path. A thousand grigeens ran toward it, but she knew they couldn't stop it. She reached for magic but there was nothing there.

Then a tiny fist punching her shoulder woke her up. She sat up immediately with her dagger in her hand.

Tobias had been the one to wake her, but the other four were looking at her carefully.

"Did I scream? Please tell me I didn't scream in my sleep." The vestiges of terror at her nightmare fled quickly, but the images and sounds remained. She shivered.

"No screaming, but you were tossing around some. Seemed to be running, or trying to." Gareth looked toward the crumpled blanket at her feet.

"I felt, more than that, you were in serious distress. Both physically and magically. Someone was trying to tell you something," Hilth said, and Solange nodded in agreement.

"I really hope what I just saw wasn't true. It felt too real. Aside from me not being able to run, that is."

Solange looked pensive. "That could have been your psyche trying to help, but instead making things worse. Are you normally a fast runner?"

"One of the fastest in the kingdom," Tobias said before Piallen could respond.

"Then I'd say your mind realized this wasn't a normal dream and added the lack of running to share that with you." She nodded sagely.

"Wouldn't that be common though?" Gareth looked around. "When I have nightmares, I often can't move."

"For others, yes. Wizards, no. Our minds are designed differently." She turned back to Piallen. "Are nightmares common to you?"

"Not at all. My sister Nevaine used to get them a lot when we were kids. She was so angry that I didn't get them that I started making them up to make her feel better. But, no, I could count how many times I've had them on one hand."

"Then someone was trying to tell you something. Tell us what you went through."

Piallen went through the nightmare, it was far shorter and less terrifying now, not being in it at the moment. But Hilth and Solange still made her repeat it three times.

"Sounds like the oracles to me. But we'll know better when we visit their temple." Solange and Hilth shared a long look. "You should be able to sleep without any problems now. I suggest we all go back to sleep."

The last thing Piallen wanted to do after that was sleep. She'd recognized the voices yelling from the burning palace—her family. But she found that she dropped off to sleep almost immediately once she went back into her bedroll.

The morning was cool and quiet when she woke. There were no signs of anyone else being up when she rolled onto her elbow. She shoved a strand of hair out of her face, then stopped when she realized it was her normal black, not the blondish color that Kendric had created.

Was she back in a dream? She tried to cry out when a dark man-shaped cloud appeared in front of her. "I wouldn't if I were you. I'm not ready to try myself against this amount of power. I have come to see who you really are, Princess Piallen. And I have answered my questions. We'll meet again." The dark cloud vanished.

Tobias twitched on the ground from a foot away and sat up, blinking heavily. "I was coming to wake you up. What happened?"

The others were stirring as well. And also appeared confused.

"Were all of you awake? I thought I was the first, and some weird dark cloud man popped up. He changed my hair." She waggled a long dark strand to everyone. "Then said he was trying to find out who I really was and that he wasn't ready to face this much power. Yet. Does that sound familiar to any evil people in your lives? And how did he get through to us, but the shield is still standing?" She felt she should be more upset about the visit, but for some reason she wasn't. Maybe it was the bit about not wanting to face them yet.

"All of us were awake, except you, until a moment ago." Kendric watched her for a while. "As for who and what?" Kendric closed his eyes and stepped back toward the shield.

Solange and Hilth rolled to their feet and also started walking toward the shield with their hands outstretched.

Gareth and Tobias shrugged and went looking for food to drag out of the packs.

"Don't eat too much, Tobias. I want us on the road quickly and you don't travel well with a full stomach." Piallen rolled up all of her sleeping materials and put them and her wizard books in her pack. She'd wanted to show the books to the wizards, but the urge to get on the road was stronger now. If it had been the oracles who had sent that nightmare to her earlier, they wanted to get her moving.

"It was Lord Thistledove." Kendric stepped back from the shield a moment before Solange and Hilth said the same name—without the Lord in front of it.

"He wasn't a lord when we knew him. But we both recognize his magic." Solange's frown indicated she wasn't a fan.

Gareth looked up from Kendric's pack. "Wait, you mean that annoying old man who hides in the library? Why and how did he get here, get through your shield, accost Piallen, and change her hair?"

Kendric even did a double take at the last bit. "You're worried about her hair?"

"No, but why did he do it? He wanted to see who she *really* was? What does that even mean?"

"Who is Lord Thistledove? And what could he possibly care or want to know about me? And how did he do that bit with the smoke?"

"Lord Thistledove is a noble who usually travels around kissing up to Chancellor Mertil. As for that smoke you described, or how he got past the shield, I have no idea." Kendric got the fire built up and then got the cooking gear out. "He doesn't have the power to project himself through a shield nor do a shadow chaser spell. I've no idea why the three of us felt that it was him."

"Shadow chaser? And don't get breakfast for Tobias and me, we need to be going. Just dried rations for us." Piallen ignored Tobias' frown. He'd live, and they needed to get moving. After they warned Astarious, she'd see if Solange and Hilth could come south for wizard lessons.

Solange bustled forward. "Don't be silly, child. You two have access to a good meal, take it." Her smile faded. "But as for Thistledove, the man was a nuisance before he became a lord, but if he's now using high-end sorcery spells such as a shadow chaser, things have changed for the worse."

"Shadow chasing is what you saw," Hilth said. "A practitioner of the spell can travel in an incorporeal state—but not for long. A strong enough sorcerer can go through shields, even powerful ones like the one you created. But he is limited as to what he can do in that state."

Kendric nodded as he used the last of the eggs. "That's probably why he changed your hair back—he didn't need to see who you were on that level, but he wanted to make it look like he had more abilities than he does."

Hilth sat on a boulder. "That he's connected to the Chancellor doesn't bode well. We've no idea if some of our abilities were taken to boost people in the Ceredigion kingdom, as I said, we never saw who took us."

"So, he could be with that army down on the plain?" Gareth asked. "Wouldn't we have noticed people from Ceredigion down there? No troops have been sent anywhere out of the kingdom."

"We might not notice if they were wearing uniforms of other lands." Kendric started swearing. "You'd been gone for a week down here? And another week before that in Hoeth?" At Gareth's nod, he started putting his supplies away. "I was ordered after Drubella by Chancellor Mertil a few weeks ago and was sent all around the country to hunt her. Someone was getting us, and probably a few others, out of the way. No breakfast for anyone, we have to get going, now."

"That's the spirit." Solange smiled. "Now as for Piallen and Tobias, you need to come with us. I do hope you don't mind us dropping your title—either of you—better not to give things away."

"We can't go with you; didn't you hear that nightmare I had? You even said you thought the oracles sent it—it was pretty clear."

"Or it was a warning that those events were what will happen if you *do* try to go back without help." Hilth nodded. "Think of it, you were stuck in place and alone. You needed help."

"If you want to come with us, fine, I will try and get my father to send assistance. After we've sorted out Mertil and Thistledove." Kendric finished packing things back up and kicked out the fire. "But we're not taking the chorogh path. It's too risky. We can travel quickly enough without it."

Solange snapped her fingers and the bedding for her and Hilth vanished. Tobias was chewing a pear, but he got his things into his pack and the pack on his back without a sound.

Hilth waved his hand and Piallen's shield vanished.

And the sound of booted feet marching down the trail was suddenly audible.

Chapter Fourteen

"Why didn't we hear them before?" Piallen got on her pack, secured her sword belt, but kept her bow and quiver out. They couldn't see the marchers, which meant even in dense woods, she'd be better off with her bow. A crossbow would be handier with armor, but she'd trained for years to find the weak places in armor with a longbow as well. Not that she ever expected to be in a situation for it, but it was good training.

"They have at least one strong mage with them, probably more." Kendric had also kept his recently acquired bow out. Although it hadn't been his to start with, he held it like he knew how to use it. "Piallen and I can cover your escape. It sounds like there are too many to fight." He nodded to Piallen with a grim smile.

She nodded back. "Agreed. Tobias, go with them."

Gareth's response was to turn into his giant snake form. "Not running."

Hilth and Solange shook their heads. "That's extremely noble of you two royals, but I believe we do have another option. It would be better that no one die today—and that no one sees who was here."

Piallen was watching where the marching sound was coming from, but glanced behind her at a whooshing sound. A patch of nothing hung there. It was as if someone had blocked out a round section of the trees, ground, and shrubs behind them. And left a pool of emptiness.

"It's too dangerous." Kendric had also looked back.

"And you two dying heroically as you save your friends, who can save themselves, thank you, isn't?" Hilth said as he motioned for Tobias to get on Gareth's back near his head.

133

Tobias climbed on board with a shrug and he and Gareth vanished into the gap in the air.

"Damn it." Kendric put his bow and quiver over his shoulder, grabbed his pack and turned to Piallen. "They have a good point, but please don't ever tell anyone about this." Before she could respond, he vanished, and a huge auburn coated stag appeared. "Get on, they're getting closer."

Piallen paused, then put her bow and quiver on her pack and climbed on Kendric. It was a good thing she was tall with long legs; she'd never seen a stag this size—Nevaine wouldn't have even come up to his back. He adjusted to her weight, then bounded through the emptiness.

Piallen had no idea what to expect, but it felt like nothing. The only thing she was aware of was where she touched the stag. It was just Kendric and her. No sight, no sound, nothing. After what felt like an hour, a circle of wood appeared ahead and they ran out.

Kendric shivered and changed into a man. Piallen was still on him so she fell on him as they dropped to the ground.

"Cute, very cute. But obviously, if you have a passenger, you do need to let them off before you change," Gareth said as he and Tobias sat a few feet over from them.

Piallen untangled herself from Kendric.

Two birds, large alsohawks with three-foot wingspans, massive beaks, and deep brown feathers tipped in white flew low over them, then landed, and changed. The larger alsohawk was Solange. Made sense, even though she was the smaller of the two when in human form, female alsohawks were often larger than the males.

"Okay, so where are we?" Piallen adjusted her pack. It was interesting that all of Kendric's belongings—and clothing—stayed with him through the change. She'd love to ask more about it, but considering how he felt about being a shapeshifter, he wouldn't be the one to speak to about it.

Maybe later she could talk to one of the others about it.

"We're not exactly where I'd hoped." Hilth scowled at the trees around them. "But we're not about to be killed by a bunch of metal-clad hooligans, so that's a start. But someone back there threw off our spell. I'd been aiming for the gardens behind the castle in Ceredigion. This is outside the castle grounds by a good hour or two walk."

"Or something on this side messed with it. The mountains have distorted spells in the last few years," Kendric walked in a slow circle. "There's resistance in that direction. Toward the castle."

"Now, don't race off. I know that was in your handsome head." Solange stepped in front of him. "I feel it too, now. There is a magical force around the castle grounds. It could be that something has happened and your father is enacting spell protocols."

"Or someone is attacking the castle," Kendric said. He had been polite to both wizards, but right now he looked ready to pick up Solange and move her aside to get her out of his way.

"And finding out which before charging forward would be a better plan." Piallen stepped next to Solange. "Without knowing enemy from friend, the battle is lost before it has begun."

Solange smiled and turned to her. "I like that one, is it one of the warrior poets?"

"It's my mother." Piallen smiled and shoved down the spark of terror from her nightmare. "She's a great strategist and often gave us quotes to remember things. It's valid in this case for certain."

Kendric took a step back and ran his fingers through his hair. "I'm glad that I was wrong about the way getting here, but according to the tales, if someone did make it work, it couldn't be stopped before it reached the destination. To my knowledge, our kingdom doesn't have the magical power to stop something like a chorogh path. Which means that the palace is under attack by someone with far more power than we expected."

"And how does that mean that it's okay to run in there blazing against such odds?" Piallen shook her head. "You have two...and a half...wizards here. Wouldn't it be better to work with them? Us?" It was great that Solange and Hilth had confirmed she had the ability to use wizardry, but she still wasn't trained.

Not to mention that years of believing she couldn't do much magic due to her leak still lingered in her mind.

"You have to get over your bias against wizards." Gareth had stayed back but now came forward. "You know I'll fight alongside you to the end, but if it comes to that, let's make it count?"

Kendric ran his fingers through his hair again with a sigh. "I'm sorry. I shouldn't have let my emotions get in the way. My suggestion would be if a bird or two were to survey the area, while we cautiously continued toward the castle."

Hilth slapped him on the back. "There you go. I'd say both of us should go. Keep out of arrow range, but we can get a better idea of the situation."

Kendric nodded and both wizards shifted, then flew off. Then Kendric continued the way he'd been headed.

Piallen followed closely, mostly in case he decided to do something heroically stupid, like leave the three of them behind. She was beginning to like Kendric, even though he had a stubborn streak and was opinionated. He would also have died to protect two wizards—people he didn't trust. She had the feeling he would do the same for anyone in his kingdom. He would make a great king one day.

"You know, this could be one of those times that I rode on your pack? If needed, I could hand you your bow and arrows easily." Tobias had started out closer to Gareth, who was bringing up the rear, but was now jogging alongside her.

"Hold up," Piallen said as she stopped to let Tobias climb up. She was quite able to get her bow quickly—she'd trained for that for months too—but she knew why Tobias was asking. He felt the same chill she did. It wasn't strong, but there was a coldness the further they went. She rubbed her arms.

"You're feeling it too?" Gareth kept his voice down as they started walking again. "That cold isn't natural."

Kendric didn't stop, but did turn. "I think we're all feeling it. It's getting harder to move forward as well. Not a lot, but the pressure is definitely there."

They continued walking, whether it was from his mentioning it, or because it was more obvious, Piallen noticed her footsteps slowing down.

All three grabbed their swords as a screeching cry, followed by a large falling shape, cracked through the silence and a few tree branches. They ran over to see it was actually two alsohawks who had crashed into a small clearing just past the trees. One helping the other whose wing was mangled by an arrow.

"Solange!" Kendric ran into the clearing. The larger alsohawk was the one injured, and she snapped her beak as they came closer. Alsohawks' beaks were large enough to take off a hand, so all three stayed back.

The second alsohawk shimmered back into Hilth, but he held his hand up. "That arrow has poison and an explosive on it. You all need to move back."

Kendric kept going. "No. I have some healing magic. I can help her."

Solange gave an odd hiss, but he kept walking forward.

Piallen shook her shoulders and got Tobias and her pack off. "I think I can help." She pulled out the wizard stone, it was glowing and pulling toward Solange. "Yup—so says the dead wizard. You two need to move back though." She didn't add *in case we all blow up,* but that was possible.

Holding the wizard stone and focusing on Solange, she could see the poison running through her. It wasn't fast, but it was heading toward her heart. The explosive element was trickier, it was tied to the arrow, which would kill her if removed. Kill all of them if it wasn't removed.

Kendric dropped down next to the injured bird—who hissed at him again. "You can yell all you want, Solange. We're helping you." His face was gentle as he touched her uninjured side.

"Why can't she speak?" Piallen asked as she kneeled near Kendric.

"The ability to speak while in a changed form is difficult," Hilth said. "She's focusing on surviving right now."

Kendric went into a trance. While still holding her stone, Piallen could see his magic as it worked to slow the poison. He was a strong magic user from what she'd felt, but he was fighting hard to keep the poison at bay.

Looking closer, Piallen saw why. The poison, the explosive, and the arrow were all linked—they were a trap. One aimed directly at Kendric.

Piallen knew he had to have felt it once he went in, but was stubborn enough to keep going. Trying to pull him free of it wouldn't be a good idea as it would most likely blow up all of them. So instead, she gripped the stone tighter, and followed his trail through Solange. The wizardry she'd used so far had been spell-based—her controlling elements to get what she desired.

This was different. She felt as if she *was* magic. She wasn't Piallen anymore, she was an elemental being. The world around her were colors never seen by the eye. She almost got distracted, then noticed Kendric was too close to the trap.

She reached for him physically to push him away as she cut his tie with Solange on the elemental level. There was a flare of anger from him, but then he was gone. "Okay, Pantiar, it's just you and me.

Help me." She felt a warm connection flow over her, but there was also an echo of...Nevaine? It wasn't her sister, but part of her left behind when she'd anchored Pantiar into the rock.

Piallen quickly stopped the poison, cut off the explosive, and removed the arrow.

She opened her eyes to see Solange turning back into herself. Piallen grinned. Granted, she'd had help, but that wasn't nearly as hard as she'd thought. Then she tried to stand up.

The world opened before her eyes and she fell into a void.

Chapter Fifteen

There was nothing. It was similar to the path Hilth and Solange had opened—but whereas that was empty but oddly comforting—this was terrifying. It didn't help that she had an odd sensation of falling. It was difficult to define, as there was nothing around her to base it off of. No wind against her skin, nothing.

But she was falling.

Faint sounds made their way to her, as if people were yelling from down a well. She recognized the people she was with; Kendric sounded the most frantic, but Tobias was close. Then Gliandra, Nevaine, Lizeth, their parents. Her friends from her first archery class. Everyone she knew was yelling for her to stop.

"This isn't where you should be. But only you can get yourself out of it."

The oracles? Her terror increased until she got ahold of herself. Her mother used to come out and visit while Piallen worked on her archery and acrobatics among the trees. Nothing important, just chatting since she knew Piallen didn't come inside much. She always knew when Piallen just needed her to be nearby.

Piallen grabbed onto the feeling of her mother. All the times she comforted Piallen when she fell out of a tree or missed a shot.

The feeling of falling stopped and Piallen became aware of the wizard stone in her hand again.

Control. This was all control. She simply needed to push herself up and out, just like she prepared for during acrobatic training as a kid. The idea of tree running—one of her favorite ways to relax—was that your weight had to be as light as air to race in the trees. Barely touching each branch as you went over them.

Right now, she needed to make herself lighter than that. She was being pulled somewhere she didn't want to go, and she needed to get out quickly.

Mentally putting her weight on her left foot, she leapt up. Or what she determined to be up, based on where her head was.

The wizard stone warmed, but it didn't feel like a warning. She repeated the move as the voices around her vanished. One more push and she shot up into the tree branches above where she'd healed Solange. She wasn't expecting it, so couldn't grab any branches and quickly fell back down.

Strong arms grabbed her as she dropped and didn't let go. Kendric held her and looked relieved. "We thought we'd lost you. You started to get up, the ground opened, and it swallowed you."

Piallen looked down expecting to see a hole, or at least churned up dirt—the ground was solid and untouched. And she was still in Kendric's arms.

"How did I come out of that? And without disturbing *any-thing*?" She probably should get out of his arms, but it felt good. And she wasn't completely certain her legs would hold just yet.

"How did you heal me?" Solange came over slowly. "I'm still stiff, but you saved me." She nodded to Kendric. "And that man holding you helped too. It was meant to destroy him, the rest of us if possible—but he was the target." She gave a small smile. "She's probably okay to stand on her own now."

Kendric gently set her down, a blush running across his cheeks. "I just wanted to make sure she was okay. She did vanish into the ground then fly back up without disrupting a single blade of grass. That's got to be hard for anyone—even a wizard."

Tobias ran to Piallen and she scooped him up. "I have no idea how I did any of it, but the oracles pointed out that I was going the wrong way. I had to go up."

"It was good you did," Hilth said. "Both Solange and I were weakened by the attack on her. We're joined, so what hurts one hurts the other. But even so, I felt nothing from you at all once you vanished. With that stone you carry, we should have sensed you."

"I wish I could tell you where I was. All I know is that once I realized Kendric was the target, I was able to save Solange. Then just, poof." She snapped her fingers.

"I don't even want to try and figure out what happened to Piallen. I'm still confused about Kendric." Gareth looked at Solange. "Why would they go after you if Kendric was the target? Why not just shoot him with the magic-poisonous-exploding-arrow." He nodded to Piallen. "They told me what it was after you vanished."

"Obviously our prince is directly protected against them," Hilth said. "Whoever they are. We weren't even over the castle when the arrows started. They hit Solange on the second round as we couldn't pull back fast enough." His eyes started to tear up and he turned away.

"It's okay, I'm still here." She hugged him tightly. "Thanks to Piallen and Kendric. But I believe we have verified that the castle is under attack. Even if they might not realize it."

Piallen put the wizard stone back under her shirt and sat on a boulder. Her legs were getting steadier, but she wasn't sure how she felt about the dirt in the clearing. She might not have actually gone through and back out of the ground, but she'd gone through something. And it looked questionable to her.

"So, they have the castle secured, but it might not be apparent to those inside, and they can't directly go after Kendric, but want to kill him. Why?" Piallen was used to being third in the royal line and even though her kingdom allowed for multiple rulers, she really hadn't been looking forward to claiming her spot. There was a good chance that she might decide not to. Providing she survived her Challenge.

So really understanding that Kendric's heir status might lead to people wanting his death was new and unwelcome.

"So he won't become king when his father dies?" Gareth looked around when no one spoke. "That's it, right?"

Kendric shook his head. "It has to be more than that. My brothers could easily assume the throne. Or my sister for that matter, if she left the oracles. As for the protection on me? This is the first I've heard of it."

Solange walked around him slowly. "You do have a protection, and I think it's from the oracles." Then she walked around Piallen. "So does she."

"Wait, the oracles are protecting me on the Challenge that they sent me on? Doesn't that seem odd to anyone?" She felt like something had changed since her adventure into the void. She found she couldn't stop looking at Kendric for one thing. He was attractive, but this wasn't the time, place, nor anything else for that kind of thinking. She took a deep breath, closed her eyes, and told her psyche to settle down.

"Are you okay?" Tobias was still in her arms and patted her face.

She opened her eyes and let out a long breath. Kendric looked normal again. Rather, her reaction to him was normal. Cute guy, but not even a romantic consideration. "Yup, fine. Just clearing a few things in my mind."

"Back to the oracles. As odd as it sounds, they could be protecting you both," Solange said. "Years before we were taken, the oracles had been growing more distant from the common people, even in Ceredigion. I know their standing had fallen in the years before that in other lands, but even in our kingdom it was happening. The addition of Jhali, Kendric's sister, to their priestesses did increase their popularity twenty years ago." She looked to Kendric and Gareth in question.

"The oracles are still honored, but I agree with Piallen, why send Astarious royals on these events to prove their abilities, and then step in to protect her? I might understand me, if they feel the throne is in danger, but as I'm the one who will destroy the kingdom, that also makes no sense." Kendric rubbed his face.

"That might not mean what you think it means," Hilth said.

"Or it could mean what we've all heard it means and Prince Kendric will doom us all. Stand still or this arrow goes through the girl." The voice came from behind Piallen. She grinned to the others, threw Tobias toward Gareth, then dropped and flung her dagger. Not as good as a knife, and she had nowhere near Nevaine's skill, but she still got the archer who spoke in the shoulder.

"I don't like being called a girl, at least not with that tone of voice." Piallen had her own bow ready to shoot before the archer's bow fell from his hands. There were six people behind him, all armed with swords that didn't match their attire. The people looked like farmers, their weapons looked like they belonged to guards or military. "I can move extremely fast and have been training with a bow since I was five. The question now becomes, who wants to be first?"

None of her companions behind her had spoken, but all seven people who'd attacked slowly lowered their weapons.

"Nicely done," the new voice was heavy and dark. "Not sure who you are, but I would take your own advice before I strangle him."

Piallen turned to see a tall, cloaked shape holding Kendric up by the throat. Kendric's arm muscles bulged as he tried to remove the person's hands, but the kicking of his legs was growing weaker.

Gareth was frozen in place, Tobias was watching from under a bush, but also looked frozen. Solange and Hilth had vanished.

Piallen dropped her bow and raised her hands. Had they been wrong about the wizards? Or rather, had she been wrong and Kendric been right? They vanished right as they were needed.

The massive person threw Kendric at her feet. "I actually don't want to see him die, not until he's finished out the prophecy. But you I don't know. I don't see a reason for you to keep breathing and I need a hostage so his highness does what he is supposed to." The shape made a motioning movement with his fingers.

Piallen fought, but she was pulled forward, like it or not. She reached for the wizard stone, but both it and her acorn amulet were missing. Kendric blinked, but couldn't move much more than that. He still tried to grab her as she was pulled past him.

The cloaked shape picked her up, then turned to Kendric. "You will go to the castle, kill your father, and assume the throne. The mayhem will fall into place as it is supposed to." He turned to the seven attackers. "You can do what you want with the other one, and that furry thing, if you find it."

Piallen felt a surge of magic slam into Kendric as the man spoke. Kendric got to his feet, but his movements were stiff, and his unblinking eyes had a bright green glow. He nodded once.

She couldn't talk but she wanted to shout as the man holding her still called Kendric closer. "Don't forget, this is your one true love. If you fail, she will die."

The longing in Kendric's face would have meaning if it were real. But Piallen felt another spell flow over him.

"I will save you, my love." The words were stilted and she really hoped he was still in there somewhere.

The spell holding Gareth and Tobias dropped and they both came running into the clearing.

The man holding her started to leave, not even waiting to see what would happen. But there was a gap in the spell holding her, so she kicked back as hard as she could.

He dropped her and she pulled out her sword.

Kendric grabbed her from behind. "Don't fight. We'll be together." He pushed her back to the mage, who magically bound her arms.

"Tsk, tsk, tsk. Whoever you are, shouldn't you be happy to have gained the love of a handsome prince?" This time her legs were tied as well, and he threw her over his shoulder.

Her last glance was Kendric standing still, watching them go, as the attackers went after Gareth and Tobias.

Piallen was trying to figure out what had happened and where Solange and Hilth had gone. They'd both been weakened by the attack on Solange, but she couldn't believe that if they had enough magic to vanish, they didn't have enough to fight back against this mage.

Or to stop Kendric from killing his father. Most likely this mage carrying her was just taking advantage of the prophecy to get the king out of the way by someone who could get close to the king.

She didn't want to think about the sounds of fighting she heard as he strode away.

They'd been traveling for about ten minutes, and Piallen still couldn't move anything, not even a finger. She was breathing, blinking her eyes, but that was about it.

"It was good of you to come along with the prince, made life easier. I had planned on tying in the friendship spell with his snake friend, but unrequited love is stronger. Sorry that you won't live through it." He kept walking in silence as if waiting for her response. Funny, since thanks to him, she couldn't move her vocal cords.

He finally continued talking. "You do have some odd magics; I will say that. It's taking far more work to keep you still than it should."

Piallen took that as a challenge and closed her eyes. She focused on slowing her breathing. Then on thinking about the spell Gliandra had given her. It seemed that skin on skin was needed to break it, and although he had her tossed over his shoulder, there was no skin contact.

She simply needed to save what energy she had, then burst out with everything she had tied into that spell. If it worked, he'd drop, and she could roll away and hopefully free herself. If not, she'd be in the same spot she was now.

She spent her time recharging and focusing on his words—he'd tied a passion connection to a compulsion spell. She was pretty sure both were sorcery spells. Not sure if that helped her situation, but she'd store it aside. Since Nevaine and Finnian had been training as sorcerers while still in the palace, Piallen had caught some of their discussions. Mostly when they came outside for a break, and she only half-listened, but there was something there, lurking in her memory.

Her captor was walking slower now and wasn't talking anymore. It was nice not hearing someone she couldn't respond to, but he might have given her more information to work with if he'd kept up his chatter.

The thing was, while she was starting to feel her body again, which hopefully meant she could move when needed—she didn't think she had enough energy to call up the wizardry spell.

The mage slowed down still more and seemed to be listening for something that she couldn't hear.

A battlemage spell and maneuver came to mind as she waited for him to move on. Many of the battlemage spells came with a full routine of physical moves as well the magic. She had been participating in the lessons, but the higher she got in the spell difficulty, the more she leaked.

She'd worn the acorn amulet since she was a baby, and she had no idea what it not being on her would do to her spell. But she needed to try something.

Her captor started walking again. He slowed down a few minutes later as he crossed a rocky, but mostly dry, stream.

Best time to attack is when your opponent is distracted. Piallen took a deep breath and focused on the battlemage spell. The wizardry one popped up in her mind as well. She hadn't meant to try for both, but she wasn't as focused as she should be.

The battlemage spell flung the man away from her, leaving her flying in the air. She was still bound but was able to tuck and roll once she hit the ground. The wizard spell slammed into the attacking mage and dropped him like a bag of rocks. But he was still groaning, which wasn't good. If the wizardry spell had worked as it should, he should be unconscious.

Piallen broke the tie on her wrists, then the one on her ankles, then ran like mad.

Chapter Sixteen

She had no idea where she was in relation to the castle or her friends. Hanging upside down while being carried had a bad effect on sense of time and location.

So, she did the only logical thing—she went up. It took a few moments to find the right tree, but the mage who'd attacked her wasn't moving yet from what she could hear, so she waited until a tree with the perfect grabbing branch was in her path. She ran as fast as she could, the effects of the spell he'd used on her were still lingering, then jumped and swung up using the solid lower branch.

Although tree running depended on the person's ability to keep the bulk of their weight elevated and therefore allowed for travel on thinner branches, that first jump needed to be solid. Some tree runners could literally run up the trunk of a tree—Piallen wasn't at that level yet.

She swung herself up into the tree and picked a different direction than where she'd been running. If the mage who'd taken her recovered as quickly as she feared, he hopefully would be thrown off once she left the trail.

She wasn't as fast as her runs back home—this was an unknown forest and she still felt weak—but the movement through the trees relaxed her. After ten minutes of running, she heard a person arguing. Loudly. She took a tree that led toward the voice, but slowed down. Stealth was no good if you knocked a branch, leaves, or pinecone down on someone.

The voice was Gareth.

"You can't do this. Damn it, Kendric, stop walking!"

Piallen almost wept when she heard a very much loved angry chitter. However, they'd done it, Tobias and Gareth had survived.

She kept moving until she was over them. It seemed like they were heading in the same direction that the mage who'd grabbed her had been going. Kendric was marching like a man with a mission, but from what she could see his eyes weren't as bright green as they'd been when that mage grabbed him. They also weren't blinking though.

Gareth and Tobias were walking alongside and trying to stop him. Gareth was carrying her pack and weapons which made her almost as happy as finding them. But if they kept going the direction Kendric was heading, chances were good they'd end up running back into the mage. Her spell hadn't worked quite as she'd hoped, and he could have recovered by now.

Piallen ran a few trees ahead of them, then swung down in front of Kendric.

Tobias raced past the other two and jumped into her arms. "You're okay!"

She hugged him tightly. "You too. I thought I'd lost you."

Kendric froze at her appearance and he blinked rapidly. Then he stumbled forward. "I...what am I doing?" He shook his head and his eyes returned to hazel.

"You were trying to rescue your kidnapped love." Gareth grinned and handed Piallen her things.

"My kidnapped love? Pretty sure I would recall falling in love and her being kidnapped." He looked around. "Where are Solange and Hilth, and did I see you just drop out of a tree?" His eyes briefly flashed light green when he turned to her, but it went away quickly and he didn't lunge for her and profess his undying love, so that was a start.

Hopefully he also didn't have an urge to kill his father.

"They took off when we were attacked. Piallen was grabbed, you were spelled to think she was your lost love and if you didn't kill the king, she would be destroyed," Gareth said. "You don't recall a thing, do you?"

Piallen ruffled Tobias' fur. "I want to know how you two survived. When I was taken, I heard you under attack."

"He doesn't recall that either." Tobias shrugged but gave no indication of getting out of her arms anytime soon. "Kendric fought. Oh, Gareth and I did our fair share, but Kendric just went in there and started fighting, took most of them out with that sword. He's quite good."

Kendric shook his head. "Nope, don't recall that either." He gave a shiver. "What broke the spell?"

"I'd say *she* did," Gareth said. "You were marching like a man on a mission, not paying attention to either Tobias or me, then she drops in front of you, and boom, Kendric is back."

"Did you use wizardry?" There was still a bit of annoyance on the word *wizardry*.

Piallen scowled. "On you? No. I just appeared, and most likely since our mage attacker tied your compulsion spell to me, that broke it. But I did try a combination battlemage spell and a wizardry one on our mage friend. I got away, but the spells didn't work like they should. We probably don't want to linger here." She wanted to know where Solange and Hilth took off to—most likely with her wizard stone and acorn amulet—but first they needed to get somewhere safe to hide. Somewhere not in the castle.

"I agree. Leaving this area would be extremely good." Tobias peered into her face. "Can I just travel like this?"

She gave him a tight hug. "I might need my hands if we're attacked, so why don't you ride on my pack?"

"Deal." He scampered around and nestled on the pack.

She'd often wondered how the grigeens, who were fairly large, could travel lightly on people. Someday she'd find out their secret, but being lighter sometimes made life easier if they rode on people.

"I think we should go that way." Gareth nodded to a thin trail to the left. There wasn't much of it, but it looked like it went deeper into the woods.

"Have you been here before?" Kendric's eyebrow went up.

"Nope, just feels less busy and we want less busy right now." He looked to Piallen. "I'm going to change into my snake form to see what I can find out that way—you want to follow me or Kendric?"

"I have no problem following a snake, but just in case there is a residual to the spell that guy put on Kendric, it might be better if he's in the middle of us." She turned to Kendric. "No offense, but your eyes have flashed green three times since you shook off the spell."

"What? They sometimes do that when I'm shape changing, or about to change, or really pissed off, none of which are going on right now."

Gareth changed and started down the trail. He could speak in that form, Piallen had heard him. But he kept silent as he went.

"Maybe that mage tied the spell he used to your shapeshifter abilities. I couldn't tell what his spell was, but I felt it—it was strong." And terrifying, but that didn't need to be said out loud.

"I'm sorry you got tied into this," Kendric said as he closely followed Gareth. He seemed to be apologizing for more than her being grabbed.

"Who knows, it might be connected to the Challenge. Us being here, not some crazed evil mage grabbing me as your love interest and then ordering you to kill your father."

"That was horrible." He glanced back. "Not the bit about you, but my father. Now that you and Gareth told me, it's starting to come back. It seemed so real and logical. I do wish I'd been wrong about Solange and Hilth though. I can't believe they took off when we were attacked."

"They might not have been able to fight." Tobias had been silent but now spoke up. "They were there in those first moments of the fighters appearing. They were gone almost immediately. After stopping by Piallen."

"What? How come I didn't notice? So, they deserted us and took my necklaces. I trusted them."

"Or they had their reasons." Tobias adjusted himself on her pack. "I don't think they meant harm."

"If I'd had my stone and my magic wasn't leaking, I might not have been grabbed. And I might have been able to cast a solid spell when I got free." She wanted training, and those two were the only wizards she knew of who were still alive. But she'd also trusted them. Even risked her life to save Solange.

And at the first sign of a heavy magic user, they stole her things and abandoned them. They, like the oracles, had a lot of explaining to do.

They traveled in silence for another half-hour until Gareth found a nice shelter. A large tree had fallen long ago, and it, plus the ones that had grown around it, created a small clearing.

Gareth turned back into his human form and swung in a circle. He could make a complete turn with his arms out, but that was the limit of the space. "Not much room, and we can't have a fire, but it'll be easy to shield and should keep us safe."

Tobias climbed off Piallen's pack and went first to the fallen tree, patted it, and went to the largest of the newer ones. He turned with a toothy grin. "They will also protect us. We are safe for the night."

That was good enough for Piallen. She took off her pack and settled in. Even though they didn't have a fire, Kendric created some of the little magical glow lights from before and piled them in the middle while they ate.

"They seem more orange this time." Piallen was ravenous and worked through an entire pack of fish jerky. Maybe it was all the magic she'd used. She had never been a light eater and had that been physical exertion instead of magic, she wouldn't have questioned her appetite. Apparently wizardry was like a long archery class. An extremely intense one.

"That's to keep them from being seen." Kendric nodded and held up his hand so one of the balls lifted slowly into the air. "The orange spell blocks the light from traveling more than a few feet. If someone is that close, they would have already seen us. But with this spell I can also shut them down faster." He snapped his fingers and all of the lights went out.

Gareth swore when the lights vanished as he'd been digging through Kendric's pack for food. "Come on, you know I never get that spell right in this form. I need light."

Kendric snapped again and the small orange lights resumed.

"You can cast spells in your changed form?" Piallen kept her question aimed at Gareth. He seemed far less prickly about being able to change shapes. "Sorry, we know nothing about shapeshifters."

"No one knows about us." Kendric spoke first but kept his eyes on the pile of orange lights. "We limit access to our people, most of the ones who are changed come to live in the castle. You missed seeing it because of the way we got here, but our kingdom is an entire valley, and the mountains that surround it are massive and deadly to cross. Few know of us, and we work hard to keep it that way."

Gareth waited until Kendric stopped, then nodded. "It does make it hard to know people from other lands. There is a fear that if information about us got out we would be hunted and either killed or experimented on. No one knows for certain the combination of wizardry that created us. But in answer to your prior question—yes, we can cast spells when changed. It feels more natural for me for instance."

"Does shapeshifting run in families?" She shook her head. "I'm sorry, but it's fascinating. A spell that is continuing to impact people not born when it was placed? That's a seriously powerful spell."

"It doesn't seem to have any rhyme or reason as to who are changed. I'm the only one in my family, for instance." That didn't seem to bother Gareth.

"I'm the only royal. Ever. No wonder I'm cursed." Kendric didn't seem angry now, just resigned. It must have been hard growing up as the only one in the royal family who was a shifter—and then to have a curse dropped on him as well.

Silence was accented by eating. Lots of eating. She hadn't been the only one who felt over-drawn.

"So, ten forms? That's got to be interesting." Tobias had eaten three pears and almost his weight in fish jerky and was rolling back against the fallen tree. His raccoon disguise was mostly coming off, but he kept washing his face to help it along.

Kendric didn't look like he would answer, then gave in with a smile. "Might as well talk about it, the shield should keep our sound muffled." He took the chunk of travel bread out of Gareth's hands—it had come from his pack after all. After a few bites, he nodded.

"When I was born, my parents already had a strong kingdom. They protected the clystikes, and welcomed them, as I said, to live in the castle. Most of our people acknowledged the changed people in principle, but when it's only a small portion of the population who are affected, it sometimes gets difficult to accept." He sighed.

"Most shapeshifters show early on, within the first year. Mine hit when I was two, and it wasn't pretty. The stag is my dominant form, almost more so than this one when I was younger. And it took a while for me to be able to control it." He gave a small smile. "My parents were shocked, but they handled it well. A stag for a son was okay. Then I added a new shape every year on my birthday for nine years. I wanted to run away and hide from everything after my tenth birthday. My sister, Jhali, is fifteen years older than me. She'd always had a religious leaning, but that day she went to the oracles and spoke to them. She offered her life in service if they could remove my changes." He shrugged. "They said they hadn't created them, so they couldn't get rid of them. But they were able to stop me from getting more."

"She sounds like a wonderful sister," Piallen said.

Kendric nodded. "She is. It was hard on all of us three years ago when our mother died, but in some ways it was worse for her. She's mostly isolated in the temple with the other priests and priestesses, she missed being around our mother, who would often visit her."

"I'm sorry for your loss." It sounded so formal, but she wasn't sure what else to say. Not to mention, he didn't look like he wanted to keep talking about his family.

"Thank you. There have been some odd things going on in the past two years with the shape changers. More are falling into it hours after birth, and not all survive. We still say only about ten percent of our population, but my father fears it might be growing."

"And it's only in your kingdom? I've never heard of your land, but I have a feeling that is deliberate."

"It is. It's impossible to stumble upon us, the mountains will confuse anyone who tries." He gave a wince. "There is a lot of magic in those mountains and many spells. But the protection one is the most helpful. It was created by Solange and Hilth before I was born. If they're not on our side anymore that protection will be gone."

"Now, don't get all doom and gloom. You really were a cheerful baby, not sure why that changed," Solange's voice came from behind them.

"Easy there, we mean you no harm," Hilth said as all of them stood and grabbed weapons. Both wizards looked exhausted.

"You left us to die, and you took my pendants." Piallen held out her sword. She was far more upset at their betrayal than the stolen necklaces, but that was easier to focus on right now.

"Now, we knew you had a better chance without us. I took these," Solange held out the two necklaces to Piallen. "To keep Mertil from getting them. That's who that mage was. He has grown terrifyingly powerful. If he'd gotten the wizard stone, he could turn it to focus spells far beyond what his abilities should be. As for the acorn? It helped us find you all by your magic leak. And was also something that shouldn't have fallen into his hands."

Piallen silently put the necklaces back on, but wasn't certain how much she believed the wizards. They did look awful though.

"How come you both look worse than when you left?" Tobias watched them carefully.

"That's a long story." Hilth shook his head. "But to sum up, we were too cocky. I knew neither of us could fight Mertil, and if he caught us—again—it would make things worse. As soon as he appeared, I confirmed that he was the one who took us twenty years ago, as we thought by his magic on those chains. But I hadn't realized that he'd sent a tracking spell after us. We dislodged it, but we're even more exhausted after fighting it off."

"We're heading to the castle in the morning. Mertil spelled me, but I'm free now." Kendric had stayed silent but still held his sword. Then he spoke a few words softly.

Piallen felt a chill as the spell flowed around them. Solange and Hilth gave sad smiles.

"As you can see, we are still us, and not under any spells. I am sorry that you had to use that one, Prince Kendric," Solange said.

"What was that?" It left a cold feeling in Piallen's soul unlike anything she'd ever felt before.

"A trilock spell. It's old and uncommon. It reveals all magic connected with a person, but it is risky to cast. Some things can be dangerous to open." Hilth nodded.

"It's what killed my mother." Kendric's face showed no emotion. "Or rather, releasing a hidden trapped dark mage killed her. But I didn't have a choice. This kingdom is under attack and I'm not letting it fall." Kendric's jaw was back to full clench. "To anyone."

Solange and Hilth nodded, but didn't appear surprised at the revelation. Considering that they'd been captured at the time of her death, Piallen wanted to ask how they knew. But the pain in Kendric's eyes kept her from doing so.

Kendric stayed silent for a few more moments, then sheathed his sword and stepped back. "You might as well join us. We'll need all the help we can get."

Food was handed to them, but no one spoke much. With a final check on their shields—Piallen's leaking magic had been what allowed Solange and Hilth to find them through the shield, now that that was resolved, the shield held.

Piallen wished she'd known about the issue before, but Gliandra had admitted she wasn't sure what all the acorn amulet could do beyond reducing the amount of magic she leaked.

Even though there was a shield, one confirmed as solid by Solange and Hilth, Kendric insisted on keeping guard. Rather, he and Gareth keeping guard. Piallen understood his rejecting of assistance by the two wizards, but she was hurt when he turned her down as well.

"It's nothing personal, but we're in Ceredigion now, so it's up to Gareth and me to keep watch."

Piallen nodded, still not happy, nor did she agree. But this *was* his land. One that she'd never heard of before. He was keeping their secrets closely to him.

She set up her bedroll with Tobias alongside her and drifted off.

The sound of hissing, and a lot of it, woke her out of her sleep. Kendric was asleep, and Gareth was in snake form keeping watch.

She had no idea why or how there were dozens of snakes just outside the shield.

Chapter Seventeen

"Gareth? Are these your friends?" Piallen had her sword out, but had no idea how to fight off snakes with it. Nor did she have any spells she could think of that would work. The one Gliandra gave her might work, but if it didn't work on the snakes, it could leave her with a bunch of unconscious friends.

And she'd still be surrounded by annoyed appearing snakes.

"Not that I know of." Gareth stayed in snake form and raised his head higher. Then rattled off something that seemed to be mostly full of long s-sounds. More hisses came from the surrounding snakes in response and he started laughing. "I think we're safe, they were coming to warn me that there was a snake spell out near the castle. They are afraid it was after me." He hissed back. "I told them thank you and asked if the spell hurt them—they said it was like a little shock, but actually tickled. They are going back to see if they can overwhelm it."

The snakes hissed once more, then dispersed.

"If it doesn't do any damage, why have it up?" Piallen put away her sword with a shiver. She had nothing against snakes, but that many in one place would make anyone uncomfortable.

"It would do damage to a giant snake. At the least stun him, possibly kill him," Hilth said. "I'd say our enemies are aware that we're out here, and what Gareth and Kendric are."

"And you two. There's no reason to think that they aren't aware you're with us," Piallen added. "Someone shot Solange down with the intent of killing Kendric." There could be two groups: one who wanted to kill Kendric and one who wanted to use him—neither option was good.

"The snakes are going to try to overwhelm the spell against Gareth on the castle, but do we need a bunch of deer to overwhelm a spell against Kendric? A flight of alsohawks for the wizards? And what about Kendric's other nine forms?" Piallen hadn't asked what they were before since he didn't want to discuss it, but it could be important now. She wasn't sure how the snakes tracked down Gareth, but no herds of deer had appeared.

"I'm not sure if the deer would respond to me, they never have in the past." Kendric handed out food from his and Piallen's packs. They still couldn't have a fire, but he seemed to have taken on the role of feeding everyone. Too bad he was a prince who was destined for the throne; he would make a great restaurateur.

"Not all clystikes are the same, and Kendric has always been the only deer. I don't believe your other shapes would respond if you don't use them very often. Gareth changes into his snake form more, so the snakes picked up on him," Solange said.

"I haven't changed into the other shapes since the first time they each appeared." Kendric shrugged. "For the record, they are: a large land tortoise, wren, small desert cat, duck, tree warbler, jackal, trilanx goat, stilfin, and an iterian rambler. I don't even know how I would switch between them. But if there is an animal-based spell aimed at me, it would be going after the stag."

Tobias was deep in his pack but popped back out. "The rambler would be handy in a fight. Not so much most of the others."

"The rambler was my final addition." Kendric shook his head. "That one I *did* try to change into after its first appearance, but all that happened was that the stag appeared."

"The stag has grown stronger than the others." Solange tilted her head. "Has there been anything odd about that form lately?"

Kendric shrugged. "No. I don't change often, but it's been fine."

"Aside from those paintings." Piallen ignored the look of annoyance on Kendric's face. He might not want to deal with them, but there was no way they'd been a coincidence.

"Paintings of a stag?" Hilth had been eating food like he'd not seen any for weeks, but he paused at her comment.

"Yes, twice." She quickly told them of the paintings.

"And they were copies of the tapestry in the castle? That tapestry is over five hundred years old." Solange was eating, but slowly, and it appeared that her right arm, the same that the arrow had gone through on her wing, was still weak.

"*Almost* copies." Gareth also ignored Kendric's annoyed expression as he jumped in. "I didn't see the first one, it was before I joined them. But aside from the hunters not having weapons, and being far closer to the stag, it was close to the same." He shrugged. "Well, for being painted on a wall in a ruined cabin. It was still clear though."

"And they both had impacts on the tall folks." Tobias lashed his tail to emphasize the lack of prior mention. "It appeared to involve line-of-sight. The first one transfixed them, the second seemed to be trying to do something, but never finished. It did slam into Piallen when she reached out to touch it magically. There was also a nightmare spell in the cave with the first one, but I'm not sure if that was connected. I think Piallen's wizard stone stopped it."

Piallen nodded. "The nightmare spell hit the two of them, but not me. As for the second painting, it was as if I'd entered a distorted reality. Knocked me back hard."

Hilth and Solange did that odd silent communication trick they did, then both nodded. "They were in Northalian, correct?" Hilth looked around. "I believe they were both a warning and a trap for our young prince."

"But they were made years, many years, before I was even born? Who did it? Why?" Kendric was involved now. He might not have wanted to bring up the paintings, or give them credence, but the expression on both Solange and Hilth's faces was worrisome.

"There were rumors when you were born. That you were the harbinger of doom. That was kept quiet by your parents, but those things travel. We were taken before you changed, but it wouldn't have been lost that you turned into the image of the spirit-born, the ysbryd carw in the old tongue."

Piallen watched them all. Like the existence of the kingdom of Ceredigion, this story was unknown to her.

Solange caught her confusion. "The ysbryd carw is an old myth. A spirit stag who has gone through death's land and survived and seeks vengeance among the living. He is seen as all powerful and unstoppable."

"Your people are really into doom and gloom." Tobias shook his head.

"Then why did they put up a tapestry with it?" Piallen was still sorting this out. She really wished Lizeth and Nevaine were here for this. An unknown kingdom, five-hundred-year-old myths, and a handsome cursed prince. They would both love it.

She would as well, if she weren't in the middle of it.

"Kendric's long-ago ancestor, Queen Jelwen, had it made by a song-weaver to honor the myth and to keep the ysbryd carw always under the watchful eyes of the hunters of Ceredigion. The skill of song-weaving has been gone for hundreds of years, but the spells used in it from that tapestry could have latched on and replicated the magic in those paintings you saw."

"In odd random places, that had I not been grabbed by the oracles to join Piallen I never would have gone to?" Kendric tilted his head back and rubbed his eyes. "I don't believe in the ysbryd carw. I am *not* the ysbryd carw. And until you can give me solid proof that those two paintings are connected to me, I won't believe that either. We're losing focus. There's a massive army waiting to possibly invade

Astarious. And there's a subtler, but just as deadly, invasion going on here. We shouldn't be focusing on myths."

"Unless the myths, as you call them, are tied to these attacks." Hilth looked between Kendric and Piallen. "She is on an important task for the oracles, her land has nothing to do with Ceredigion, yet the oracles included you on her adventure. Why? I doubt that was happenstance. Somehow everything we're seeing is connected. And you two are meant to help each other—and your kingdoms."

Tobias nodded. "That makes sense. Kendric can do things that Piallen can't, and the reverse. Those oracles, always up to something."

"They have reasons; not sure what they are, but they have them," Piallen said. "I really wish the stipulation of not finding out about past Challenges until you've completed one wasn't in place. I know their reasons, but I don't agree. Especially when these Challenges might be affecting more than just the challenger. Knowing what had gone on before could really help. But I agree with Kendric, if those paintings have no bearing on the current situations, we can't focus on them. We need to stop whoever is attacking or has attacked the castle, then get a fighting force together to help Astarious. Now."

Solange frowned. "I doubt those paintings had no meaning, and the fact that they appeared where Kendric shouldn't have been lends more credence to that—they might have only appeared after you were nearby, even though they seemed to be old. However, time is important." Her look to Kendric said she wasn't dropping it completely, just for now.

Kendric ignored her look. "We need to get into the castle, but we need to see what is going on inside there before we plan our attack. I don't want to go in blind, but we might not have a choice." He looked around the group. "Or sneak invasion, as is more accurate. We're not a very imposing force. One undertrained wizard, two worn out ones, a snake shifter, a grigeen, and me. We need to use stealth."

"I believe Solange and I are recovering, thank you. We look this way because we're old." Hilth did look more robust than he had the prior night, and so did Solange. "But, regardless, stealth is still the best action. Mertil overpowered us once and he did the same to all of you."

"Can I see the spell books you have?" Solange held up her hand as Kendric opened his mouth to complain. "They might help us. You four plan the invasion, Piallen and I are going to see if we can boost that untrained wizard status." She grinned. "Can't make you a wizard overnight, takes years for that—but we can at least get a few spells into you."

Kendric shrugged then closed in with the other three as he drew a diagram in the dirt.

Piallen was good at strategy, but she had to figure Kendric was as well. Besides, having some wizardry would help against that mage Mertil. She didn't intend to be captured by him again. Or allow anyone with her to fall to him.

Solange led her a bit away from the others and created a new shield. "Just so that we don't overtax the first one, and I definitely don't want anyone outside to hear us."

Piallen pulled out the three spell books, then the protected page of the spell that Gliandra had given her. "My friend Gliandra gave me this. She's not a wizard, but knows things. She said one of her order entrusted her with it. I've made it work a few times."

Solange smiled. "I recall her! She's a unique magic user and must be the last of the Illusterati from Laiandra originally. They died out hundreds of years ago—it's good to know she survived."

"I thought she wasn't a wizard. How old is she?" Some magic users could extend their lives, but the wizards were the only ones who oft times survived over a thousand years.

"She's...complicated. But I'd say she's possibly as old as me." She patted Piallen's hand. "This is a rare and solid spell, from a book lost to all except for this page. Keep it in your arsenal, but only use it when there is no other option. And watch using it against something large, like an army with many magic users. A strong mage could slip in during the casting and steal the spell once it's cast, using it against you and your people."

"Even if they're not a wizard? Don't wizardry spells only work for us?"

"A strong enough mage could do it. They couldn't create this spell without wizardry, but they could usurp it once it's cast."

Piallen shivered. She'd used it against Drubella, a strong mage from all signs. The terror she could have caused if she knew to grab Piallen's spell away from her was terrifying. And she'd used it against Mertil. Luckily, he hadn't grabbed it. Or maybe he couldn't because she managed to squish it together with the battlemage spell.

"Okay, now, put that one away, and let's see what else you have."

Piallen handed her the book Nevaine had given her. "My sister had been trying to read this one."

Solange nodded as she glanced through the pages. "This one has a great launch into wizardry—it would be almost impossible for anyone not with wizardry in their blood to read though. Let's see the other two." She handed it back.

"These two appeared in the pack the oracles sent me." Piallen handed them over. "Not sure where they came from, but Nevaine was having more wizardry books sent up from the university, maybe these are some of those? I have no idea how the oracles gather what they put in the packs—or how they get the packs to us."

Both books were close in size to the one Nevaine had given her, but were thicker.

Solange looked at the first cover, a dark green book with faded golden writing. Then she held it up to Piallen without opening it. "What can you read?"

Piallen had handed them over without trying to read the covers, but squinted at the symbols now. As with Nevaine's book, they transformed into letters she could read after a few moments. "Trials and losses. Spells for the kindred." She reread it twice. "Yes, that's what it says, but I have no idea what it means."

Solange pulled the book back. "The kindred is an ancient term for shapeshifters, even older than myself. Clystike is the Ceredigion term for that word."

"Shapeshifters were around that far back? How come we've never seen any? Or even heard about them outside of a few obscure children's stories?"

Solange looked down. "There have always been kindred, but before they appeared in the Ceredigion people, they had mostly vanished." She looked up with tears in her eyes. "Hilth and I were two of the last, we fled to the valley that became Ceredigion to escape it. The others were killed by terrified mobs."

"That's why Ceredigion is a sealed county." She understood Kendric's concerns more now.

"Yes, once it started appearing in the kingdom, Hilth and I strongly encouraged the rulers at that time to close off the kingdom for the safety of all. But now I'm afraid being locked like they are is doing more damage. I won't say anything to Kendric until we've resolved whatever is going on in the castle, but there's a stagnation here that wasn't before. Hilth and I helped create the mountain barriers to protect their people, but something's gone wrong in the past twenty years since we've been gone. The mountains feel sick." She shook her head and forced a smile. "But right now, we need to get a spell or two under your belt. I think this book might be a good start."

Time seemed to slow down as Piallen worked with Solange on the spells. Aside from the title on the green book, not all of the spells were aimed at clystikes, nor did they seem to have much to do with trials or losses. Piallen had a feeling that wizards not only had their own language, they had a unique way of looking at things. And that would take much longer to sort out.

The first spell was simpler than the one she'd been using from that page. It was a flash spell. That was pretty much what it did, flash a blinding light. The spell wasn't hard, but controlling how wide the flash went, was. Solange had kept her own spell up so that while she and Piallen could see where the light went, it wasn't blinding to them, and no one else could see it.

"It's a rudimentary spell, and won't permanently disable your enemies, but it will disorient them." Solange nodded. "Now for one that might be controversial, considering who Hilth and I are, but I fear will be needed in one way or another."

Piallen understood better when Solange explained what the spell was. The atharraich spell. It could transform a clystike against their will. And it worked both ways, freezing their ability to change back for one ancron—Solange said that was about an hour and a half. At first Piallen wasn't sure how helpful that would be against an enemy. But if they were being attacked by clystikes, it could be. Changing the form of a dangerous clystike in mid-fight back to human would disorient and weaken them.

After her fifth practice, using Solange as the test subject, Solange held up a claw then Piallen changed her back to human.

"At the very least, if you did that a few times, you'd throw off their will to fight. I have a massive headache." Solange smiled. "But it was worth it. The kindred master spell, or atharraich spell, is under your command now."

Piallen nodded, it was a scary spell in what it could do to the shapeshifters. But she knew why Solange had picked that one—they might be up against shapeshifters when they got into the castle. If that former Chancellor, now an evil mage, Mertil, had been able to capture Solange and Hilth, taken over Kendric, and grabbed her, he probably had a way to control shifters. Especially if they were a ready resource in the castle.

It felt like they'd been working on it for hours, but a glance up showed that Kendric was still going over the initial plans. "One more?" Piallen actually wanted them all in her head now. She really wasn't a patient person, but even she knew that wasn't possible.

Solange tilted her head and watched Piallen, then nodded to herself and flipped through the book. Finally she set it aside and picked up the last book, a deep orange one with deep russet writing. "Can you read this?" She held the front cover up to Piallen.

This one took longer than the other two, but eventually the symbols transformed into words she could read. "The Long Road? A little cryptic, isn't it? And how does that translation trick work, are the words changing because I'm a wizard, or is my mind making them appear in my language?" Piallen gave her back the book. It would be nice to go through it, and the other two, in a more leisurely manner, but right now they were trying to save people and kingdoms.

"The long road is what we call lifetime spells. They need to be replenished and strengthened regularly. For most wizards it's about half a year's time to replenish one of these spells, some longer, some shorter. It's a good idea, once we get you fully trained, to check the ones in this book at least monthly. You'll know if they're fading." She opened the book but didn't look down. "As for you reading the words, mostly it's in your head. Any non-wizard would just see the symbols. But our minds change them for us."

Piallen nodded and watched as Solange skimmed through the book. Another glance over to the others showed them in a similar position as before. "Are you or Hilth messing with things? They haven't moved much." She pointed to Kendric and the rest.

"Hmmm?" Solange kept her finger where she'd been reading as she looked up. "Oh. I've sped us up, Hilth is keeping the others from noticing. In our time, we've been here for two hours. Kendric would have been ready to drag us off if we took that long. For them, it's just been a few moments. Now, I think this one might be another good idea. It's simply called a lock spell." She handed the book with the page open to Piallen.

This one had an image across from the spell of a group of fighters standing still as another group attacked. "No other ancient name? Seems pretty straight forward compared to the others. It locks people in place I presume? Handy."

"No other name, and that is the basics of what it does. But it goes deeper than that. It can freeze your opponent by locking all of their joints in place. Held long enough, it will kill them. There are warnings with this one though. It only works when the opponent is moving quickly, if they are already stationary, it doesn't do much. And, like your sleep spell, it can be taken from you if you are up against another wizard, or too many powerful mages. If it's taken and turned against you, you will die, even if you're not moving."

"Sounds cheery. But also sounds like something we might need. Can you and Hilth cast it?"

Solange shook her head. "Neither of us can now. Once, yes, but that was long ago. We are both well over a thousand years old and have outlived all of our wizard cohorts. We're still stronger than a standard mage for the most part, but the heavier wizardry spells are beyond both of us."

That was a scary point. Piallen was grateful for Solange being honest, but she didn't like the idea that she might be the most powerful magic user they had in this fight. It was as if she'd been told she was the best archer in the army after only two days of practice. She wasn't ready and there were too many ways for things to go wrong.

"Now, now. I didn't mean to disturb you, but you needed to know the truth. Don't worry, we have plenty of spells still. Providing that we all survive liberating the castle, and saving your kingdom, we will gladly train you."

Piallen gave a small smile. "We just need to get through those two things. Easy."

Solange laughed. "That's the spirit. Okay, let's start on this one. Being sped up like this isn't good for any length of time." She held up her hand. "And it's not one to be used in battle. I saw that on your face. If there are too many people moving about you could end up merging with another—you'll both die horrible deaths." She nodded to reinforce her words.

This one took longer as the spell words kept trying to slip out of Piallen's mind as she worked it. No wonder it had to be refreshed. After a dozen tries, she finally got it to work. Solange rubbed her knees and nodded.

"That's as good as we can get it for now. Don't worry, we might not need it."

Piallen grinned then almost fell over.

"Sorry, I should have warned you, we're back in normal time. That just hurts more and more each time I use that one." Solange stretched and allowed Piallen to help her to her feet.

"I feel bruised. Was it the wizardry spells I was practicing or the time one?"

"Both. Wouldn't have been my first choice, but we had few options." Solange dropped her shield and they joined the rest.

Kendric got to his feet. "All done with wizard training?" He only had a slight twitch at the word *wizard*, which was an improvement.

"Done with three spells." Solange turned to Hilth. "I taught her the lock spell, the flash, and the atharraich. I don't want to push things and all of those were in the books she had."

Piallen watched both Kendric and Gareth at the name of the kindred spell. She wanted to tell them what it was, but a spell that was designed to go against their kind by wizards probably wouldn't be well received. Neither of them reacted to the term.

Hilth had been watching them as well, and he didn't look happy. But he only nodded. "Might I take a look at those books? We're going to wait until closer to the eight o'clock bell to go in. We're only fifteen minutes from the castle."

"That was a surprise even to me." Kendric started putting away the food. "We'd been more disoriented than I thought when we came here."

Piallen handed all three books to Hilth, but he quickly gave her Nevaine's book back. "I'd keep this one in the bottom of your pack." He looked ready to say more but a quick shake of her head from Solange stopped him.

Piallen finished putting away her things and found Tobias staring at her.

"What?"

"Trying to see if you look different." He narrowed his eyes then shrugged. "No one in the pack will believe that you're the first wizard. You look exactly the same."

"Maybe I could work on getting some bright robes and a sharply pointed hat?"

"Yes! That would be...you're teasing me." He turned to Solange. "Don't wizards dress up?"

Solange looked down at the dark clothing both she and Hilth wore. "Sorry. There were some wizards who wore flashy attire, just as there are for any type of person. But it's not required. As the first new wizard, I'd say she can dress however she'd like."

Tobias shook his head. "Such a waste." He shoved a few food bags back in his pack. "I'm ready."

"We still have about ten minutes before we want to head over. We need to get to the back wall at the exact moment the bells hit eight." Kendric turned to Piallen and Solange. "There is a brief moment when the spell around the castle drops in one single location, only for thirty seconds. It's at the back wall near the stables."

"Isn't that something you'd probably like to fix?" Piallen asked. She knew up until Lizeth's Challenge and all of the problems around it, they'd been a lot laxer about that level of security.

"It would have been, had we known about it." He gave Gareth a look.

"I meant to tell someone, but then I was out and about, and it's really not visible, nor is it large enough for most people to get through."

"It's a snake hole? In the wall?"

"Yeah. But it also cuts through the main shield at the weakest cycle for the shield—eight in the morning. Hopefully those other snakes have weakened the anti-snake spell there by now. I asked them to focus on that spot. As long as they have, I'll go through and release the lower pig door. You'll all have to duck, aside from Tobias, but at least you'll be able to get inside."

"Okay." There were questions but she felt it might be better not to ask. "Once we get in, what's the plan? I thought you wanted to have someone scout first?"

Kendric shook his head. "I did. But then I realized that getting in early in the day would be better since most people sleep in on All Eves Day—which, Gareth reminded me, is today. Plus, if the shield cycle is weakest at eight, another thing I didn't know about, that is our best option. There will be plenty of people up once the noon bells hit and most people don't work on All Eves Day, so staying out of their way is a good idea."

"I suggested waiting until tomorrow." Tobias sighed. "I was out-voted."

Kendric shook his head. "I don't think we can afford to wait. Not only for my father and our kingdom, but if we're going to save Astarious. We need to move fast to do both."

Hilth nodded. "The leaders of that army in Northalian kept Solange and I controlled magically, but seemed to have forgotten we had eyes and ears. The attack against Astarious was planned for two days from now, but our being taken should move things back as they lost a lot of their magic force."

"Or it could speed them up." Solange patted Piallen on the shoulder. "Again, you need to know the truth. There is a chance that they will attack sooner, even though they are weaker, in desperation that Hilth and I could move against them. But here is where we are now and what we need to stop. If Mertil is working with the Northalians, and since we now know he's the one who kidnapped Hilth and I, then it must be assumed that he is planning to control the clystikes of this kingdom as a fighting force to add to the Northalian army. Clystikes are fighters by nature, no matter what they turn into. And they are extremely difficult to kill when changed."

A dark look crossed Hilth's face. "That's the main reason the spell to increase clystike births was created. A cocky wizard found a hidden valley with magic rich mountains and a young kingdom, and cobbled together a spell to build more clystikes. His plan was to make an army that could take out any country it went against. When he was defeated, the increase in clystikes slowed down, but it was still higher than anywhere else in the world."

"Under no circumstances can we allow my people, clystike or not, to be under Mertil's control." Kendric looked like he would defend them alone if he needed. He clearly wasn't happy about being born a shapeshifter, but he wasn't going to let others suffer. He narrowed his eyes at Piallen's smile. "What?"

"You're going to make a great king, that's all. My parents are strong, yet fair, rulers, and will stop at nothing to protect their people. You will be too."

He blushed but smiled. "Thank you. I'm sure you'll be a great ruler as well."

She adjusted her pack and weapons, standing near a boulder so Tobias could climb on her pack. "Probably not." She grinned. "I'm impatient, stubborn, and not fond of staying inside. But both of my sisters and their husbands will be wonderful. I'll just stay out of their way. Even if I become heir, there are no rules that say I must ascend to the throne. Not sure I'd like being queen."

Kendric didn't look like he knew how to respond to that, so instead took the lead on the trail with Hilth and Solange a bit behind him. Gareth stayed back near her.

"So, if your sisters will rule, what will you do?" Gareth was taller than her and she realized that she'd gotten used to him in snake form. Looking up was odd.

"I don't know, to be honest. I never really thought about it. That will probably change when things have settled and I learn wizardry. Solange said it takes *years*."

The tone of her voice was clear and he laughed. "Didn't it take years to learn archery? Swordplay? I know how good Kendric is with a sword, he told me that you more than held your own."

"Yes, but those were fun lessons. I don't know that spells of any kind are going to be fun." She also wasn't looking forward to being treated differently because of her new status. Staying out in the woods most of the time meant avoiding most court people—that would change once word got out about her being the first new wizard.

But right now they needed to work on saving people. First Kendric's, then her own.

It was amazing that she hadn't noticed the castle when they were coming in, it really was quite close. Unlike the palace back home, which, while capable of defense, was mostly tall and airy, this castle was solid and screamed defense. An army could dash itself against those thick walls for months and still not get in if the people inside had enough stores to wait them out.

And yet there was a single hole, a way in with limited access. First thing she'd do when this was over and she was home, was personally check every side of the palace for weaknesses like that. And close them.

She still wasn't sure about this plan, but it wasn't her castle, nor her people. She would crawl in through a pig door if it got these people on her side. Part of her still wondered if she was really on her Challenge, regardless of what she'd heard in her head on her arrival, but the other part didn't care. Now that she knew about the fighting abilities of the clystikes, and their difficulty to stop, she agreed they needed to keep them from joining the Northalian army. Getting them to help defend Astarious was in the back of her mind, but that needed to wait. It sounded like Kendric was thinking of their regular army if anyone was to assist Astarious—the risk of exposing the clystikes to outsiders was too high.

She'd take any help she could get from anywhere.

They slowed down as they approached the heavy wall. It was massive and at least three stories high, and from what she could see, five feet thick. The massive bricks on this side seemed to gleam with strings of metal in them. She reached out to sense magic and felt none, but it was probably shielded.

Gareth grinned and changed into his snake shape, then paused in front of a drain with a crack in the grate. His tongue flickered out as he tasted the air. "The other snakes removed the spell here, well, wore it down most likely." Just as the bells started chiming, he went inside.

Piallen froze at the sound of a dark magic spell being spoken behind them. She threw up a shield as she spun, but was blown back against the castle wall.

Chapter Eighteen

Her head was ringing, but she didn't black out. There were ten weary looking guardspeople standing in front of them, with a cloaked man in the center. Judging by his finger movements and spell muttering, he was a sorcerer, and he was preparing another attack. Her friends were also shaking their heads and Kendric looked ready to charge.

"No!" Piallen was watching the sorcerer and saw his smile as Kendric stepped toward him. "That's what he wants." Her shield wasn't as strong as the one she'd done before and she was afraid that he could tell. Tobias chittered from atop her pack, but didn't get down. Solange and Hilth closed in on either side of Kendric, but made it look like they were supporting him, not stepping in to grab him if he charged the sorcerer.

Kendric stayed put, but didn't look happy. "Limin, how are you even here? You were banished three years ago—there's a spell to keep you out of the kingdom." He still looked like he wanted to run the man through personally.

Piallen let out a silent whistle. Three years ago was when his mother had been killed by a spell gone bad. A dark magic user who had been exposed when she cast a revealing spell. That would explain Kendric's fury, if this person was that sorcerer. It was impressive that they had a spell to stop someone from coming in, even though it failed. Why they hadn't killed him or locked him up was another major question, but not one to ask now.

She knew that once Gareth opened the small pig door from the other side, they needed to get through it quickly. And they couldn't have people know they were here. Keeping an eye on the sorcerer and his guards, Piallen moved sideways to the others. She dropped her voice. "I need all of you, even Tobias, to touch my skin. Now." She held out her left arm. Tobias reached down to her face, Solange and Hilth grabbed her arm. Kendric was last but he put his hand over hers.

She spat out the words to the sleep spell.

The sorcerer laughed at first, then his guards fell, and a moment later so did he.

"That delay was disturbing." Piallen still counted it a win, but now, knowing the dangers of that spell, she wanted it to be more accurate. Maybe it had to fight through a shield from the sorcerer.

"You're still learning. You did well." Solange smiled as everyone let go of her arm. Tobias patted her cheek where he'd been touching it and adjusted himself on her pack.

Kendric's eyes narrowed. "That was a wizard spell, wasn't it?"

"Yes, and it saved us. So, I'd say it was a good thing I'm a wizard." It felt odd but good to say that and Piallen would have added more but the small door, made out of the same stones as the wall, pushed open, and Gareth waved them over.

Kendric motioned for everyone else to go as he stalked toward the fallen sorcerer.

"I wouldn't." Hilth's voice was calm but had an edge to it. "He wants you specifically. He's not working with any others. Don't give him a way to get inside your head."

Piallen was almost to the door but turned at Hilth's voice. Both he and Solange had hands up for a spell, but they were aimed at Kendric, not the fallen sorcerer.

Kendric looked ready to argue, then clenched his fists and stood down. "Can you keep him there? I know no one of this kingdom can kill him, but I don't want him to wake up."

"Piallen's spell is solid. It will hold them like that for at least an hour. I can't do more than that," Solange said softly. But neither she nor Hilth released their spell stance.

Kendric nodded then stomped toward the gate. Piallen crawled through as he approached. She probably should have gotten Tobias off her back first, as he muttered and chittered as things got too tight, but whatever had just gone on with Kendric and the wizards distracted her.

How had that sorcerer made it so an entire kingdom couldn't kill him? That was an interesting and horrific spell.

Gareth had changed back into his human form and motioned to her from the side of a building that was sheltered from the rest of the castle.

"What happened?"

Piallen told him about Limin, and Kendric's reaction.

"Not good. Limin had his own agenda and even though it wasn't proven, it's believed he contributed to the spell backlash that killed the queen. They tried to kill him, or at least lock him up after she died, but he'd spelled himself to make it impossible. The king was too distraught at her loss to be rational and when the chancellor suggested banishment, he gave in." The look on his face showed what he thought of that.

Kendric, followed by Hilth and Solange, came through the small door with the wizards spelling the door shut behind them.

"No one can get in this way, but we can get out quickly if needed." Hilth nodded.

Whatever had gone on with Kendric and the sorcerer, he wasn't focusing on it now. "We still need to figure out what's happened, but we're going in with the assumption that the castle is under an attack of some kind. I'd originally thought we should split up to see what's happening, but with the appearance of Limin, I think it's best if we stick together."

Gareth nodded. "It's too quiet out there. Even for it being All Eves Day, there should be guards doing their rounds if nothing else. Listen."

Piallen didn't know what the daily castle activities here sounded like, but if she were in the palace right now, she'd say something was wrong. There was no chatter from the morning people, the chefs and staff, as they went about their business, no guards, nothing. Not even any birds.

Tobias jumped off her pack and slowly went around the wall. He came back with his tail and the fur on his back poofed. "There's a spell. It's moving about the castle and putting people to sleep. Not like Piallen's, it's weaker, but if it keeps moving it will keep everyone down,including us."

"A solin spell. Trickier to use because it can turn around and hit the spell caster as well." Hilth nodded. "But we can block it for a while. However, taking it down will be better done once we find the one who cast it." He closed his eyes and placed the tips of his fingers together.

Solange put her hand on Hilth's wrist. "Everyone touch his hands, you too, Tobias. Don't worry, you won't need to stay in contact like this, but it will make the spell stronger."

Piallen thought the similarity between Hilth's spell blocking a sleep spell, and the wizardry sleep spell that she knew was interesting. But she'd store those comments and questions aside for later.

A slight tingling went through where her hand touched Hilth's, then he nodded and they all stepped back. "The one who cast it is strong. I'll know them when we find them, but there wasn't enough signature to sort it out before. We have less than an hour to find them and reverse their spell or get out of the castle."

"My bet would be Mertil, but we'll deal with that when we find him. I need to see what's happened to my father. Be careful, since whoever is working with Mertil won't be expecting anyone but their own people walking around," Kendric said. "We're going to take the servants' way into the throne room." He didn't wait, but turned down another outer walkway, opened a nondescript wooden door, and slipped inside. They dropped their packs off in a small storage room that Solange spelled shut, then they went up a steep stairwell.

Piallen stayed behind him, and Tobias kept running alongside her as they went up the stairs.

The stairway was narrow and completely silent. Piallen fought off a chill. She hoped that the people of this castle were simply asleep and not dead. If the one behind this wanted the clystike as fighters, they at least should still be alive. Hopefully he didn't find it easier to kill the rest.

Voices above them a few moments later were startling since it had been so quiet everywhere in the castle grounds. Kendric paused until they'd caught up to him, but even then didn't go further. Too bad he said he had little control over his other shapes, a cat or bird would be a handy spy.

The voices above them got louder and footsteps were clearly heard coming onto the stairwell.

Piallen and the rest of the magic users all held spells in their hands. Tobias stayed against the stair wall and tried to shrink in on himself. Everyone seemed to be holding their breath as the steps increased then left. Hopefully they got out of the stairwell at another floor and weren't just waiting. But it had sounded like only one person, so even if they were waiting, they could be overwhelmed.

Kendric waited a few more moments, then nodded and continued up. He went slower this time and paused to listen, but they found no one at the next floor. He nodded and kept moving.

They kept slowly going up until Piallen felt she was just going to run past him and charge into the top room with her sword waving, when Kendric stopped.

This elaborate door was clearly an entrance to a royal room, even though it was still in the servants' stairwell.

Kendric tilted his head, then motioned for Gareth to step forward. Gareth changed into his snake form, then leaned against the door for a moment. His tongue flickered and his eyes closed. He pulled back and changed back into his human self.

Gareth kept his voice low. "The king is there, so is Mertil, I know his voice. There are others, at least three clystike, too difficult to tell how many beyond that."

"We have to get my father." Kendric's jaw was back to full clench and he almost looked ready to fight them all if they disagreed.

"Agreed," Solange's voice was low, but clear. She reached forward and clasped Kendric's shoulder. "We have to save everyone. And we will."

Kendric took a deep breath and seemed to re-focus. "Thank you. Is everyone ready?"

Piallen shrugged, plans were made to be changed and there were limits to what a small group could do against an entire castle. Wizards helped their side, but knowing they weren't as strong as they'd once been sort of offset things in her mind.

She mentally checked on the wizard spells she had ready. She did know a few magic spells that weren't too affected by her magic leak, but Solange had suggested not trying to cross them—that's what happened before when she ended up unintentionally mushing battlemage magic and wizardry together. It weakened both.

When everyone nodded that they were ready, Kendric sent a thin trickle of magic into the lock on the door and a soft click was heard. He shoved open the door and dropped low as a bolt of magic shot over his head. Piallen and the others had also dropped, she actually rolled to the side of Kendric and used her flash spell. It was simple but effective, as the cloaked mage, Mertil she guessed, who had been sending spells at them, stumbled back.

Two wolves and a large cat, most likely the clystikes that Gareth had sensed, also stumbled as the flash of her spell disoriented them. A tall gray-haired man with a sharp face like Kendric's sat slumped in a chair that was wedged in the corner. He was pale, but looked to be breathing. Three castle guards were piled around him. They didn't seem to be alive.

Piallen went to use the flash spell again when an odd coldness hit her. There was no magic to grab. All the spells, magic and wizardry, were out of her reach.

"You were almost as easy to get this time as before. Won't be doing the same trick to me again, though. Now what is this?" Mertil moved forward to grab the chains on her neck as he magically lifted the pendants into the air. None of her friends were moving so whatever spell he was using had hit them as well.

Not Tobias though.

Tobias had been down by her feet but jumped up and bit Mertil's leg. He released the man's leg immediately then jumped to the unconscious king and stood on him, facing the rest of the room and growling.

Mertil stumbled forward in pain, grigeen teeth were long and sharp.

"What have you done?" The familiar voice came from the open doorway. Drubella.

Chapter Nineteen

Piallen couldn't turn around but saw Drubella as she came into view. Still short, but far more of a killer look in her eyes now. She'd hidden it well back in Astarious. "The princess made it. I knew the deer-boy would get his magic together eventually and grab you. Honestly, I was counting on him killing you, thinking it was me in disguise, but you can't always get what you want."

Piallen worked her jaw free, but stayed silent—the wizard stone was warming now. Mertil had backed off when Drubella came in, so she might have a few moments to get the wizard stone to do something. Anything.

"Now, I guess you don't get a pretty dress, but maybe we can find another use for you." Drubella turned on Mertil. "Providing that you didn't mess things up. What are you doing? We need to take control of the clystikes in the kingdom and kill the rest. We had a plan to take over Ceredigion."

"No. I agree on the clystikes, but I've joined with another. We have bigger plans than just controlling this valley." Mertil raised his hand and a bolt struck Drubella in the chest.

She stumbled, but recovered with a growl. "I made you who you are, you grabbed those wizards and had no idea what to do with them. Where are they now?" She sent a spell, but it was deflected by Mertil's shields.

Piallen was slowly regaining movement and turned her head just enough to see that where Solange and Hilth had been was now empty. And that the window they'd been near was more open than before.

Piallen appreciated that sometimes people had to change the plan and, after her first reaction, she didn't think the wizards had abandoned them. But not knowing what their agenda was didn't help.

Mertil snapped his fingers and the three clystikes jumped at Drubella. "I don't need you to control the clystikes. I gained control over them myself." His glance toward the king said it wasn't just his power that gained the control, he was using the king's magic, and possibly more, for his control.

Drubella fought but the clystikes were too strong and soon had her pushed against the open window. "You can't do this. I brought you the Astarious princess. I made *you*." Her magic wasn't making much of an impact on the clystikes or the mage. The cat clystike jumped at her, taking a blast of her magic in the face. Both of them fell out of the window.

Mertil went to the window to watch her fall, then turned with a shrug to Piallen. "Princess? Well, not sure how helpful you'll be when your kingdom has fallen, but as a magic user I can still use you. Those Offialians aren't the brightest, but their machines to drain magic are exceedingly brilliant. Now, where was I?"

Piallen recovered enough movement to grab the wizard stone and spit out the lock spell. She wanted to focus it only at Mertil as he ran for her, but Gareth yelped as his arm froze when her lock spell nicked him. It couldn't have done much damage since he wasn't moving when the spell hit and it was only his arm. But he fell over.

Casting her lock spell had removed the spell Mertil put on her and the others. But she'd hit both Kendric and Gareth with her own spell. Piallen ran to them and touched their hands to release Gareth and Kendric as two alsohawks flew in through the window.

Both changed to their human forms just as Kendric was about to cut off Mertil's head.

"No! You can't." Hilth grabbed Kendric's hand. "The sleeping spell on the kingdom will never go away if he dies. He has to release it."

Piallen dropped the wizard stone back under her shirt and shook her head. "He won't do it." She stepped closer to the mage as the two remaining clystikes circled her but didn't attack.

Solange stayed near the door. "Mertil, you can't win. You've actually already lost. While you were focusing on maintaining control of the clystikes, we were freeing the guards. They will be slow to recover, but it will happen."

"He linked control of the clystikes through the king, that's going to be harder to undo." Hilth went to join Kendric near his father.

"You can't win. I won't allow it." With a yell, Mertil tore through the lock spell on his joints, and ran out the window. Piallen went after him, but, unlike Drubella, he didn't fall, instead he changed into a large vulture and awkwardly flew off.

The two clystikes collapsed, both still alive but unconscious.

"Did anyone know Mertil was a clystike?" Gareth looked out the window as well.

"No. He hid it well." Solange shook her head as she went to the king's side. "We still have to get the spell off the rest. King Brae as well. Mertil is gone, but his spells are still in place—weaker, but still active."

Piallen came back from the window. "Why didn't my lock spell hold? Shouldn't he have been unable to move?"

"He broke his joints to get free," Hilth said as he and Kendric lifted the king up. "His change into his bird form removed the pain, but when he becomes human again it will return. We need to get the king to bed, he's not doing well."

The room they were in opened to a long hall and the royal private chambers. King Brae was tall like his son, but more solid. His face seemed to be getting paler as they went.

Piallen wished she'd added a healing spell to her collection, but she and Solange were mostly going after the ones she could learn quickly and that would have the most impact on the people they were fighting.

"I can try to heal him, but I don't think it will be enough." Kendric had some healing magic, but from the look of terror on his face he was afraid of trying it on his father.

They got the king onto the bed and Solange went to his side. She stood there with her hands over him and her eyes closed for a few moments. She finally opened her eyes and stepped back. "I know we don't have much time before that sleep spell gets us, but this isn't going to be quick, and I'm going to need help. We have to break the spell on the clystikes first, then the one on the rest of the castle population will be easier to break."

"I thought you said you'd freed the guards?" Piallen had wondered when and how, but she knew that was what she heard.

"I lied." Solange grinned. "Sometimes that's just enough to throw people off." Her smile dropped. "Kendric, your healing helped save me, but for this you'd be too emotional. Piallen will have to help me with this spell. I have the knowledge, but no longer the strength." She tilted her head as she peered at Piallen. "Maybe that's part of the reason you appeared now, since Hilth and I are slowing down."

"Bah, we'll deal with that later. I never could do the healing spell she's talking about, so it's up to you two." Hilth turned to Kendric. "I know you're not fond of wizardry, but it's the only thing that can save your father and the clystikes. They are linked too closely; if he dies, they will as well. Possibly even those of us not linked to the spell."

Kendric nodded and looked toward Piallen. "Please, whatever you can do, save him. Save them."

Piallen let out a long breath—no pressure there. It was nice to not see fear and anger at the idea of her being a wizard, but she was terrified if something went wrong. She didn't have a clue as to what this spell was and knew there was no time for Solange to teach it to her. "I'll do my best." She gave Kendric a hopefully positive smile before stepping next to Solange.

"You'll do fine." Solange patted her hand, but her smile was small. She was worried too. "Now stay there, as I say the words and focus it on the king, you just hang on and add power. Hold my right hand and focus on the channel between us." She started to close her eyes, opened them again and looked to Kendric, then tilted her head. "A family tie can't hurt and your own magics might be able to call your father back to us. It should be safe since you won't be doing any healing. Take Piallen's other hand, she won't need hands to focus her magic."

Kendric took her hand but looked doubtful.

Piallen echoed that doubt but knew doubt could destroy a spell. She squeezed his hand. "We will save him, concentrate on that."

She pushed the fear of that roaming sleep spell, not to mention any clystikes who might be up and operating under Mertil's orders, aside. Helping funnel wizard magic to Solange was her center. She felt Kendric's fear flow through their hands and tried to calm it. But she knew how she'd feel if it were one of her parents dying in front of them. He calmed down and his fear turned to hope.

Solange dropped into her spell quickly. Piallen could almost see it in her mind, but it was like catching the edge of a whispered conversation—there was something there, but not anything she understood. Riding on the back of Solange's magic, Piallen felt the damage done to the king. The spell controlling the clystikes was based on their loyalty to him, and while the spell controlling them didn't come from him, it was leaching magic and life from him to keep it running. Had it lasted much longer, there would have been nothing left of him.

Solange was fast, drawing on Piallen's power and Kendric's love for his father to sever the ties of the spell and help lead King Brae out of the dark hole his mind had become.

The spell Mertil had cast was fast too. It fought back like a living thing, rebuilding the connections and pushing the king's mind back into the dark and empty place. They were losing him no matter how much power Piallen added.

An image of a lovely woman, one with hints of blond and red in her long dark hair flowed from Kendric. That got the king's attention, but his sorrow was horrific. Kendric pushed harder and more images, happy ones of their life together, passed through to the king.

The king started coming back. Like Kendric, he was a magic user, and his magic joined them to cut the ties to the spell.

"Thank you." The voice that spoke was rough and weak—but still there.

It took a moment for Piallen to realize that the words were spoken out loud.

"You made it back, thank the stars." The king was slowly getting some color back as he reached forward to grab Kendric. "He told me you were lost."

"He lied, your majesty." Solange looked tired but pleased.

"Solange?" The king looked to where Hilth and Gareth stood. "You have returned to us at a dangerous time."

"We were kidnapped by Chancellor Mertil. But we were saved." Solange turned to Piallen. "Might I present Princess Piallen of Astarious?"

Piallen was usually the last one to go on diplomatic missions or meet with visitors to the palace, but she pulled herself together and curtsied to the king. "I'm honored to meet you, King Brae. Hopefully, once this crisis is over, your kingdom and our kingdom can be friends."

"Thank you for bringing the wizards back, and I believe saving me as well. I am familiar with your kingdom, but I didn't know they were known for beauty and grace as well as strong magics." He patted her hand. "I believe you've already met my son?" His grin was broad even though he was still pale.

"I have indeed, thank you." Piallen felt a tug on her leg and looked to Tobias. She reached down to pick him up. "I would like to present my friend, Tobias. He kept you safe while we fought off the attackers."

The king's eyes went wide as Hilth and Kendric piled up the pillows behind him so he could see without straining. "A grigeen? My friend, you are nothing but myth in this land. I am honored to meet you. And thank you for protecting me."

Tobias preened and did a bow from Piallen's arms. "I am honored to meet you. Maybe some of our people can come here someday."

Hilth went to the window. "We don't have much time. The spell over the clystikes is broken, but the sleep spell is still active."

"How are we going to break it if Mertil was the one who cast it?" Gareth had been standing back, but his question was valid.

"A certain wizard-in-training, with help." Hilth nodded to Piallen. "Help from all of you, except the king. I'm sorry, we can't risk it. And your stone, Piallen." He looked around the chamber. "Was Mertil in here? Or mostly the throne room?"

"He would have stayed in the throne room. I don't know at what point I became unconscious, but I know that. Only people approved of by myself or my family can get through that door—no matter how strong they are." His glance between Kendric and Piallen was brief but noticeable.

"I'll stay with the king, you're all stronger magic users than me." Gareth pulled up a chair next to the bed, and noticeably set his sword across his legs.

Piallen and Tobias followed the two wizards and Kendric out to the throne room. "What are we looking for?" There seemed to be a delay in her words, like something was slowing them down. "The sleep spell is coming." She forced herself to fight it, but she had no idea how long it would take to fully knock them out.

"Keep moving and stay focused," Hilth said as he stomped around the room. "We need something that Mertil touched magically."

Piallen pulled out her necklaces. "He was trying to get these, never touched them with his hands, but he did lift them up with magic."

Solange was closer, so she took hold of the pendants. "These should work. He didn't grab the pendants, but his magic is all over the chains. I think we can do it. Together." She motioned for Kendric, Hilth, and even Tobias to come around Piallen.

"Tobias, can you get on her back? The rest of us need to circle her. Piallen, hold both pendants but let their chains hang free."

Piallen waited until Tobias was on her back, harder without her pack on, and the other three had gone around her. Then she raised the pendants in the air.

"Now, follow my words, and concentrate on the chains." Hilth rubbed his hands together then started chanting. All of them repeated the words even though Piallen had no idea what they meant. Both pendants warmed as she held them—which she hoped was a good thing.

Hilth's words started slowing down, and Piallen felt her eyes drifting shut. She stomped her feet in order to stay awake. If they fell, this kingdom would remain unguarded and asleep until Mertil or someone else came back to take over. It might not be her kingdom, but she wasn't going to let that happen.

Hilth took a deep breath and repeated the words louder. There was a cracking sound—one that felt like it went through everything, then the pressure to fall asleep vanished.

Hilth held up one hand as he stopped the spell, then smiled. "We broke it. Considering that I still feel like I just want to sleep for a few days, I think we made it just in time."

They turned to go back into the king's chamber, when the sound of a lot of feet in armor running up the stairwell hit them.

Chapter Twenty

Drubella had shut and barred the door when she'd joined them, but from the sounds coming from the other side, it wouldn't hold for long.

"Who's out there?" The king was trying to get off his bed, and Gareth was politely trying to push him down.

"You need to stay there, your majesty, we did run into Limin outside, and he and his people might have gotten in," Solange said as she began to close the door to his room.

"No. I'm strong enough to stand. With help. I can't fight, but I'm not going to be struck down in my bed." The snarl on his face told Piallen where Kendric got it. The king probably clenched his jaw a lot too.

"He has a point. I'd feel the same." Kendric slipped past Solange and he and Gareth helped his father up.

"They're almost in." Tobias remained in the throne room but was staying near the hallway to the bed chamber.

Solange joined Hilth in the front room and Piallen went near them. Her spell options weren't great, but if she had to, she'd knock everyone out and sort things later. Tobias must have guessed what she was thinking as he stayed next to her and put his paw on her calf under her pants. She, Kendric, and Gareth also had their swords out. The king sat on his throne and looked like he wished he had a sword also. Right now he looked fine, but having a sword and dropping it would ruin that illusion.

The door splintered open and two armored guards shoved their way in. "In the name of the king, stand down or be run through." The first one bellowed loud enough that had the sleep spell still been in place he could have awoken half the castle.

"Do you not recognize your prince? Or me?" The king didn't stand, he probably couldn't, but he lifted himself higher in his throne. "You draw weapons against the royal family?"

The second guard looked from Kendric to the king, then back. "We'd been told Prince Kendric was a...traitor...your majesty. That he'd come to kill you."

"Chancellor Mertil told you that?" Hilth was still holding a spell crackling in his hand. "The same Mertil who killed three of your order?" He pointed to the guards lying near the throne. "The same who tried to twist Prince Kendric to do his bidding, and failed? Think carefully before you answer. I'm old and don't have the patience of youth."

Piallen narrowed her eyes and stepped closer to the king. She didn't think that a sleep spell would do his weakened condition any good. Perhaps she could get close enough to touch him before she threw her spell.

Tobias shuffled over as well, still hanging on to her calf.

"Our orders were given by the captain, not five minutes ago." The second guard was looking at the dead guards lying near the throne, but appeared confused. His sword wasn't up, but he also hadn't put it away.

"The same captain who died defending me? I know you see him there. He and his two companions died to save the crown. The one that is still on my head."

Piallen looked back. The king hadn't had his crown before, but he did now. Tobias grinned from the throne and scampered back to her. He'd obviously found it.

"I apologize, your majesty." The first guard bowed to the king, then turned to Kendric. "And to you, your highness."

Both guards sheathed their swords and stepped forward as more guards from behind came in and did the same.

Hilth had dropped his flashy-looking spell, but moved back along the wall to watch as the guards came in. Solange smiled to them, but did the same. Obviously, neither were taking chances.

"Then who was it that I spoke to? I see with my own eyes my captain on the floor, but I also know I spoke to him moments before we came up here." The guard approached the throne, but stopped when Hilth stepped forward.

"I'd say it was Limin. He must have broken out of the spell and got inside the castle. He's not a wizard, but a well-trained sorcerer can trick the eye for short periods. Or Thistledove. He was up to something." Hilth nodded.

"We found Thistledove just minutes before the fake captain approached us. But he ran off before we could speak to him." The guard nodded. "Might we remove our fellow guards, your majesty?"

There seemed to be a number of people working toward taking over this kingdom. While they might have been working together at some point, that wasn't the case anymore.

The king still held himself rigid but gave a small nod. "Please do so and make sure they are treated with honor. They died protecting me against great forces."

The three dead guards were carefully carried out and then the one who'd first broken in stopped and looked at the door with a wince. "I will have this repaired immediately, your majesty."

"I believe I can fix it, if that's okay?" Solange looked to the king.

"Please do so, thank you. Guardsman Gath, I will need guards posted at the bottom of the stairs and on each floor. Both on that stairwell, and the official entrance. I will be in consultation with my advisors and am not to be disturbed."

Guardsman Gath glanced around the room, stopping at Tobias. But he simply nodded and carried out his orders.

Piallen watched as Solange rebuilt the door splinter by splinter. Her hands moved quickly as she spelled the pieces back into place. In less than a minute the door was as solid as before.

"Can you teach me that? Does it work with other things besides doors?" Piallen wasn't sure if it would have a fighting use, and that's what her spells had been aimed at so far. But this one was cool. And could be handy at some point.

"Yes, once we get your full training lined up, I believe you could master this one. Some wizardry is more nature based, relying on the natural order of the world. Your abilities would do well in that area."

"As opposed to me, who mostly blows things up." Hilth laughed. "I can do other things as well, but she's right, you'll be good at both."

Piallen shook her head. "Once we stop the Northalian army and save my kingdom that is. Can we get back there the same way we came here?"

"I believe so, we should be able to use the chorogh path again. There are limitations, but we should be fine."

"I would like to hear more of what has happened. And speak more to our fine grigeen friend." The king had slumped back down in his throne once the guards left and the door had been repaired. He looked even paler than before.

"You need to be resting, where are Rhys and Donall?" Kendric went to his father.

"I can't rest, not now. We were invaded, and that can't go unchallenged. I sent your brothers to the oracles' temple. I told Donall it was to protect the priests and priestesses."

Kendric laughed. "Good idea, you know that he would fight going otherwise. He's stubborn."

"All of my boys are." The king's smile matched Kendric's.

The king conceded to move to a long low chair instead of his throne, but he refused to go back to bed. They took turns filling the king in on everything from Kendric trying to magically grab Drubella, getting Piallen instead, rescuing Solange and Hilth, to their attack in the forest outside of the castle. King Brae's face kept getting grimmer.

"None of this is good and I fear it does sound like this army is aimed at Astarious. I know we don't have a treaty with your kingdom, we don't have one with any of them, but we shall try to help where we can. The first objective is to stop that army before it leaves Northalian. It's always better to keep your opponent out of the field, than have to defend one's home."

"That sounds like something my mother would say." Piallen smiled. "Would it be possible to go to the oracles' temple before we leave? I feel they are more involved in things than my family believes." She briefly explained about the Challenge and the fact that the oracles had sent Kendric along with her.

"Interesting, I'd love to hear the history of this Challenge once we have stopped the attack. It will take me a while to get the army together, if Solange and Hilth can assist, in case we have any more duplicates in the ranks?" At their nods he turned back to Piallen. "Then yes, please make it quick though. Kendric and Gareth can escort you and Tobias."

Piallen nodded and went for the door. Gareth and Tobias were behind her, but Kendric paused before his father. "I know it's something we hadn't talked about, but I'd like to gather a group of fighters from among the clystike. I believe they will help push things over for our side."

Piallen and Gareth both stopped. The shock on Gareth's face was probably on her own. Kendric didn't like being a clystike, and keeping them secret from the rest of the world had been this kingdom's plan since they first started appearing.

The king looked startled, but recovered quickly. "A small group, but they all have to fully understand that if they are captured in battle, we might not be able to save them."

Kendric nodded and passed Piallen and Gareth. "Let's go."

He took the lead as they left the castle and headed down a sheltered path in the woods outside the walls.

"The oracles don't think it's safer to be inside the castle walls? Well, normally?" Piallen asked.

Tobias hadn't asked to ride on her back, which was good since they'd left their packs behind. He seemed happy to scurry alongside all three of them, making chittering noises when he felt they were going too slow.

"No, they claim they need to be separate. Even though they are in our land, they aren't part of Ceredigion. And they are probably far safer than the castle is, even before our invasion." He nodded to a slim white tree as they passed. Piallen felt a flow of questing magic pass over her.

"Are those magic defenses? Oh, they are very nice." Tobias was more excited than a small child in a bakery. He bounced to the first white tree, then stayed off the path to rub against them all. The trees were a few feet from the trail and seemed to be about five feet apart. Piallen had never heard of or seen such things, but maybe they could duplicate them back home.

"They are." Kendric dropped back into whatever thoughts he was working through, and even Gareth seemed lost in thought, so Piallen just enjoyed the walk.

The oracles' temple was really a compound of smaller buildings. The people going about their business were definitely human. Hopefully Kendric's sister would be able to facilitate a way to get the information—and her questions—to the oracles themselves.

"Prince Kendric, your sister and brothers will be glad to see you." A tall older man in gray robes approached and bowed deeply.

"Priest Fallin, I'm glad to see you are doing well." Kendric's genuine smile lit his face and he gave a small bow. "These are my companions, Princess Piallen and Tobias of Astarious, and I believe you know Gareth."

The priest nodded to all of them, but then came forward to take Piallen's hand. "I am honored to meet a challenger. The oracles foresaw your arrival but were unsure on exactly when it would happen. Please, leave your weapons on that bench and come with me." He turned and led them to the largest building in the group, one with elaborate columns and subtle designs painted on the tall walls.

Piallen wasn't fond of being unarmed, especially after what they'd just gone through, but there was a peace here.

Gareth saw someone he knew and waved. "I'm going to go catch up with Jhali, I'll tell her you'll be by in a bit." The look on his face said that priestess or not, Gareth had a thing for Kendric's older sister.

The stunning woman was working with three others in a garden and stood at Gareth's arrival. She had light blond hair that reached mid-back, deep brown eyes, and almost looked happier to see Gareth than Kendric—although she did wave to him as well.

"Your best friend and your sister? Is that a thing?" Piallen kept her voice low as she didn't want to offend the priest if their calling included celibacy.

"He's had a crush on her since we were all kids. He's helped her get through losing our mother as well. And no, the oracles don't require their people to be celibate." He grinned as they went through the main door.

The hall was huge, and yet intimate at the same time. Priests and priestesses nodded as they went by, and more than one looked ready to run and hug Tobias—or at least pet him.

Tobias looked ready to run to them as well.

Piallen waved him off. "Go. I'm sure if you need to be there, the oracles will make it happen."

He didn't even wait until she'd finished speaking before taking off.

Priest Fallin turned as Tobias ran to greet two men and a woman. "They are sorely missed, the grigeens. Now that they are back in the world, perhaps some can come here."

Piallen was going to ask how he knew about that, being as cut off as they were, then shook her head. Oracles. "They are trying to relocate packs throughout the land, if Ceredigion opens its borders, maybe some could move here."

Sadness briefly crossed Fallin's face, but he recovered quickly. "I'm sure something can be arranged. Please come into the room of silence, the oracles await."

Piallen froze. She figured the priests and priestesses would speak for the oracles—not that they would reach out directly. Even Kendric looked concerned and slowed down.

"There is nothing to worry you, Princess Piallen. The oracles just wish a more direct interaction with what they have to say." Fallin paused. "To both of you. Alone."

"The oracles only appear to the priests and priestesses. That's always been the case." Now Kendric stopped walking. "And what has this to do with me? It's Piallen's Challenge."

"One that you are included in for a reason, Prince Kendric. Please, enter." The priest stood in front of a small, yet ornate door.

"You're not coming with us?" Piallen had grown up hearing about the far distant oracles who influenced things, lead the Challengers on their journeys, but didn't speak to others directly. In person.

"No. They wish to speak to you both in private. I will go visit with Tobias." He gave a small bow, then left.

"Do we knock? Just walk in?" Piallen stepped next to Kendric, but he hadn't moved toward the door.

He ran his hand through his hair. "I have no idea. If I had time, I'd go ask Jhali about this—it's never been done. At least not since I've been alive." He took a step forward and knocked on the door. It wasn't a forceful knock at all, but the door gently swung open.

Piallen flinched when she heard the same chime that had announced the start of her Challenge. Kendric stepped forward, so she followed.

The chamber was small, with soft padded benches along the walls.

And there was no one there. There were also no other doors and no windows.

Piallen jumped when the door swung shut behind them. "Okay, I'll admit this is making me nervous." She kept her voice low, there might not be anyone else in there but that didn't mean no one could hear them.

"Do not fear, child, there is only goodness for those who serve the oracles. Your sisters and those in your family before them have all served us well." The voice came through first, then three ghostly shapes drifted through the walls. "Now it is time for your sacrifice."

Chapter Twenty-One

Piallen scrambled back toward the door and Kendric held his hand up for a spell.

"Sacrifice? What is this?" Kendric moved so that he was blocking Piallen.

She figured if those oracles, or whatever they were, could go through a solid wall, going through him wouldn't be a problem. But she appreciated the sentiment. She stepped around Kendric. "Who are you to call for my sacrifice?" She automatically reached to put her hand on the hilt of her sword, before remembering they'd left their weapons outside.

Instead, she reached for her wizard stone. She had no idea if these were truly oracles or not, but she wasn't taking chances.

"It is okay, Pantiar's stone doesn't need to be involved. There are many kinds of sacrifice, not all require a fighting defense. Please, sit, both of you. We mean you no harm."

Piallen sat, but didn't release her hold on the stone.

Kendric remained standing. "What kind of sacrifice?"

"Your lives, but not as you think. We have been encouraging changes that needed to happen but that we could not do directly in other people. Most of it through the Astarious royals. Here is our last stand, if you will. The mountains surrounding this valley protect us, but we aren't what we once were. Things went wrong. We've tried to fix them, but now we need to directly ask for help. The prince who would end his kingdom and the first wizard, you are both called on to surrender your individual lives and join as one."

Piallen's mind took a split second to catch their meaning. "You are saying we are to be married? We barely know each other." She got to her feet. "I know my sisters both came back with the loves of their lives, but it takes more than a handsome face to make me fall in love in a week." She turned to Kendric. "No offense."

He shrugged. "None taken. I feel the same. Not to mention how could us being married help you?"

"It's not to help us, but your kingdoms, and the world. It's very complicated. But Kendric was the prince to end his kingdom—as it is. There is a stagnation in the land, it's been building so subtly that we didn't notice it until recently. We can't fix it, so you and your people must."

"Well, it was noticed at your birth," a second oracle added. "Time is different for us than for you. But this kingdom must be cleansed, and then opened—no more hiding."

"What has that got to do with him and me?" Piallen was certain she was missing something big.

"Together you two will find a way to save this land, and bring back the wizards to the world, as they were meant to be. Like the grigeens, they are essential to the balance of the world."

"I'm not being a wizard brood mare." Piallen turned on her heels. "That's it, I'm out." She pushed on the door, but it didn't budge.

"You wouldn't need to be. As more wizards come into the world, more will follow. We could make it very comfortable for you both."

Piallen was attracted to Kendric, he was handsome, kind, and honorable—he also had a good sense of humor when he wasn't clenching his jaw. But she needed far more time to fall in love. But a feeling flowed over her and she turned to Kendric. It was as if they'd known each other for years.

"No." Piallen broke free of the spell and stepped back. "Is *this* my Challenge? Is this what you've become? Are we just playing pieces you move around the board?" Her family had followed the oracles, and these Challenges, for hundreds of years—some people never returned. And this was what it was for? So she could marry someone she barely knew?

Kendric shook his head as he also pulled away from the oracles' spell. "My sister believed in you."

"We are not handling this well. It has been eons since we have even been in this form, let alone bodies as you have. We apologize. We will not force anything, but know that you will need to work together to save both kingdoms, and many more. It would be easier if you two were mated, but it won't be forced. This has gone beyond any Challenge; we are fighting to save this world. Not for us, we're past that, but for you."

Another oracle moved forward. "We did not mean to upset you, either of you. We also apologize that Prince Kendric grew up with a misunderstood curse, it was not meant as such—he is to *change* his kingdom, not destroy it. Go forth and listen to your hearts. Save who you can."

All three turned and went back into the wall before either Piallen or Kendric could speak.

The door popped open, but Kendric turned to her. "Are you okay?"

"I'm annoyed and pissed, but aside from that, I'm fine." She tilted her head. "Are you okay? Whatever they were trying to force between us aside, they did leave you with a grossly misunderstood curse for your entire life."

"True. I don't think they mean badly, but they need to work on their communication."

They walked out into the main chamber to find Gareth, Tobias, and Jhali waiting. Jhali ran to Kendric and hugged him. "Was it good news, little brother?" She beamed to Piallen. "You must be Princess Piallen, I am honored to meet you."

Kendric stepped back from his sister. "Did you know what they were doing?"

"Not fully. Even to us, the oracles rarely appear in that form. But they said you would be arriving with your queen." She wrinkled her nose as she took in their faces. "And that's not what is happening. I'm sorry."

"I have nothing against your brother, but we did only just meet a few days ago. I'm not marrying anyone at this point," Piallen said.

"But he does have such a lovable, cranky face, doesn't he?" Jhali reached up and shook Kendric's jaw.

"That's enough of that and any future matchmaking. But the oracles did tell me that my curse was wrong, that it meant I would change the kingdom, not destroy it. And that we need to cleanse the mountains and then open our kingdom. They said we're stagnating and it will eventually kill everyone in the kingdom."

She nodded and motioned for everyone to follow her outside. "The part about your curse I hadn't heard before, but the other has been a topic for the last few months here. We've been working on finding a way to stabilize the clystike situation. We can't change people back, but we can protect the ones being born. Perhaps even reduce the number born, although as Gareth pointed out, many clystikes like being who they are and might not want to deprive someone else of that. But the mountains must be cleansed." She led them to a table loaded with food. "For now, eat. I fear you all have a heavy path ahead of you. Now, what news of our father?"

They sat and discussed the attack and the massive army forming in Northalian.

Jhali's scowl was a mirror of both her father and her brothers'. "Mertil and Limin grew too bold. I can't say that I am surprised about Thistledove, there was always something disturbing about him. And I never did trust Drubella." She nodded to Piallen. "You're lucky she only marked you as a decoy and didn't do more. The oracles are losing their ability to see the world and some people are able to block them. She was one. But it is a joyous thing that you brought back Solange and Hilth, as well as you being a wizard yourself."

Two boys, both with dark brown hair, hazel eyes, and Kendric's jaw, came running up. The taller one was probably close in height with Kendric and had that gangly teenager look. His eyes lit up when he saw Piallen.

"I am Prince Donall, and quite pleased to meet you." His bow was more of a nod and the emphasis on his title was clear.

Kendric looked up from his food, then shook his head. "Donall, please meet *Princess* Piallen. And she's not impressed by you being a prince."

Piallen kept from laughing and gave a polite head nod to the younger prince. It must be odd to not have any interaction beyond one's own kingdom—especially at sixteen. "I am honored to meet you."

The younger boy next to him looked with wide eyes at Tobias. "Is that real?"

Tobias flashed his teeth in a mostly-there-grin. "I hope so, or all this food has been wasted. And I don't believe in wasting food."

"Rhys, meet the princess and her grigeen companion, Tobias. Now both of you sit and eat."

"You sound like dad." Donall kept watching Piallen as he dropped into a chair. But it didn't stop him from amassing a huge pile of food.

Rhys slid down as close as he could get to Tobias without sitting on him. "How do you talk? Is it a trick? Magic? Are there strings?"

"How do *you* talk?" Tobias peered into Rhys' face. "It's the same, really. Although can you do this?" He popped a shell covered nut into his mouth, crunched twice and spit out the shell.

Piallen laughed, he used to do that a lot when she was young—until she decided to copy him and almost choked. Granted, she'd only been six at the time. Rhys was nine, so probably smart enough not to try it.

Jhali looked at Rhys and shook her head. "Don't."

Rhys put down the nut he'd grabbed then went back to asking Tobias a million questions.

"How soon will the army move out? There's no way to get them across two kingdoms and into Northalian quickly." Jhali might be a priestess, but she was still a princess of Ceredigion.

"Wait, the army is marching?" Donall dropped his focus on Piallen. "I get to go, right? I've trained."

Kendric and Jhali shared a look, she nodded to him.

"They are marching to help Piallen's kingdom, and honestly any others who might be in the path of this army if Astarious falls. You'd have to talk to our father, but he might need you to stay. He was injured in the recent attack and will need help."

Donall rolled his eyes and looked between his two older siblings. "You're just saying that. He's fine."

Jhali took Donall's hand. "He's not. I felt it, just as I feel if anything happens to you three. It's serious, Donall. And right now, our kingdom is facing changes far beyond anything faced before. You need to step up, but it might not be what you think it is."

Even Rhys looked away from Tobias at the tone of her voice. "He's okay, though, right?" The fear in his eyes reminded Piallen that he'd only been about six when his mother died.

"He will be. He has two wizards looking after him." Piallen smiled. "They won't let anything happen to him." They would also be going on the trip to stop the army, but Rhys didn't need to hear that.

Tobias got to his feet. "I would love to see more of this place, do you think you could give me a tour?" He loved food and walking away from a feast was unheard of. Unless a child needed him.

Piallen smiled but said nothing.

Rhys nodded and grabbed some cookies. "Let's go. I have a lot of places no one else even knows about." He nodded to his siblings, then they left.

"That's a kind grigeen. Rhys still hasn't recovered from our mother's death." Jhali turned back to Kendric. "Now, about this battle?"

He told her about his plan to gather a small group of clystikes and use a chorogh path. But admitted trying to find a fast way to move the rest of the army was stumping him.

Piallen looked around. "How does the chorogh path work? I know it's opened and closed by clystikes only. And that only they can travel it, but what magic is making that happen? Is there a way to modify the primary concept of the path to let someone else travel it if created and held by clystikes?"

Jhali answered before Kendric. "The magic of the clystikes is unique. I don't know that it can be replicated in others."

Piallen got to her feet, sometimes pacing helped work things out. "The oracles mentioned that the wizards returning was as important as the grigeens—we're part of nature in a way that is different than others. But clystikes are part of nature as well and existed outside of this kingdom long ago. The mountains that create the field of magic here worked to help increase the number of clystikes here when they vanished everywhere else. What if a wizard and a grigeen lent their help to allow non-clystikes to use the chorogh path, just once?"

Donall was back to staring at her. "You're a...wizard?"

"She is, so don't mess with her." Kendric grinned at Piallen. "I think we'd have to talk to Solange and Hilth, since they are both wizard and clystike. But maybe there's something there."

"The oracles don't mention connections unless they have a reason. I'll go back to the castle with all of you. I want to see father and speak to Solange and Hilth." If Jhali was startled by Piallen's revelation, she didn't show it.

Donall was still processing it. And still eating.

Gareth had added his parts about the attack, but had stayed silent since then. "When do we leave? We have a kingdom to save and ours to fix."

Piallen gave him a smile. "Thank you. I agree, the sooner we leave the better." She forced aside the tendril of fear that it was already too late. They had to be able to stop the Northalian army.

Jhali went to change clothes. Donall and Gareth went to hunt down Tobias and Rhys.

"You're looking worried. Hiding it, but it's in your eyes," Kendric said as they waited.

"It's just...this was supposed to be a simple Challenge. Something to show that I could be counted as heir. Now it's saving our kingdom...and more." She looked up to meet his eyes.

"We will do this. Then, I'll come back here and Ceredigion will fix whatever is wrong with our magic. Then, hopefully, I'll get to visit Astarious."

"You'd better." Piallen stepped back. "I will be extremely upset if you don't visit. You don't want a wizard mad at you. Could end up a toad."

"Deal. Not the toad, I don't need yet another shape." He was laughing though. Maybe he was accepting who and what he was—or at least making strides in that direction.

The others returned and they quickly went back to the castle. Again, everyone was silent, mostly because of the concern the siblings had about their father.

They went to the main entrance for the throne room and, as ordered, there were pairs of guards on each landing. They all gave short bows as the royals went up.

"I take it they still haven't found Limin?" Jhali kept her voice low as she spoke to Kendric and Piallen.

"Most likely not. And Mertil is still out there. He was injured, but he's also a clystike with wings—he could have gone far," Kendric said as a guard at the top held open the door.

Piallen had been hoping that King Brae was doing better than when they left, but if anything, he looked more fatigued. Solange was sitting next to him, but Hilth was focusing on something out the window.

Jhali and her two youngest brothers ran to their father and Solange moved out of the way.

While King Brae worked on assuring his children he was fine, Piallen, Kendric, and Gareth pulled Solange and Hilth away to bring up Piallen's idea.

Solange and Hilth looked dubious at the plan.

"They failed to mention grigeen assistance," Tobias said with a grin. "This grigeen, that is. I believe that we could open a chorogh path long enough to get the army to Northalian."

"With what spells? I just don't think we have the time to experiment." Hilth shook his head. "The army is assembling, but it will take two weeks, at least, to reach Northalian."

"Which is why we have to try. If it fails, it fails. But two weeks is going to be too long." Piallen knew the army couldn't move fast and while the clystikes were supposedly fierce fighters, they would be too small of a group to take on the full force they'd be facing. "Maybe try to cobble together some support spell from my books." She wasn't usually the brainstorming one, but there was a part of her that knew there had to be a way. "The oracles gave me those books for a reason. Yes, I've used a few of the spells, but there has to be something else we can use."

Their packs were piled against a wall now, so she went and dug out all three books. "Do either of you have a preference?" She held them up to Solange and Hilth.

"It seems that youth is trying to win over old age, my love." Solange picked the original book from Nevaine with a smile.

"I believe you are correct." Hilth took the orange book. "Thank goodness for youth who never know what is impossible." He grinned at Piallen.

It only took a half-hour to pull something together that, in theory, would extend a chorogh path to allow non-clystikes to use it. Actually, it would still need a few clystikes. One on each end, to open and close it, and one per each group of twenty non-clystikes to fortify the connection. Piallen, Solange, and Hilth would also be spread out among the army in-between the clystikes to act as guideposts for the spell.

If it worked, it would allow the horses and their riders to pass through the chorogh path. Or it could dump everyone out in the middle of nowhere. Or worse.

Rhys and Donall had been sent to their rooms with guards to bring what they needed to stay in the king's chambers. Limin and Mertil were still unaccounted for and guarding all of them in one spot would be easier. Jhali was also staying but from the look on her face it was more based on her concern over her father's health than fear for her own safety. All of the oracles' priests and priestesses had different abilities—hers was healing.

Once the younger royals left, the debate started. King Brae had almost had the life sucked out of him by the spells Mertil was using, but he had enough energy to argue.

Piallen had a feeling Kendric would be the same—luckily, in this case, he was on her side.

"It's too risky. If you strand the army somewhere, we'll all be in a worse situation than if we let them leave tomorrow morning as planned. Two weeks isn't optimal, but they will get there intact. And without draining a bunch of wizards and mages."

All of the clystikes were magic users of some kind, but it wasn't clear if they became clystikes because they were magic users or if being a clystike made them magic users.

"Your Majesty, I'm in agreement with those who thought this up," Gareth said. "The size of that force facing Astarious can't be underestimated. From what Piallen has told us, while Astarious is strong, it can't hold against that without help. We have to stop it, as you yourself said, before it reaches them."

The king tilted his head. "One of you, go over the entire thing again."

Kendric beat the others to the punch and succinctly mapped out their plan. Gareth was calling the clystikes who lived in the castle together in less than an hour. Kendric would explain the plan and the risks—he would only take volunteers. They estimated they would need fifty clystikes to cover the just under a thousand military personnel. The rest of the Ceredigion forces were spread in the mountains and would take too long to pull back. With the magic load spread out, the drain would be minimal on all of the mages and wizards. If everything went according to plan.

The plan would only go forward if they got enough clystike volunteers.

"Still the same, still reckless. But what of our grigeen? What does he say?" King Brae appeared to have been testing Kendric, and the rest, on their knowledge of the plan—and willingness to see it through. He did smile at Tobias though.

"I will be riding in the front. What Kendric failed to mention was that he would lead the path and the charge, with Piallen a third of the way behind him. I will ride on him and focus the magic around us." He rubbed his paws together. "I relish the challenge."

"Has he done anything like this before?" The king turned to Piallen.

"Nope. But has any of us? Even for Solange and Hilth, we're going beyond anything they've done." Piallen knew how hard it was for many royals to switch their way of thinking quickly, but there wasn't a choice.

"And, when this is done, I can promise that my people will come and help you clean this valley." Tobias wrinkled his nose. "The magic stagnation created by those mountains is growing stronger. It will take a few years of being even more cut off than you currently are, no visits, even for your spies." He nodded to Gareth. "But my people can make it happen."

Piallen knew that it would be up to the grigeen pack counsel if they helped, not Tobias. But she also knew how much grigeens valued nature and restoring it. If these mountains were that corrupted, the grigeens would help.

Not to mention, that when he really wanted something, Tobias could be extremely persistent.

The king nodded but still appeared to be thinking things through. "Please make our guests comfortable, then speak to the clystikes. I would like to speak to Solange and Hilth alone now. One way or another, we will send forth our army to face the menace in Northalian—tomorrow."

Everyone except the two wizards left, with Jhali leading the way. "I have a perfect guest room near my chambers. It should be fine for you and Tobias." She grinned down as he trotted behind her. "Thank you, by the way. My father grew up fascinated with the myth of the grigeens. Your words will help him make a difficult decision."

They crossed over a bridge to another tower where Kendric and Gareth bid their goodnights. It wasn't that late, but there was no way to know how long the clystike meeting would go.

Jhali waited until they were going down an elaborate hall. "How do you feel about my brother?"

Piallen laughed. "Up until the oracles pulled that incredibly awkward stunt, I'd say I liked him. He and I got off to a bad start, but under that terseness, he seems to be an interesting man. But I'm not going to become his queen after knowing him only a few days."

"The oracles are a strange group, and I say that as someone who will be devoted to them until the end of my days. They forget what it's like to be human, or as close as they ever were. Even though belief in them has dwindled in other lands—at least according to what they tell us—they have still been trying to guide and protect. They might not last much longer, which could be years or decades with their timelines. But their wish to help is genuine. They just saw what you and Kendric could bring into the world." She laughed at Piallen's face. "Not potential children, but changes. I gathered from them that your sisters already instigated some." She opened an ornate door to the guest room and invited Piallen and Tobias to the elaborate seating area.

Piallen explained more about the Challenge as they sat in the guest room. Her pack had already been moved in.

Tobias chipped in whenever he felt she missed something, but mostly nibbled on a fruit bowl.

Jhali stood. "I am sorry, you will have a long day ahead of you tomorrow and I'm talking your ear off. Thank you for our talk though." Her face stilled. "Please watch out for Kendric. He is a fierce fighter and mage, but sometimes forgets that he is also flesh and blood. Even a clystike can be killed."

Piallen gave her a hug. "I will. Gareth too."

"That obvious?" Jhali had almost gotten teary eyed, but laughed. "It is to everyone except him. He can't believe that I return his affection. After this is over, I'll be working on that. Thank you for watching out for both." She pulled Piallen's head down and kissed her forehead. "The blessings of the oracles upon you." Then she reached down and did the same to Tobias. "Sleep well, both of you."

Piallen looked through the wizard spell books, and it took almost an hour to find what she wanted. Hopefully, she'd have time to tell Solange and Hilth her plan and show them the spell in the morning. The orange book held a way to shut down a mage-portal. Something that sounded an awful lot like what they would be facing. It also had a lot of warnings about its use. She'd warn Solange and Hilth in the morning, but she wouldn't tell Kendric. She couldn't take the chance he'd try to stop her.

Piallen intended to stay awake for a while, after she'd memorized the spell, and sort out her head. Those oracles had messed with it, and she wanted to know what she really felt about Kendric. But as soon as she and Tobias had tumbled into the massive bed, she was asleep.

Until a loud pounding on her door made her shoot wide awake.

"Princess! We're under attack!"

Chapter Twenty-Two

Piallen had changed before she went to bed, but into another set of her fighting clothes. She was grateful for that now as she ran to the door, but held off opening it. "Where's Prince Kendric?"

"I'm here, so are Gareth and the clystikes."

Piallen opened the door and ran back to get her boots on. "What's happened?"

"Limin is coming back with magic users. He must have snuck out while they were looking for him earlier. Most are still on their way down from the mountains, but we need to get our fighters out of here now."

"But can we leave the castle defenseless?" She knew they had to stop the Northalians in order to save her people, but she wasn't going to sacrifice one kingdom to save another.

"No. It would have been, but the military in the mountains have been chased out by mysterious creatures and just arrived. They saw Limin and his group." Kendric turned to his sister with a smile.

Jhali smiled. "The oracles might have had something to do with that. It's as close as they could get to direct intervention."

"Chased out by...never mind." Piallen grabbed all of her weapons, then tossed on her pack. "You coming, Tobias?"

He was cramming his mouth full of fruit and some jerky from his pack. He slipped his pack on and nodded while still chewing.

"My father is letting us go with your plan. Solange and Hilth are waiting with the soldiers and clystikes." Kendric gave a wide grin. "You ready to test that theory of yours?"

Piallen nodded as they ran down the corridor. "Yes; but it's not just mine. Solange and Hilth helped come up with it too." She fought down a flutter as they ran. Not only would this be her first true battle, but it was running off a plan she was involved in creating. Once they got there, the captains of the army, as well as Kendric and Gareth, would stage the attacks, but being involved in this part was wild.

It was still dark; the light of the sun was just starting to show over the far mountains. But the army and the clystikes were ready to go. As Kendric and the rest came toward them, they all changed. There were a few larger birds, like Solange and Hilth's alsohawks, but most of the ones here were bears, wolves, and large mountain cats. There were two other large snakes, and they greeted Gareth as he ran by and changed.

"The hopes of not only our kingdom, but another, rest upon all of you." The king was standing on a balcony, and it looked like Solange was augmenting his voice. "Go knowing that this fight will show the world who we are." He nodded and the army moved their horses in line. The clystikes were almost as regimented as they counted off soldiers and took their places.

Kendric bowed to his father and changed. His stag form was extremely impressive, even more so being the only one. He turned to Tobias. "Ready?"

Tobias looked up to Piallen. "Don't get killed." He had his fierce face on, but also looked like he might cry.

"I'll do my best. You stay safe. Stay with Kendric." She smiled as Tobias ran and got on Kendric's back and they rode to the front.

Solange and Hilth were already in their places and wizard magic crackled off of them as Piallen went ahead to her spot. She chanted the spell in her head and felt the same energy the other two wizards had flow from her.

Kendric gave a yell and the chorogh path opened.

It took a bit longer than it should have to get started, as the first horses weren't sure about the path of nothingness. But once they went through, the rest followed. It felt choppier than last time, but she figured her nerves were probably contributing to that. She had worked long and hard to be as proficient with weapons as she was—going off into a real battle, with untested wizard magic, wasn't a good feeling.

They'd only seen the battlefield from high on the mountain, but their chorogh path opened up on the plain itself. They were still far enough away that they weren't dropped right into the other side, but seeing it on this level really pointed out how many soldiers the enemy had.

Kendric would lead the charge of the clystikes down the middle, with the captains from the horse soldiers splitting off with their companies along the sides. Kendric and Gareth took charge of the clystikes and Solange and Hilth, who'd crossed the path in human form, changed and flew up to observe.

Piallen ran toward Tobias who'd jumped off Kendric's back once they arrived and was mostly working on staying out from underneath everyone. "Good job, we made it."

"I was going to say the same." Tobias looked around. "I tried reaching out to my people while we were on that path, it has a component of mental communication to it that I thought I might be able to use. But I don't know if they understood. Would it be bad if I rode on your pack?"

Piallen smiled. "By all means, I can't imagine going into battle without you." Even though she wasn't a clystike, they'd decided that she and Tobias would fight with them, as they fit in better than with the horse soldiers. Once Tobias was in place, she jogged up to the clystike group.

Mostly it was Kendric reminding them that if they got captured, a rescue might not be able to happen.

A huge brown bear laughed. "Tell us something new, Prince Kendric. I think we've been spotted."

The Northalian army probably hadn't been expecting anyone at this end of the plain, there was nothing but a nasty looking desert. Piallen's eyes weren't on the same level as the alsohawks circling above them, but even she could see confusion and disorganization in the actions of the Northalian army as they turned to face the new attackers.

The Ceredigion horse soldiers all charged forward. Archers from the back waited until the enemy was close enough, then started firing. Piallen was impressed, firing on horseback took a lot of skill, even more so with a longbow.

Kendric kept the clystikes in place as the two alsohawks dropped down and resumed human form.

Hilth shook his head as he looked off into the distance. "They're building a portal on the other end of the plain. We'd hoped that without us that wouldn't be an option for them—we were wrong. It's not completed yet, but even far above, we could feel it."

"I'm not letting that happen." Kendric tossed his head back and bellowed. "We have a new target! Get through that army and shut down that portal, at all costs!" Roars, growls, and other assorted sounds followed. He turned to Piallen. "Can you keep up? You could ride on me, but you won't be able to fight."

Now that she'd gotten over her nerves, she found that she did want to fight. Not to mention that she couldn't imagine riding Kendric would help his fighting either. "I think I can keep up. Right, Tobias?"

He patted her head. "Always. Charge!"

Kendric turned and led the way. Gareth and the other two snakes had gone on the outside of the enemy army; Kendric was going through the middle.

Screams came from the direction the snakes went.

"Is Gareth poisonous?" She asked as she kept pace with Kendric.

He turned with a grin. "Extremely; all the snake shifters are." He broke off, lowered his head, and charged into a Stiklin. The Stiklin tried backing up but got thrown into the air by Kendric's antlers, and stomped by the clystikes following him.

They kept running. Not only had the Northalian army not been expecting an attack, and one coming from the desert, they were not expecting a pack of wild animals, and were running away in terror as the group of animals ran for them.

And heading directly into the path of the Ceredigion horsemen.

Piallen had kept her bow over her pack, as there was too much chaos to even try shooting, so she only had her sword. She had to slice an Offialian who ran toward her, but aside from that, she mostly ran.

The Ceredigion captains wheeled their troops around for another charge. Only about a third of the Northalian army were on horses, and they didn't move nearly as well as Kendric's people.

Solange and Hilth had stayed in human form and had commandeered two horses from the enemy. Both were firing spells, to add more confusion and take down the enemy.

Piallen watched but didn't join in. She didn't trust her spell throwing and running any more than she did her archery and running. Not in this mess.

The wizard stone gave a warming flash and a spell bounced off a shield she didn't know she had. Judging by the satisfied feeling coming from the stone, it was trying to save her, and itself.

"What was that? I thought it was too hard to carry a shield while fighting and running," Tobias said in her ear.

"So did I. I think the stone did it. Is that a riderless horse?" Piallen was fast, and had done far longer runs than this, but if she wanted to save some energy for fighting through to that portal, she needed a horse. The one near her was running wild and appeared to be one of the Ceredigion mounts.

"Yep, let me try." Tobias made an odd sound that sounded like a horse, sort of.

The horse slowed down and seemed to calm a bit. Piallen dodged over to it and jumped on its back. Not a graceful attempt, and both she and Tobias almost fell off, but she was on the horse, and got it turned to follow the clystikes.

"Easy there, you'll be fine, these are friends." She rubbed his neck as he ran. Considering the looks of terror on the faces of the few Northalian horses at the groups of furry predators charging their way, it was a good thing that the first horse she found was one from Ceredigion. He still looked a bit wild eyed, but he ran alongside Kendric and a large wolf without pause.

"Thank goodness; I don't think they have the portal up yet." Piallen yelled as they ran. Then she swore. A giant ring flared to life at the end of the battlefield, and the army was vanishing into it.

Chapter Twenty-Three

"Kendric! The portal is open! We have to stop them." Piallen bent low over the neck of her horse and felt Tobias cling tighter as they sped ahead. Kendric lowered his head and kept pace. Most of the Northalian army had come to face them, so they weren't close to the portal when it opened. But there were still enough soldiers going through to cause problems. It would be a disaster if any more got through—she had to close it.

Piallen had memorized the mage-portal closure spell, but hadn't told anyone else about it since they'd had to leave so suddenly. Solange and Hilth were fighting toward the back, so it was up to Piallen to close it. And hope it didn't take her down with it.

She'd been so focused on getting to the portal she hadn't been paying attention to where the enemy archers were. The arrow strike to her side had enough force to knock her off her horse. Tobias sailed over her head, but it looked like the arrow had missed him.

Piallen felt the arrow as she tumbled off the horse, only a lot of training kept her from breaking her neck. Her roll saved her life, but she felt the arrow snap and go deeper.

Kendric spun back as Piallen's borrowed horse tore past him. Piallen struggled to her feet, her left arm hung uselessly, and throbbing pain and heat radiated from her side. She stumbled as her knees buckled. She didn't fall, but there was little strength in it. Her tuck and roll hadn't been as successful as she'd hoped. Breathing was also becoming an issue—the arrow had managed to get through her ribs and strike her lung—or it was poisoned.

A rider in Northalian garb charged toward her but was cut off by Kendric as he charged him with his antlers down.

Kendric's eyes were huge as he whirled back to her and for a moment, she thought he was going to change back to human, but he came alongside her. "Can you get on?"

She tried to at least drape herself over his back, but couldn't do it.

A pair of hands came from behind and gently lifted her onto Kendric's back. It was Gareth and he changed back into a snake as soon as she was on Kendric.

"Where's Tobias?" That took a lot of breath she didn't have, but she didn't see him. Judging by her rapid decline—she was sure there had been poison on the arrow. Civilized armies never used those, as they could end up poisoning their own people. Clearly, the Northalian kingdom didn't care. Her fingers on that side were numb now.

Kendric was already running for a break in the fighting and a small grove off to the side, but Gareth turned toward the fighting.

"I see Tobias, don't worry, I'll bring him to you." He could move extremely fast as a snake, and the last she saw was him darting toward a bundle of fur bouncing across the haunches of horses.

Piallen blinked as Kendric got them to the grove, but black spots were obscuring her vision and there was a nasty rattle coming out every time she breathed.

Kendric changed into his human form, but twisted as he did so that he could catch her. He gently laid her on a spot of grass, but kept her injured side up. "I'm going to have to heal you first, then get the arrow out—I can feel the poison from here."

"Let me go. Stop the invasion." It took a lot of energy to get that out, but she needed him to hear her. She was losing consciousness and he needed to save her kingdom—not her. The numbness was covering her entire side now. It was moving too fast.

"No. We can still save your land, but I'm saving you first." He positioned her against a tree stump so she didn't have to lie face down but he could still get to the injury. "Not going to lie, it's bad. But I have healing magic, I can do this." He was talking more to himself than her.

"You have to save them, please." Piallen wanted to get up and shake him. She didn't have a wish to die, but even worse would be living without her family.

He moved so that she could see his face. "Again, no. I can't let you die. *I won't let you die.* Now hold still."

His strong hands shook for a moment, then steadied as he held her back on either side of the burning stick of pain that was the arrow. His focus was on the poison that had coated the tip. She was fading in and out as the magic flowed through her. The world felt dimmer as his spell narrowed down to where the arrow was, then failed. The numbness had been pushed back a bit, but not enough.

"Let me go." She needed him to listen to her. The arrow probably wouldn't have been fatal on its own, providing she got healing. But she was dying from the poison.

"No, he's not letting you go. You need to live." Tobias was near her head but sounded far away as he turned to Kendric. "Focus on how you feel about her as you send the healing, trust me." Tobias' paws touched her burning skin, spreading coolness.

Piallen would have objected, that grigeens didn't *do* magic, they *were* magic. But after a few moments, Kendric's spell of healing came back and this time there was a warmth and fire to it. He was calling to her spirit to stay as much as he healed her injuries. The numbness and the pain from the poison faded, then vanished. Then the arrow came out, but surprisingly didn't hurt at all. It was just a sensation, nothing more. Tobias must have been doing something as well—she felt him too. And even Gareth was lending support.

Then she blacked out.

"You did a good job, now let me finish. The poison they used can leave a marker for another attack." That voice was Solange and she was extremely close to Piallen's head as she regained consciousness. Piallen didn't have the strength to open her eyes, she was tired and just wanted to sleep.

The plus side, she still didn't feel any pain. Hopefully, that was a plus side.

Solange's cool hands rested on her shoulder and side and coolness flowed over her. Then a jolt hit her and her eyes flew open.

Piallen took a deep breath and there wasn't a rattle nor cough. Her lung was fine, her arm was fine, even her knee was fine. Kendric gave a weary but relieved smile from where he sat on the grass. Gareth and Tobias sat next to him. Solange stood near Piallen.

The sounds of battle were silent.

"It's over?" Piallen scrambled to her feet. "Soldiers got through the portal; we have to stop—" She saw the battlefield as she got up. The fight was still going, but it was so slow it was almost frozen in place. She turned to Solange. "I thought that was a dangerous spell to use in a crowd? Or, say, a battlefield."

"It is. Extremely so, and when you learn it, do *not* do what I just did." Solange shrugged. "Kendric was healing you, but it was going too slow, and you were slipping away from us. I was flying by, looking for all of you when Tobias flagged me down. There was no way I was letting the first wizard die in her first battle if I could help it. Plus, we're far enough out of the way of the fighting, that our time difference really wasn't an issue." She narrowed her eyes. "But still, don't do it."

Piallen smiled and nodded. Most likely, once she learned this handy spell, she'd use it when needed. Just as Solange had.

"She saved you." Kendric sounded as tired as he looked, but smiled.

Solange shook her head. "*You* saved her, I just finished up. If you weren't all lined up to be king someday, I'd suggest you go into a career as a healer. You have a caring soul under there."

Piallen looked around, she'd felt all of them, but Kendric had done the most, even if he didn't listen to her. To be fair, now that she wasn't dying, she realized even if he had left her, he couldn't have closed the portal—the spell was a wizardry one.

"We have to close the portal. I am so grateful to all of you for saving me." Her eyes lingered on Kendric. "But we have to end this here."

"Thought you might want this." Gareth held out her sword. "You apparently failed to hang onto it when you fell off your horse." His eyes held a lot of emotion, far more than his words.

"Thank you. And I believe you saved Tobias as well." She put her sword in its sheath. It would come back out soon enough. "I can't thank you enough for that."

Gareth looked embarrassed, but Tobias puffed up his chest. "I was saving myself, thank you." He gave a twitch. "Okay, Gareth saved me from trying to save myself." He gave a fang-filled grin to Gareth. "Thank you, my snake friend."

Gareth gave a regal nod.

Solange changed into her alsohawk form. "I need to go back and help Hilth, I hope you save your kingdom!" She lifted up into the air with unnatural speed, there would be no archers fast enough to shoot her this time, and the speed up spell disappeared.

The sudden noise from the battlefield slammed into Piallen. "We need to get back out there. I have a way to close that portal but might need some help getting there."

Kendric got to his feet and went out toward the battlefield; he came back leading a horse. "I know you're fast, but let's get you there intact and not exhausted." He handed her the reins. "Just no more arrows, okay?"

She grinned and swung into the saddle. Tobias jumped up as well, and Kendric and Gareth changed forms. Together they raced back into the battle.

Kendric and Gareth stayed on either side of Piallen and Tobias. Every once in a while, a soldier or enemy mage would try to block them and either Kendric or Gareth would zip off to clear the way. Gareth's movements made it look like he barely touched the ground—and he might not be. Piallen had to admit having a large poisonous snake and a huge stag as defenders worked well.

"Look out!" Tobias' yell in her ear came at a time when both Kendric and Gareth were fighting off more attackers.

Piallen turned to see two mages coming for her on horseback—their spells crackling around them. Limin and Thistledove.

Chapter Twenty-Four

Piallen swore under her breath; she needed to keep trying to go for the portal, but those two were going to catch her long before then. "You might want to see about joining the other grigeens, this could get ugly."

Tobias snorted. "No way am I leaving you to have all the fun. Besides, I brought back up." He waved his arm down in front of her. Clait's collar was doubled and pushed up to his shoulder. "It might have helped me help you when you were trying to die. It just gave me a shock when those two came into sight. I don't think it likes them."

Piallen laughed. She knew the collar was too small for his neck, but it was good to know Tobias figured out a way to use it. "Does it have a shield of some sort? It's doing something." An opalescent circle appeared as Limin released a spell, the circle flared brightly, then the spell vanished.

"She didn't tell me it did that!" From the sound of his voice, Tobias wasn't planning on giving it back to Clait now if he could help it.

Limin didn't slow down and behind him Thistledove was trying to spell a knife. While riding on horseback.

Piallen had only seen Thistledove once, and that was more as a smoke shadow than anything, but he appeared to be far more bumbling sycophant and less dangerous mage right now.

Thistledove threw his knife, but his aim was poor and the throw was weak. Piallen smacked the knife aside with her sword and sent back a focused flash spell. Not the best option in better circumstances, but better than ending up crossing her magic spells with the wizardry inside her.

The flare she sent was nothing compared to the full version she'd let loose in King Brae's throne room—it would be too risky to their own people to use that here. But it was enough to startle the horses of both mages.

Thistledove was dumped off and his horse ran from the battle-field. A pair of Ceredigion knights took care of Thistledove swiftly. They didn't take betraying the kingdom well.

Limin maintained control of his horse and kept coming.

"Hang on to the saddle, Tobias, and keep ahold of that collar!" Piallen didn't grab her pendant, but there was a familiar warmth from it. Limin might not be a wizard, but the wizardly artifacts didn't like him.

It was too risky to try the lock spell; the troops from both sides were around them. Might as well see how that shield from the collar helped a full attack. Limin was too dangerous to leave roaming around and he knew who she was.

Piallen charged forward as Limin started moving his fingers for another spell. The finger movements were definitely more like those of sorcerers than magic users.

She charged him and leapt off her horse to tackle him as he tried to get the words of his spell out. Tobias hadn't stayed on their horse but came racing over. Limin tried to roll away but Piallen punched him in the jaw. A few times. Then she pulled his face close to hers and whispered the lock spell.

Panic widened his eyes, then he froze.

"Move!" Tobias pulled on Piallen's tunic to get her out of the way just as two horses ran right over Limin. Whatever spell he'd been about to say had died with him.

Piallen scrambled to her feet, grateful to see that her horse was battle trained and hadn't gone far. She scooped up Tobias, dodged a few skirmishes, and got them back on the horse.

The portal was close, but there were still fighters going through.

"Yah!" She kept an eye out for Kendric and Gareth but the fighting was chaotic. Hopefully both of them were okay and they'd meet again someday.

She was within a few yards of the entrance when she was attacked and swept off her horse by a pikeman she had managed to miss. The pike didn't go through her or Tobias, who jumped off after her, but the horse did take off, leaving her in the dirt. Battle trained or not, she didn't blame the horse. For an excellent horse rider, she was annoyed at being unhorsed so much in this battle.

She jumped to her feet and swung her sword as the pikeman made another pass, knocking him and his pike aside and unbalancing him enough to lose control of his horse.

She'd almost died once today; she wasn't letting that happen again.

Piallen dodged as yet another soldier ran for her. The clystike army that Kendric had brought was cutting a swath through to the portal. Solange had returned to help Hilth keep the enemy mages on task at the other end, but there were still too many soldiers running for the portal. And Mertil was still here somewhere—hopefully not on the other side of that portal.

Even though Solange had sped up time for Piallen's healing, there had still been too many enemy soldiers who'd made it through. The Ceredigion forces were focusing on stopping the fight here, but they might have done better to run through the portal.

A rumbling sound came from the right and a flood of grigeens ran around her as they raced off a low cliff from the mountain and onto the plain. They went after the soldiers heading toward the portal and jumped on them as well as their horses.

Tobias was still hanging on her back as he yelled. "They made it! These are the ones from our side of the mountain—the ones I tried to contact when we were on the chorogh path." There were hundreds of grigeens and they were fiercely attacking the soldiers.

Piallen dodged around the grigeen/soldier battles and ran for the portal. She had to destroy it. Having Kendric's people come though would be great—except it meant allowing more of the enemy to come through as well. She couldn't take that chance. "I'm going to end this, but we could end up anywhere." The spell to close the portal that she'd seen had been simple, but it looked like the one casting it didn't always survive.

She been trying to ignore that part.

Kendric ran to her, changed into his human form, and grabbed her arm. "Let me come with you, too many have gone through already."

Piallen smiled and touched his face. Regardless of the meddling of the oracles, she might have been falling for him—and that was before she saw the real him while he was saving her life. But the Ceredigion kingdom needed to be locked down, no one in or out until the stagnation lurking in those mountains could be lifted. He was crucial to making it happen and freeing their land. "You can't. You might not make it back home. You have to be there."

There was a very good chance that she wouldn't survive what she was about to do and even if she did, it would be years before she ever saw him again—*if* she saw him again. "But first I need to do this." She grabbed him and kissed him. He responded immediately and his arms pulled her closer. She wouldn't recommend kissing during a battle, but it did get the adrenaline moving. He looked as dazed as she felt when she pulled back. "Now go save your land." She pushed him away as hard as she could and ran for the portal; Kendric was fast, but not as fast as she was. She said the spell words to shut it down as she and Tobias hit the entrance. And the world went black.

Chapter Twenty-Five

The darkness vanished and she felt like she'd been tossed on the ground and run over a few times.

"I think she'll live." Tobias patted her cheeks as Piallen mentally tried to confirm that all of her body parts were intact. She didn't open her eyes yet as that seemed too hard.

"And I thought I liked to make an entrance," Lizeth's voice was good to hear, but Piallen still didn't want to open her eyes to see her. "You two flew through the air. It's amazing you both weren't killed."

"The portal had a bit of a kick when she closed it." Tobias stopped patting her cheeks.

"We're under attack. Ouch." Piallen finally opened her eyes but it felt like every nerve in her body was simultaneously on fire and ice cold. Movement wasn't easy. The good news was that she and Tobias survived. "Is the portal gone?" Pain or not, Piallen rolled to her feet and reached out magically. The portal's magic signature had been unique and was gone. That was good.

But the feeling of a lot of magic users and non-magicked fighters coming their way through the woods, wasn't.

She looked around, trying to figure out where they were. Lizeth and Tobias had a few dozen grigeens with them, and from what she could tell they were on the edge of the grigeen forest.

Lizeth had been crouched next to her but got to her feet and touched Piallen's shoulder. "Easy there, we're facing an attack from whom? Aren't you still on your Challenge?"

Tobias shrugged. "I couldn't say yes or no. Things are a bit muddled."

"I think I'm still on it. But we're under attack from a combined army: Northalians, Laiandrans, Stiklins, and even a few Offialians.

231

We tried to stop them but some got through. I'd say a lot of them from what I'm feeling."

Lizeth sang a soft spell song. Then started some very unladylike swearing. "You're right. They're still back a way, but there's a large force coming our way. We have to get back to the palace. Can you run?"

Everything still ached, but Piallen nodded.

"Then let's go, and if you can pass me do so—tell our parents, I'll be right behind." Lizeth turned to the grigeens around them. "Can you warn your people? It's far worse than we thought."

All of the grigeens, except Tobias, nodded as one and ran off.

"We were looking for a disturbance in the forest. Something had called the mountain grigeens away, but this wasn't what we'd expected," Lizeth said before she started running.

"Those grigeens were coming to help us fight in Northalian. To-bias contacted them." Piallen stayed alongside her sister as her body slowly returned to normal. She was glad she'd cut off the portal, but was still surprised at how many enemies had made it through, based on what she felt. After a few minutes her body felt recovered. She nodded to Lizeth as she and Tobias sprinted ahead.

Vestiges of her nightmare slammed into her as she approached the palace. But this time there were people there and ways to fight.

"Princess Piallen?" The front door guards both looked surprised.

"Yup, me. Can't talk. Parents?" She slowed down, finding where they were would be better than racing around the palace.

"In the main throne room." Both guards jumped out of her way as she raced past with Tobias fast on her heels.

Her parents were in their monthly nobles' conferences when she shoved open the door. "We're under attack!"

Her parents looked surprised, but recovered quickly and waved her forward. They didn't send away the five nobles they'd been talk-ing with, however.

"What? The oracles didn't tell us you were back." Her mother didn't come down from the dais, but looked ready to.

"I'm not. I mean, I'm here, but I don't think my Challenge is over." She quickly explained about the invading army and the portal. Ignoring the growing paleness on the five nobles' faces.

"Get the army and guards ready. And all of the mages." Her father didn't question her. But he did wave to the nobles. "Get moving, you'll be fighting too." The nobles looked around unhappily then jogged out of the throne room.

"And someone get Gliandra," her mother added before she ran down to hug Piallen.

Nevaine and Sean came running into the throne room as everyone else ran out.

Piallen explained what was happening as she took off her pack. "I only have my sword and bow; can I borrow a few knives?" she asked Nevaine as she adjusted her sword belt.

Nevaine handed her three without question. "But I'll understand if I don't get them back. This is your Challenge?" There were a lot of questions in her eyes, but she clearly knew right now wasn't the time.

"I think so." Piallen shrugged. "Not really sure." She looked up as a heavily armed Finnian, Lizeth, and all of the foresters came running in. Thirty foresters weren't an army, but all of them were well-trained and well-armed. They also knew the woods far better than the invaders who were running through them.

Sean smiled as a group of eighty or so battlemages came in right behind them, then he turned back to Piallen. "Now, what can you tell us about what we're facing?"

Piallen repeated a brief version, then started for the door. "They came in near the grigeen forest, but I don't think we have time to wait for the army. The mountain grigeens found a way through the mountains and are fighting the army left in Northalian." She knew the enemy would be moving quickly, and she needed to get there now. Not to mention, the Astarious royal army would be on horseback and would quickly catch up with the battlemages and foresters who were on foot.

Sean nodded and Piallen led the way. Within a half hour, flashes of her dream hit again as she heard the fighters marching forward. And a wall of grigeens stood in front of them.

Not this time—now she had help. She couldn't use her two strongest wizard spells, there were too many strong magic users in the attacking group and it would be bad if one of them grabbed the spell. She was more protected than before, but still not enough to risk it.

The battlemages took the lead and Piallen stayed near Sean and Nevaine. Lizeth, Finnian, and the foresters spread out behind. Lizeth sang a low spell song as she ran, adding a mist to the area.

The attackers charged the grigeens, not noticing the rest of them. Piallen glanced to Sean. His smile as he muttered words and flicked his fingers said it was thanks to him. Nevaine wasn't far behind and she was casting a spell as she ran as well. Between those two and Lizeth's song for mist, the entire group was practically invisible.

Grigeens were far better fighters than their size would indicate, but they were being overwhelmed. Tobias, Scruff, and Clait raced forward to help them.

The battlemages yelled as they sprinted forward, with Sean and Nevaine dropping their hiding spells and leading the charge. Lizeth lowered her song, just enough to send a bit of confusion to the attackers, but not enough to cause issues with the fighters on the Astarious side. The mist she'd created was lower now and drifting around the enemy forces.

Piallen yelled as well, even though she wasn't a fully trained battlemage—it felt right.

The foresters engaged on the other side.

The fight was close, but soon they were joined by the first wave of the royal army on horseback, led by the king and queen, both in full armor. The attackers were strong, but when all the forces from the Astarious side were in the fight, the attackers were slowly being pushed back and defeated.

Then a new wave of enemies appeared.

Piallen had only seen one portal while in Northalian, the one she'd shut down. But there was another group coming their way from the north. There must have been two, but somehow, she and the others had missed the second one. Or someone had reopened the one she'd shut down. Creating those portals wasn't easy and the odds of their enemies having been able to create a brand new one since she closed the other were slim.

Then she spotted a familiar cloaked figure leading the second group at the front. Mertil.

"Fall back! We need to regroup!" The king had to yell it a few times before the battlemages and foresters pulled back. The royal army paid closer attention and held back after the first call.

Piallen knew how the battlemages and foresters felt. If the enemy got past them, they would not only destroy the palace, they would destroy Astarious. Her sisters and their husbands looked as unhappy about being pulled back as she did.

Gliandra looked furious as she came up to them. "We have to keep fighting; they can't be allowed to win." She turned to Piallen. "Where are the wizards?"

Piallen didn't stop moving, but almost dropped her sword. "How did you know about them?" She knew Solange had recognized Gliandra's name, but didn't realize there might be more to it.

"I felt their presence with you, it's a long story, not important. But they should have come here with you." Gliandra kept looking around as if she'd somehow missed the wizards.

"They were at the far end of the attacking army and keeping much of the focus on them. I had a chance to close the portal, so I took it." Piallen hoped her friends were okay, but she'd had to do what she could to stop the enemy from coming here.

The two groups of enemies joined forces and the fight became one-sided. The Astarious forces were still fighting as they fell back, but each step was lost with lives.

Sean ran to the king and queen with Nevaine right behind him. Neither the king nor queen looked happy at whatever the other two were saying but they eventually nodded. Sean and Nevaine raced off with the rest of the battlemages.

"Where are they going?" Piallen got to her parents. Gliandra was keeping pace, but almost seemed to be floating an inch above the ground. Considering that she often used a cane, there was obviously a spell involved.

"They're going to circle the enemy and try and split them from behind." Her father nodded behind her. "Finnian, Lizeth and the foresters are going around the other side along with the grigeens."

"I should be with the battlemages."

"You need to stay here. You'll have enough to fight, trust me." Gliandra's eyes were sad as she put her hand on Piallen's arm.

"Our side won't win, we're still outmatched." Sending the other two groups around would slow them down, but not defeat their enemies.

"We need the wizards," Gliandra said softly.

"We probably do, but I have no way to reach them, and they were fighting for their lives last I saw." Piallen watched as the fighting continued and her people continued to lose ground.

"You still have the wizard pendant? Use it. Call them. You need friends to stand with you." Gliandra was watching Piallen, not the fighting.

Another flash of her nightmare hit her at those words, but she took out the pendant. "No idea how to reach them, but I'll try." She closed her eyes and focused on the stone, on the long-dead-wizard connected to the stone, and on Solange and Hilth.

Nothing.

Chapter Twenty-Six

The air stilled around them, but there was nothing from Solange and Hilth. "I told you, I can't..." Piallen stopped speaking as a familiar patch of emptiness opened in front of them. A chorogh path.

Her father started pulling back his soldiers to attack it but she shook him off. "That's not a portal, it's a path for people on our side. Unless I say so, no one strikes *anything* that comes through. No matter what." Piallen ran closer to the portal to block her own people if need be. If Kendric and his clystikes were with Hilth and Solange, there could be a lot of shapeshifters coming through.

Her father yelled the command to stand down and Piallen reached the entrance to the chorogh path. Two alsohawks flew over her, followed by dozens of clystikes who changed form back to human as they came through. It looked like most of the ones who'd committed to the battle on the plain had survived—and were willing to fight for Astarious. Gareth led them through, but changed out of his snake form immediately. Like the rest, he had a lot of weapons on him—they preferred to fight in their clystike forms—but none of them looked ill-prepared in their human ones either. The last was the red stag.

Kendric stayed in his stag shape for a moment, just long enough to close the path behind him, then shimmered back to his human form. He was also heavily armed, more so than he'd been when they left for the battle. They must have known they'd need to fight in human form and taken what they needed from the Northalians. "The wizards said you needed help. Sorry that I took their word over your command to stay away." He grinned and hugged Piallen tightly, then stepped back. "We won't let your people fall."

The king got his army in a defensive line and held their ground against Mertil and the enemy. Piallen watched Mertil for a few moments, but he was fighting with a sword, not magic. Something had changed but she didn't know if they had time to find out what.

Solange and Hilth circled the forest battles, then landed near the king and queen and changed back into human forms.

Gliandra ran to them. "Took you long enough. Now, shall we get this done?"

The three nodded to the king and queen, then Solange and Hilth each took one of Piallen's arms.

"We have wizardry to do and a battle to win." Gliandra was beaming as she kept up with them.

"You're a wizard too?"

"Wizard adjacent, but it'll do."

Piallen nodded to her parents and ran with the others. Hilth took the lead and seemed to be partially following the path the battlemages had gone.

If her parents had anything to say, their words were lost as the clystikes, still in human form, ran along with the wizards.

"I take it you stopped them in Northalian?" Piallen asked Kendric as they ran side by side. She'd really thought she'd never see him again, but was grateful he'd come. If he was upset about her passionate farewell, he gave no sign of it.

"The rest of our regular army is mopping them up, but their mages have fallen." He frowned. "Or come here. I think Mertil came through the second portal. They had a smaller one hidden at the edge of the battlefield. When you collapsed their other one, they started going through the new one."

"I saw Mertil near the front, but he wasn't casting spells though. Shouldn't the clystikes change form?" They'd been fighting in their shifted forms when she left Northalian, but they all stayed human now.

"I was worried about what your people might do if a bunch of wild animals joined in. But once we get closer to the invaders, we will change. Most of your troops are toward the front, so we'll circle around to the back."

"I'll do my best to keep the clystikes safe from my people." They were following the direction the battlemages had gone. Out of all the fighters on their side, that would be the group who should be more accepting of fighting side by side with shapeshifters.

She hoped. She darted ahead to Nevaine and Sean and quickly told them about the clystikes and not to be surprised if animals joined in on the battle. Their eyes widened, but both nodded.

And then they led the battlemages toward a splinter group of combined enemies. Northalians, Laiandrans, and Offialians all banded together. No Stiklins, which was good.

Kendric motioned to Gareth and he led a small group of clystikes to follow. They changed form as they went.

"Why isn't Mertil using magic?" Piallen turned to the wizards. They hadn't used it either.

"There's a spell over this forest, it's stopping stronger spells. And it's one that I'm still trying to find the source of. That's why we haven't used wizardry yet—possibly why Mertil hasn't either. Nothing more than a simple cantrip will go through." Solange shook her head.

"But I've seen mages on both sides use it—sorcerers too," Piallen said as they ran. There had been magical attacks in this forest before, granted nothing as large as the current battle.

"Aye, but this is something deeper—it's triggered to darker magics and wizardry. I'd say it's something generated by the grigeens." Gliandra was definitely using magic to keep up with them, but didn't seem to be having any problems. "Your friend Mertil is probably using dark magic. Rare in this part of the world, but not unheard of."

Piallen looked at Gliandra—she didn't seem upset at all by the situation. "Why did we need the wizards? No offense, I'm glad that you all came, but if we can't use wizardry?"

"You can. We just have to wait for the grigeens to dismantle their spell." Gliandra shook her head. "It's an old one, and one I didn't know was in place. The first comers here put it up against the attacks that took the rest of their people."

"Pantiar."

"Exactly. He did what he did to save the grigeens from various sources, but the grigeens here just knew that their people were missing—not that it was to keep them safe. They had a stronger concentrated magic long ago and blocked evil wizards and dark arts with a unified spell. Mertil must have tried a powerful dark magic when he got here and the grigeens' spell kicked in, blocking magic and wizardry." Gliandra looked up at a group of grigeens coming toward them. "Thank you for coming. We need you to release your spell, it's limiting the wizards."

"We can't break it." The lead grigeen was one of the council members, but not someone Piallen had seen more than once or twice.

"You have to. The wizards can't work," Gliandra said.

"Neither can Mertil—he's not a wizard, but he's got some serious power. We might be better off without him being able to tap into it." Piallen knew they didn't have time to debate this and right now the clystikes were helping to stabilize the fight, but that might not hold.

"But their other mages are still fighting—they might be on his side, but clearly aren't using dark magic. And there's a chance Mertil will find a way around the spell." Hilth had been standing with his eyes closed, but turned back to them. "And the battle is turning against us. We can't get more fighters here. We have to break the grigeens' spell."

The grigeen council member shook his head. "We've tried. It was tied to the one who trapped our people. Without them here, we can't undo it."

Tobias tugged Clait's collar off of his shoulder and gave it to Piallen. "You still have your stone, right?"

Piallen held out the wizard stone as she took the collar. "So, we try to trick the spell?"

"Can't hurt. Well, hopefully it can't hurt." Solange held out her hands and took the collar and the stone. "There should be a third relic that Pantiar left, I can feel it. Oh, Pantiar, you sneaky devil." She looked up as Sean came running back to them.

"What? Someone called me back here. Why is Tobias looking at me like that?" Sean looked battered but was more annoyed at being pulled back from the fight than anything.

"Your pin, I've heard of it. The one the wizard gave you?" Tobias held out his paw.

Sean shrugged and took off a stick-pin from the inside of his vest. "I wouldn't use it, it seemed to kind of take over. I kept it to remind me not to get too cocky." He handed it to Solange. "I'm not sure what's going on, but we're starting to fall back again." He nodded to Piallen and ran back to the fighting.

"Okay, who called him back here?" Piallen looked around as Solange held all three relics together. Or rather, two relics and a stone.

"I'd say the ghost of Pantiar, or something connected to him." She bent down to the grigeens. "Now, focus on these and try to release the spell again. These relics were connected to the one who trapped your people—although he did it to save you, in his mind."

The battle was shifting, but the grigeens, aside from Tobias who just watched, all started chanting. And chanting louder. It seemed like the same chant, but done in a loop.

Piallen was about to ask Hilth to help her move the entire group further from the fighting when Solange jumped. A massive shield came from her hands, followed by a line of flame—aiming right at the enemy forces. The flame forced the enemies back at least for the moment.

"We're through! The spell is broken!" She yelled as both the flame and the shield fell, but a wave of power flowed over them as the grigeen spell was released. "Let's go get that mage." She tossed Piallen the stone and the two relics. "You should use any spells at your disposal, these will keep him from taking them from you." The snarl on her face said she'd be doing the same.

They ran toward the front, skirting around the battlemages and clystikes. Piallen put the necklace with the stone on and pocketed the other two items. She'd ask about that pin of Sean's later. Right now, it and the collar seemed warm, and she got the feeling they both wanted to fight. Somehow, she didn't think that was a great idea. Sean was someone who appreciated a good spell, but he didn't trust the pin, probably with reason.

Mertil was bearing down on the army and lightning crackled from his fingers. It would have been better to have broken the grigeen spell when they were in a better position to release their own, but time wasn't on their side.

Solange and Hilth rose in the air, but not as alsohawks—they were using wizardry to fly up. Neither went high, not much higher than Piallen's head, but it gave them a great angle for spells. Both sent out focus blast spells to the approaching army. So focused they knocked the soldiers off their horses, leaving the animals to run free.

Piallen really hoped she was able to master both of those spells at some point—and she was grateful their enemies didn't appear to have battle trained horses.

A group ran for her, managing to skirt around the clystikes and battlemages. Piallen crouched a bit, held her sword steady, and grinned. There were six of them and only two were on horseback. Seeing her with a sword, and alone, they charged.

She took a step back and released the lock spell. It hit the ground fighters first, then the riders. The horses were missed, but not happy, and bucked their frozen riders off and ran. Smart horses.

Piallen walked to the soldiers but none of them moved. Alive, but not going anywhere. She was still upset about Mertil getting out of her lock spell in the Ceredigion castle, but these didn't appear to be going anywhere.

Solange and Hilth both changed into alsohawks and flew higher as the fighting came closer. It looked like the battle was turning and that Mertil's group was now struggling. Piallen was still near the clystikes and they were definitely holding their own.

One of the big cats turned and jumped a battlemage. It was only through a serious spell and fighting combination that the battlemage survived. The cat was injured but still growled at the battlemage, ready to try again.

Chapter Twenty-Seven

One by one all of the clystikes started to turn on the battlemages, including Gareth and Kendric. They all moved stiffly, as if they were trying to fight a compulsion spell, but they were moving. At the very least they would have lost the clystikes and possibly the battlemages. It was enough to turn the battle again.

Piallen ran into the center of the clystikes—then looked around them. Mertil was nearby and chanting a spell. His focus was completely on the clystikes and a small grin told her he was the one controlling them. Piallen called up the atharraich spell, the kindred master spell that forced clystikes to change forms. She didn't have time to try and counteract Mertil's spell in any other way. Not optimal as clystikes were stronger in their non-human form, and Solange and Hilth might still be flying, but she didn't have a choice.

She cast the spell.

At first it seemed like nothing happened, then all of the clystikes froze and changed back into their human forms. "Don't hurt them! They're spelled!" She yelled to all of the battlemages, but mostly to Sean and Nevaine.

The battlemages returned to fighting only Mertil's soldiers just based on a pair of nods from Nevaine and Sean.

The clystikes all looked stunned. Piallen had seen them change back and forth with ease, but this forced change was different—it also looked like it had been painful. They tried to turn back, but failing that, drew their swords and fought the enemy army. The compulsion spell Mertil put on them to fight the people of Astarious was broken.

Whatever the spell Mertil had put on them had been, it must only affect them if they were in their changed form. Kendric fought an attacker but his eyes kept going back to her. Explaining this spell to him wasn't going to be fun, but it might have saved all of the clystikes—the battlemages as well.

Mertil turned to her and threw another spell. She held up her stone; the other two relics were still in her pocket but she felt them respond as a shield went up in front of her. The urge to throw fire was overwhelming and not related to any spell she knew, magic or wizardry based. But once Mertil's spell fell apart against her shield, she sent fire his way.

It was weird throwing a spell she didn't know, had never seen, and didn't have a clue where it came from, but seeing the terror on Mertil's face as he frantically blocked the flames was worth it.

She ran toward him, swinging her sword at anyone who tried to get in her way. The flames kept hounding him, but he drew his sword as well.

The clash of their swords jarred her arm, but she pressed back. The flames eventually died but neither she nor Mertil reached for magic. To do so would mean the other one would probably run them through before they got the spell out.

Piallen fought to disarm him. King Brae had asked that he be brought back alive to stand for his crimes, if it could be safely done. Mertil got a tricky shot in and sliced her sword arm. Then he stepped back and started an ugly sounding spell.

Piallen switched her sword to her other hand, and ran him through before he could finish. She'd trained to fight, or shoot, with either hand once she had started her battlemage training. It was something that Nevaine had been trying to get her to do for years. Most opponents wouldn't expect it, and it would keep you fighting longer.

Although the spell died on his lips, another one flowed over everyone. Solange and Hilth, still in alsohawk forms, came flying in as a sense of peace flowed from them.

The fighters from Northalian all collapsed where they stood, and Solange and Hilth changed back into their human forms.

"I'd tie them all up quickly. Or whatever you plan to do. That spell won't hold more than a few minutes. We couldn't cast it before, as Mertil was protecting them." Solange yelled toward Sean and Nevaine. She and Hilth looked drawn—whatever that spell was, it had cost them.

Most of the battlemages quickly tied the enemy soldiers up as another group ran to tell the remaining Astarious forces.

Piallen shook her head. "I was afraid I'd killed you both when I cast the atharraich spell. But I didn't have a choice."

"We were out of range from getting a full strike of the atharraich spell—and as wizards we probably could have fought the change off anyway," Hilth said. "You did the right thing."

"Is that what you used?" Kendric had first gone to confirm that Mertil was dead, then came over to them. His face was neutral but his jaw was tight.

She ran her hand through her hair. She knew this wasn't going to be fun—but it had to happen. "Yes. It wasn't right, it looked painful, but I didn't have a choice. Your people and the battlemages would have destroyed each other. And our side couldn't have recovered from that." She could understand how pissed he and the other clystikes were, but it was better than being dead and the battle falling to Mertil.

Kendric looked around as the last of the invaders were tied up, then nodded. "You did the right thing. But could you release it? It's giving me, and probably the others, a massive headache." He smiled but rubbed his head.

Piallen looked to Solange and Hilth. The spell Mertil had cast should have vanished when he was killed, but better to make sure. They both nodded and she released the atharraich spell. Many of the clystikes went back to their animal form, but Kendric stayed human.

Gareth also stayed human as he walked over. Like everyone, he had some injuries, but nothing serious. "Still alive, that's a plus. But I had to bite too many people today—it's going to take days to get that out of my mouth. Might need a few serious trips to the pub."

Nevaine jogged over to them while Sean conferred with the battlemages. "The enemy are tied up. Is everyone here okay? Our parents are sending in the healers."

"I'm fine." Piallen looked at the slice in her arm. "I guess it would be nice to get this taken care of eventually though. Good thing I can fight equally well with both hands."

Nevaine darted forward and carefully hugged her. "That's my girl!" Then she looked around. Sean was barking orders to gather the fallen enemies, the live ones, into one spot. "Okay, we might want to keep your shapeshifting friends together for now. The battlemages were fine with them, but not sure how the rest of them will react until things are explained to them." She turned to leave, then spun back and held her hand out to Kendric. "I am so sorry, I'm Piallen's sister, Nevaine. Thank you, all of you." She looked to Gareth and the other shifters. "For coming here and fighting for us."

"I'm Kendric, and you're welcome." He grinned as he shook her hand. He also didn't mention he was a prince or where he was from. They'd just fought, and some had died, to save Astarious, but he still kept his secrets.

Nevaine nodded and turned away, but not before she gave Piallen a sly wink.

A healer jogged over and quickly spelled and bandaged Piallen's arm. Then he fixed a nasty gash on Gareth's leg.

Kendric held out his hand as the healer approached. "I'm fine, but thank you." When Piallen raised her eyebrow, he was limping and twinged if he moved his right shoulder too fast, he shrugged. "I'll be fine. They should go help someone worse off."

Gareth looked up and shook his head. "I once saw Kendric almost have his arm torn clean off by a wild boar—said it was nothing. Never believe him."

Piallen folded her arms and gave the healer a nod to check Kendric.

"Torn ligaments in both the right leg and shoulder." The healer tsked a bit as he ran the spell to heal them—ligaments could take a long time to heal on their own—and Kendric kept his scowling to a minimum.

The clean-up was efficient and didn't require Piallen to join in. Once the surviving enemies were taken away to be locked up and questioned, Piallen's parents came to where Piallen stood with the clystikes. Most had switched back to human, but a few of the cats stayed in animal-form.

Her father nodded to Kendric. "I would like to formally thank you and your people for what you did by coming here. The losses your people had defending our country will never be forgotten."

Piallen stepped forward with a shake of her head. "Sorry, it's been a long day. Prince Kendric of Ceredigion, please meet my parents, King Keven and Queen Chila." Secrets only went so far.

Both parents looked surprised, but it wasn't clear if their response was more at Kendric being a prince or the name of his kingdom.

"I am honored to meet you both. My father, King Brae, sends his regards and we are all grateful that we could help."

"I am honored that your people came forth," the queen said. "I'd heard myths and rumors of Ceredigion; I am from Pax originally. Your shapeshifters are quite impressive, we will make sure the stories of them are dealt with however—unless your land is coming out of hiding?"

Kendric's smile was stunning. "Not yet, Your Majesty. And we appreciate that you'll keep the truth of our people muddled. We do hope to be ready to come forth in a few years, but will remain even more closed than we have been until then. I know my father will be pleased to meet you when that time comes."

The king and queen made official small talk for a bit, then excused themselves as a group of palace mages needed to speak to them. Gareth went to check on the clystikes. Their injuries had been addressed by the healers and it would soon be time to leave.

Solange, Hilth, and Gliandra joined Kendric and Piallen.

"I'll read my wizardry books and any others that my sister can get for me," Piallen said. It wouldn't be the same as having the two wizards here training her, but she knew it was vital that they go back to help heal Ceredigion.

"I can help a bit with that. I'm going with them as well. I'll be back here; this is my home now. But I'm needed there." Gliandra smiled. "But I can help you with any support you might need. We were discussing the shields that will be in place around Ceredigion, and I've created a way to get letters through. You'll be able to contact any of us." It would be odd not to have Gliandra around the palace, but Piallen understood.

"That would be great. I have to say that learning wizardry without support wouldn't be fun." Piallen kept looking away from Kendric. Letters would be nice from him too, but not sure that either of them was the type for building a long-distance relationship.

"You know, three wizards would be better to orchestrate this massive cleaning than just two old and aging ones." Solange looked hopeful. "The kingdom will need a lot of work to recover and we can train you as we go."

"I can help, but not on the level that you can," Gliandra said.

"There's work here too. That last battle did damage to the forest and breaking the grigeens protection spell will cause unknown results—some could be dangerous. Trees will need to be replanted, and more." Piallen was surprised at how she felt, but she was terrified to leave.

Hilth started to say something, then shook his head, and gave a small smile. "You have to do what feels right. If you will excuse us, we need to make our farewells to the king and queen."

Kendric waited until all three were out of earshot before taking her hands. "Come with me. Not just to become a wizard, but because I want to know you better. The oracles had their reasons to try and put us together—and while I don't like being told what to do, I admit they might have had the right idea. We could see if there is more than friendship?" His hazel eyes were warm as he looked down at her, but there were questions there too. "That kiss indicated that there might be?"

Piallen shook her head but didn't pull her hands away. "I can't leave my family, my kingdom. You have to go clean up your kingdom, take care of the stagnant magic, and resolve the clystikes. I know that. But what would I do there?" A little voice in her head that sounded a lot like Tobias pointed out that there was a lot she could do to help Ceredigion—as well as sort out how she felt about Kendric. But this wasn't just a few weeks—it was at least two years. She could write to her parents and sisters, but being away from them for that long was hard to even think about. Even though both Lizeth and Nevaine had their own lives, they still came back to the palace regularly.

"Train our archers? Teach our foresters that odd tree running thing you do? Learn to be a wizard? Whatever you want. We could even build you a shack in the forest, so you won't have to come inside much if you don't want to." He rubbed her arms. "I want to see what might be really between us."

She was drawn to Kendric, that wasn't a question. He was handsome, smart, honorable, and had a decent sense of humor when he wasn't carrying the entire kingdom on his back. Unfortunately, finding out what the oracles had been trying to do by bringing them together had made her doubt her own feelings. But that kiss had been real. Not sure she would have done it if she knew she'd see him this soon, but it had been genuine on both sides. "I don't know." She looked over to her parents, sisters, and their spouses. They were saying goodbye to Solange, Hilth, and Gliandra, who was sitting on a bear shifter of all things. The spell to open the chorogh path to non-shifters couldn't be used again, at least not for a while. No one had enough energy to run it again. All three waved before the wizards became alsohawks and they and the bear went into the path. Solange and Hilth had promised to come back when the valley was cleansed and fully train Piallen, but that they would also write back and forth as she worked through the books. Gliandra had promised to keep in touch.

Kendric's smile faded. "Then this is goodbye. The valley needs to be shut and will stay that way for at least two years as it is cleansed. I'll never forget you." He leaned forward and gave her a slow kiss. Then he pulled back and rubbed her jaw with his thumb. "We'll take care of the grigeens." A group of grigeens had already traveled through to Ceredigion, they'd been excited about a new land that needed them so badly.

"Are you seriously going to let him leave?" Tobias marched over and sat on his back legs in order to fold his arms and glare at her.

"I wouldn't." Her father said, as he and the rest of the family also came over. Sean and Finnian each held huge packs that floated a foot or two above the ground. Including one that had a familiar quiver and bow over it.

"Is that my quiver and bow?" Piallen knew that the bigger issue was why it was there and how they had gathered her things so quickly. But simple questions were easier right now.

Lizeth and Nevaine ran forward and engulfed her in a massive hug.

"I'm her other sister, Lizeth. It is wonderful to meet you." She gave her best smile then held up a finger. "But if we could have just one moment, if you don't mind." She and Nevaine pulled Piallen away.

"What's wrong?" Nevaine asked. "It's clear you two are drawn to each other, and it's not like you're being sent off as a long-distance bride. If you two develop into something stronger, great. If not, you come home a fully trained wizard."

"There really isn't much to lose." Lizeth kept watching Kendric with an admiring grin.

"I'm not even confirmed as heir yet." Piallen needed to mentally grab onto something. She wasn't typically a patient person, but this was too fast even for her.

The king heard that part and turned to the queen. "I'm confirming Piallen as third heir—and you?"

"Also confirming. There you go. And those packs have almost all of your belongings. They're spelled to float so even Tobias could bring them."

Her parents hugged her with her sisters joining. There were a lot of teary eyes but many smiles as well.

Piallen bit her lip as they all walked back to Kendric. "I'll write. Often. If Gliandra says she can get mail through the shield around Ceredigion, I believe her. Tobias, are you sure about this? You can't come back for two years."

Kendric smiled to her family and Tobias. "At least two years. Those mountains are deadly right now."

"I'm fine." Tobias grabbed the handles for the pack with her bow on it. "Many of my people already left to relocate there, I'm needed to keep them in line. We will go far in helping heal the land." With a bow to the king and queen, he trotted into the chorogh path as the massive pack floated behind him.

Kendric turned into his stag form and turned to her. "Will you join us, milady?"

Piallen grabbed the handle for the second floating pack, waved goodbye to her family, and climbed on his back. "You're stuck with me for a while." This was the craziest thing she'd ever done, but it felt right all of a sudden. There was no way to know what might happen in two years, but it was worth taking a chance.

"I think I'm okay with that." With a bow to Piallen's family, he strode into the path.

Epilogue-two and a half years later

Piallen straightened her dress for possibly the fifteenth time. "Are you sure I look okay?" Dresses still weren't her thing, and she felt awkward in them.

Lizeth gave a huge guffaw then winced. "You look jaw-droppingly stunning, littlest sister. But the babies don't like me laughing so hard." She patted her extremely round stomach.

"You know, we could have held off this wedding until after they're born." Piallen looked down at her sister. Only Lizeth could still look gorgeous at over eight months pregnant with twins. She hadn't said anything, but when she arrived a few days ago, she'd felt strong magics from the unborn babies. Better to wait until Solange, Hilth, and Gliandra could confirm.

"I suggested that too, but she outvoted both of us. Let me fix the veil." Nevaine dragged over a step-stool, pulled and tugged on Piallen's veil, and used about a dozen pins just on one side. There were already a bunch of them and Piallen had grown leaner in the past two years and the dress had been adjusted when she first got back. The pins still needed to be removed.

"You've been gone far too long. I didn't want you to vanish off again if we delayed it. I want to see you married before your niece and nephew are born. *Queen* Piallen."

"You two were the ones who convinced me to go to Ceredigion. As for the queen bit, that's going to take some getting used to." Piallen still wasn't sure about being a queen. King Brae had survived the attack on him, but was left extremely weak, so he stepped down and gave Kendric the throne their first month there. Kendric proposed to her eighteen months ago in the middle of the woods on a clean-up walk through. He also pointed out that she would be Queen of Ceredigion as well as heir to Astarious.

Just weird. She went from being not even sure she wanted to be an heir to being both heir and queen.

"And a wizard." Nevaine was more excited about that than the marriage or Piallen being queen before her.

"I still can't train you to become a wizard, you know. It is in our blood, apparently, many generations past. But no one else is showing it beyond me at this point."

"Oh, I know. I just want to sit and go through those books. You translate, I'll analyze." Nevaine grinned and gave a wink. "After your honeymoon, that is."

Lizeth stepped back with tears in her eyes. "This is it, we're all confirmed heirs, and after another hour, we're all married to some pretty amazing men." The tears rolled down her cheeks.

Nevaine didn't get down from her step-stool but tossed a bit of lace to her sister. "Dry your eyes, it's the babies who are doing it." But she was blinking a bit more than normal as well.

Piallen looked down at her dress. She still wasn't a fan, and warned Kendric of that repeatedly, but her wedding gown was stunning. Long, pointed gems twinkled in the bluish white satin. The narrow gems were a deep blue-black that almost matched her hair. They'd been made by Solange and Hilth at Piallen's and Gliandra's urging. "I was going to wait until after the 'I do' part, but as you two are getting all emotional...just act surprised at the wedding."

She waited until they both looked at her, then touched the gem that was near her left shoulder. A beautiful song came from all of the gems. Then it ended.

"They have a spell song in them?" Lizeth's tears were forgotten as she started looking at the gems and softly singing to them—they echoed back.

Nevaine looked at the gem closest to her. "Are they shaped like knives? It's not noticeable at all from a distance...but up close?"

"Yup. I wouldn't be here without both of you. I wanted you both to be in my dress." Piallen smiled. "But no hugs! Not until all the unpinning is done."

A soft knock at the door almost caused an issue as Piallen started to answer it.

Nevaine put her hand up. "Pins? I'll get it."

"Hello, I'm Kendric's sister; I just wanted to give Piallen a bridal gift."

"Jhali, please come in." Piallen stayed in place but introduced her sisters to her soon to be sister-in-law.

"I've heard so much about you over the past two years, I feel like I know you both."

"And we've only heard good things about you." Lizeth went and engulfed her in a hug. "Isn't it lovely?" She dabbed her eyes.

Nevaine stepped away from the dress and hugged Jhali as well. "You're one of the family too, now. Ignore Lizeth, those babies are making her weepy."

Piallen held out her arms. "I'd hug you but I have pins. I'm so glad you made it." It had been debatable if Gareth and Jhali would make the wedding. The oracles had decided that with the protections around the valley gone, and the valley cleansed, they wanted to send more of their people out to survey the kingdoms around them. Just to take a better sense of what the world was like.

As the head oracles' priestess and her husband, Jhali and Gareth had been the first on the list to go out as ambassadors once the kingdom was ready. But the oracles had seen the importance of them being at Kendric and Piallen's wedding and held back on when they needed to leave.

Piallen smiled as Jhali helped to remove the pins and adjust the gown along with her sisters. Her family had extended and being away from the palace for two years had helped make her stronger in more ways than just becoming a wizard.

She'd worked hard with Kendric, the wizards, and Gliandra—who still never clarified how she was wizard adjacent—to clear the stagnated magic. It had been created by the spell placed on the clystikes and had built slowly over the years. Introducing clystikes to the rest of the world would be a slow process, but Astarious was already starting a program to bring some into the kingdom for their education, as well as to help the Astarious people understand them. It appeared that the closing of the Ceredigion kingdom had stifled clystike births outside of it. Like the return of wizardry, there was a chance clystikes could appear in other lands.

"And she's drifted out again." Nevaine stood in front of Piallen and from the look on her face had asked her something.

Piallen laughed. "Sorry, what was it?"

"I asked if you were ready to go get married to some random king guy." Nevaine grinned and motioned around. "Your matron of honor and bridesmaids await."

Piallen patted down her dress, no more pins, and tossed back her veil. "I like the look of veils, but not fond of hiding behind one." She grinned as they started for the door. "And catch me if I faint, okay?"

Lizeth laughed, grabbed her stomach for a moment, then relaxed with a grin. "Nope, we're good, no babies yet. But let's keep things moving."

The throne room was decorated within an inch of its life, mostly because there was a king involved. Piallen had preferred something subtle, but the nobles and chancellors would have nothing to do with it. She was marrying a mystical king from a formerly hidden land—one that now held interest for all. She'd fought a bit more until Kendric mentioned that his father would love some fanciness too.

In the past two years, King Brae had become a second father to her, and often joined in on teasing Kendric. In her eyes, King Brae could have whatever he wanted, so she backed down.

But this decorating was beyond her wildest fears.

All wall spaces were filled with banners from both kingdoms and a third type showing the two linked together. There were enough flowers that sneezing, quickly stifled, could be heard throughout the massive hall.

The music started and first Jhali, next Nevaine, and then Lizeth slowly walked down the aisle. Tobias was standing up as one of the best men, along with Gareth, and Kendric's brothers.

Piallen was focusing on moving her feet forward and didn't look closely at the front until she was almost there.

Kendric was stunning. He was normally striking, but this was above and beyond. His suit was made of a deep green color that at first appeared black. The cut was so perfect, there must have been magic involved in its making. But his massive smile and the light in his hazel eyes as he saw her was the part that stopped her.

The oracles had pushed them together—and it had taken a while to get past that—but the feelings they had were real.

She regained her steps, stopped, and turned to face Kendric. But she only partially heard the words the priest of the oracles said. She and Kendric repeated their short vows and both pairs of hands were unsteady as they exchanged rings.

"Might I present, King Kendric and Queen Piallen, husband and wife. You may now kiss."

The kiss was amazing, scorching, and unshakeable.

Kendric tilted his forehead toward hers as they finished their kiss. "I think you're stuck with me."

Piallen grinned. "I think I'm okay with that."

And they ALL lived happily ever after.

The End

Dear Reader,

Thank you for joining me on a Piallen's adventure! I hope that you enjoyed this third and final trip into this world and these three sisters. As always, I appreciate you for coming along on the newest escapade.

If you want to keep up on the further adventures of any of my characters, make sure to visit my website and sign up for my mailing list. I only post about once a month unless there is a special sale or new release. http://marieandreas.com/index.html

You can also sign up on Amazon to follow me and they will keep you updated. Marie Andreas Amazon[1]

If you enjoyed this book, please spread the word! Positive reviews are like emotional gold to any writer. And mean more than you know.

Thank you again—and keep reading!

Marie

---

1. https://www.amazon.com/Marie-Andreas/e/B00SX81KIM/

About the Author

Marie is a multi-award-winning fantasy and science fiction author with a serious reading addiction. If she wasn't writing about all the people in her head, she'd be lurking about coffee shops annoying total strangers with her stories. So really, writing is a way of saving the masses. She lives in Southern California and is owned by two very faery-minded cats. She is also a member of SFWA (Science Fiction and Fantasy Writers Association).

When not saving the masses from coffee shop shenanigans, Marie likes to visit the UK and keeps hoping someone will give her a nice summer home in the Forest of Dean or Conwy, Wales.